"Last stop, Miss Clement."

He caught her under her arms as she slid from the saddle, although he was careful to hold her well away from his body.

For which she was vastly grateful. It was simple enough to be prudent from afar, but in close proximity to her handsome Tatar, it was quite a different matter. How strong he was, she thought, as he effortlessly held her at arm's length and carried her to the pavement. No doubt he was all hard, taut muscle beneath his sheepskin capote—an image of him sans coat and shirt suddenly leaping into her mind. Which *would not* do, she sternly reprimanded her wayward senses. How could she possibly allow herself to consider such wanton behavior when the world was literally going up in flames!

The moment her feet touched the ground, she immediately took a step back, intent on putting distance between herself and this provocative stranger. Why he struck her sensibilities so profoundly was unclear. She was not normally susceptible to male virility alone. A polite, well-mannered good-bye was in order, she concluded. And that would put an end to her untoward feelings. But while she uttered all the requisite courtesies and expressions of gratitude, embarrassingly, she delivered them in a breathless tumble of words.

Under his amused gaze, her voice trailed off, her embarrassment abruptly evaporated and she said with cool affront, "You find this entertaining?"

"At the risk of offending you further, I do." He grinned. "And I sincerely thank you for the pleasure."

AT HER
SERVICE

SUSAN JOHNSON

BRAVA

KENSINGTON PUBLISHING CORP.
http://www.kensingtonbooks.com

BRAVA BOOKS are published by

Kensington Publishing Corp.
119 West 40th Street
New York, NY 10018

All Kensington Titles, Imprints and Distributed Lines are
available at special quantity discounts for bulk purchases for
sales promotions, premiums, fund-raising, and educational or
institutional use. Special book excerpts or customized print-
ings can also be created to fit specific needs. For details, write
or phone the office of the Kensington special sales manager:
Kensington Publishing Corp., 119 West 40th Street, New York,
NY 10018, attn: Special Sales Department, Phone: 1-800-221-
2647.

Brava Books and the B logo Reg. U.S. Pat. & TM Off.

ISBN-13: 978-0-7582-0946-7
ISBN-10: 0-7582-0946-0

First trade paperback printing: March 2008
First mass market printing: December 2012

10 9 8 7 6 5 4 3 2 1

Printed in the United States of America

Chapter

1

The Crimea, February 1855

On a cold, frosty morning just outside Sevastopol, Hugh D'Abernon, Marquis of Darley, rode over the crest of a hill and saw her for the first time. She was standing beside a green lacquered carriage, holding up the hem of her sable coat to keep it out of the mud, watching her servant shoveling the muck away from one of the carriage wheels—or what once had been a wheel. It was shattered beyond repair.

Her red-gold hair gleamed in the sunlight, and even from ten yards away, her beauty was striking. Not that lovely ladies were of particular interest to him at the moment; he had an assignment to complete. But he had to admit in this theater of war a woman of her stamp was rare and, by definition, memorable. She was some noble's wife, no doubt. Some very *rich* noble. That sable coat she wore was fashioned from the rarest and most costly golden pelts.

Moments later as he neared the carriage that had apparently bottomed out in one of the wretched holes on the nearly impassable road, he drew his horse to a halt. Even more stunning at close range, she looked vastly out of place in this muddy waste-land—a beautiful, sloe-eyed Della Robbia Madonna far from the Medici. But rather than voice his thoughts, he doffed his wolfskin hat and said, po-litely, "May I offer you a ride into town?" He spoke in French—the language of the upper classes in Russia.

She'd been watching him for the past few min-utes, having turned at the sound of approaching horses. "Thank you, I would appreciate a ride." She too spoke in French, although she could have an-swered him in Tatar as well—in the event that was his native tongue. The large, dark-haired man had the swarthy skin and aquiline features of the local popu-lace. He was also dressed like a Tatar, but his fluent French suggested his choice of clothing could have more to do with the weather than his heritage. "The roads are worse than usual after last week's thaw," she offered with a smile, speaking the Tatar dialect of the region, testing his authenticity. These were danger-ous times, and she was involved in dangerous under-takings; *trust no one* had become her motto. "Ibrahim warned me about making the trek today." She shrugged faintly. "And as you see . . ."

"No doubt Ibrahim didn't wish to argue the point with you. A lady is always right, is she not?" Hugh replied with a small smile, his Tatar as impeccable as hers. He raised one brow slightly. "Do I pass muster?"

She smiled back—a mannered smile that gave

nothing away. "One acquires a certain wariness," she said, reverting to French, "with opposing armies in the field."

"Very sensible of you. Personally, I wish nations wouldn't go to war on such flimsy pretexts, but then"— he shrugged—"nobody asked me. In the meantime, since we are caught in the middle of this dubious endeavor, allow me to introduce myself." He bowed faintly from the saddle. "Gazi Maksoud from points east," he lied.

She dipped her head, her hands still occupied with keeping her coat out of the mud. "I am Aurore Clement from Alupka."

"A neighbor of Prince Woronzov, then."

"Yes. My estate borders his."

She didn't say my husband's estate or my father's or brother's. He found himself oddly curious about her when in all his years of wandering the globe, he'd never been inclined to question anything more than a female's availability. Was it because he was bone tired from having gone without sleep for days? Had he been living rough too long? Perhaps it was nothing more than the sight of a lush woman that suddenly conjured up pleasurable thoughts of clean sheets, soft beds and softer flesh.

Wrenched from delectable fantasy by the brisk cadence of her voice, he returned to the stark reality of a chill wind and mud as far as the eye could see.

"Ibrahim, carry out that case of wine, then wait here with our supplies. I'll send out someone with a new wheel as quickly as possible." Turning to Hugh, she added, "You don't mind transporting my wine, do you?" Aurore glanced at the string of pack horses behind him, led by two Tatars.

"No, of course not. Let me carry you over this bog." Dismounting, Darley plowed through the mud toward her. "I'm afraid I can't offer you a side saddle."

"It's of no regard. I've ridden astride most of my life."

He must be more tired than he thought; his brain was interpreting her response as double entendre. A lovely image though—her riding him. It almost made him forget this senseless war and the fact that he hadn't had a hot bath for a week. "I apologize for my stench," he murmured, half lifting his hand in demur as he approached her. "We've come down from Perekop without stopping."

"You needn't apologize. The superficialities of society hardly apply in these grievous times. In fact, after having visited the hospitals in Sevastopol, one realizes how trivial politesse is in the face of such human suffering."

"A harrowing sight, is it not?" He always distributed a portion of his provisions to the hospitals, his charity extending to the common soldier regardless of their allegiance.

"Indeed. My brother lies in hospital in Sevastopol."

"You should get him out as soon as you can," he said, lifting her into his arms, trying to ignore the soft warmth of her thighs on his forearms, the contact of her plump breasts against his chest and arm. "The hygiene in the hospitals on either side is deplorable," he added in an attempt to shift his attention from her closeness.

"I've been able to secure a small room for him outside the wards. We've cleaned it as well as we could, but the moment Etienne can be moved, we will do so." Her words at the last were slightly breathy for his arms had tightened around her as he navigated some difficult ground, and pressed hard against his body, she experienced a heady rush of pleasure.

He shot her a quizzical look.

"The wind is cutting," she lied, controlling her voice with effort since her pulse was still racing.

He just grunted in reply, carefully picking his way through the slop.

Regardless the impropriety, perfectly aware that she should be concentrating on more important things, nevertheless, Aurore found herself scrutinizing the handsome stranger from under her lashes. His features were quite stunning beneath the wolf-skin hat pulled low over his forehead: fine cheekbones, straight nose, lush sculpted mouth, firm chin. Not to mention the dark stubble shadowing his jaw afforded him the rakish air of an adventurer—which he surely was, plying his trade in this dangerous no-man's-land.

Hugh, too, understood a certain aloofness was required—more pertinently, that his mission required he be on guard. But her beguiling scent drifted into his nostrils, the Parma violet fragrance triggering long-ago memory, reminding him of better times, sweeter times and youthful amours. Christ, he silently expostulated, he needed a drink, some sleep or a stern talking to; carnal memories from the past he could do without right now. The sooner he put distance between himself and that unnerving scent of violet, the better.

While Hugh was struggling to ignore not only her but her perfume, Aurore was taking note of a hint of cologne emanating from her escort. Well aware that male cologne was not a Tatar amenity, she instantly questioned the discrepancy. Even as a number of possible explanations raced through her mind, she masked her suspicions with conversation. "I thought Ibrahim and I knew every pothole in this wretched road since we make this trek almost daily," she murmured. "But apparently not—as you see. If my foolish brother hadn't joined the French forces"—she smiled ruefully—"but he did, of course." Another smile. "In our position he should have remained neutral. Although I'm extremely grateful he was captured instead of killed"—she quickly crossed herself—"and General Osten-Sacken has been exceedingly gracious about Etienne's rash behavior. We always bring the general a few little luxuries in gratitude."

"Then we are both pursuing a similar agenda, although mine is purely for profit," Hugh replied, grateful for her conversation. He needed distraction from his increasingly lurid thoughts apropos the lady in his arms. "We bring the officers small luxuries as well—brandy, cigars, chocolate, caviar, pate, an occasional letter, things of that nature. Ah, finally—here we are," he said, relieved to have reached his black charger. He was not by nature monkish, and the lady in his arms was taxing his nonexistent virtue.

"I apologize for being such a burden," she said, misunderstanding the relief in his voice.

"Nonsense." He smiled. "You are nothing of the kind."

She suddenly noticed that his eyes weren't brown like most Tatars, but a luminous gray-green, and when he smiled like that, a seductive twinkle was only marginally disguised.

As he lifted her into the padded saddle, she shook away the deviant consequences of that improper gaze. Seductive or not, she would not be tempted.

"What length stirrup do you prefer?" he asked. "European or local?"

His voice was businesslike; she would do well to command her sensibilities with as much mastery. "Local," she replied crisply, determined to steel herself against bizarre temptation. "I was born and bred in the Crimea."

"I wasn't entirely sure with your French name and your brother's allegiance to France," he said, pulling up one stirrup. Tatars rode with short stirrups.

"Catherine the Great wanted vineyards planted in the region and my grandfather and others were lured from France by generous land grants. Our family has been here for over fifty years. Let me give you a bottle of our wine when we reach Sevastopol." Aurore smiled politely, in control once again of her sensibilities. "It's quite good."

"Yours is a family business then." He moved around to the opposite side of his charger.

"It was—or is; only Etienne and I remain." She shifted her leg as he reached for the second stirrup buckle, wishing to avoid contact when she was not normally so prudish. "My parents died of a summer fever two years ago."

He looked up. "I'm sorry."

She made a small moue. "The void remains, but our household is like family; Etienne and I are not alone." She felt the need to disavow her vulnerability, although for a woman of independence, her impulse was peculiar. It must be the war, she decided, rather than admit to a less palatable reason having to do with this stranger's seductive allure. She'd been working too hard, she thought. Fatigue made her more susceptible to emotion. Having known a number of handsome men, she couldn't be attracted by his looks alone. Although, his power and size were something quite out of the ordinary. How would he feel . . .

Stop this instant! she chastised herself. That she was even *considering* the amorous pleasures such a man might afford was reprehensible in the midst of this fearsome war. The death toll had already been enormous—from cold, from lack of food, from shell and rifle shot. Even Etienne had just narrowly escaped death, she reflected, a sudden shiver racing up her spine.

Feeling a hand on her boot, she jerked back only to look down and find Gazi looking up at her.

"Would you like a tot of brandy?" Her shiver had been unmistakable, as was her sudden jump at his touch. Not that skittishness in this war zone was abnormal. "A little brandy is good for the nerves," he said with a smile.

"Thank you. Some brandy would be wonderful." She exhaled softly. "I often wish I were a thousand miles away from this miserable war."

"I agree," Darley muttered as he pulled a silver flask from the pocket of his sheepskin capote.

"Do you think any of the rumors of peace might be true?" she asked like a child might, wanting the impossible.

"I doubt it," he gently replied, having recently seen the plans for the Allied spring offense. Uncorking his flask, he handed it to her. "I find when I am less lucid, I also care less." He winked. "Drink up."

"A byword for survival in these difficult times, I agree." She lifted the flask to her lips, drank and returned it to him with a grateful smile.

"Better?" he said.

"I am definitely less lucid."

He grinned. "Which is the point." After taking a

long draught himself, he replaced the cork and pocketed the worn container. "Now that we're suitably fortified against the stark realities," he said in a weary drawl, "shall we push on through this quagmire?"

She met his half-lidded gaze. "You sound as tired as I."

"I haven't slept for a while—unlike the damned generals who sleep soundly in their comfortable beds while the less fortunate freeze in the trenches."

"Yet you supply the general staff with luxuries." Her brows rose in query.

He shrugged. "One has to make a living." Grabbing the reins of her horse, he turned and strode toward his own mount. Reminders of the incompetence of the British command always rankled him. Raglan surrounded himself with relatives and sycophants, never made a decision unless forced to and deluded himself that he was fighting a gentleman's war. Not that his resentments could be voiced, Hugh grimly thought. But at least he was doing his part to bring up-to-date information to the British staff; whether they acted on it intelligently was beyond his control.

Reaching his horse, he gracefully swung up into the saddle, half turned and said, "I'll lead your mount through the worst of this mud."

Aurore could have replied *I can ride perfectly well,* but she didn't. Instead, she yielded to his authority as though she were some helpless young chit, when even as a child she'd never acceded to the role. She *must* be in dire need of sleep, she decided, when she was too enervated to assert herself on so trivial a matter.

Not that she would be retiring early tonight either, she thought with an inward groan. General Osten-

Sacken always insisted she come to dine when she visited her brother. But immediately after dinner, she intended to go back to the room she rented in the only hotel that hadn't been damaged by the Allied bombardment and promptly go to bed.

Which thought should *not* have invoked images of her powerful, strapping Tatar joining her there. Good heavens! This was not the time to be contemplating an amorous rendezvous! In all seriousness, she *had* to resist his preposterous allure, *control* her aberrant, outrageous desires and *stay* on task. She was in Sevastopol not only to visit Etienne but to do her duty for France.

Tired or not, weariness notwithstanding, Gazi's great beauty aside, she *would* remember her obligations and responsibilities.

Even as Aurore was constraining her improper impulses, a similar scenario was playing itself out in Hugh's brain. He, too, chided himself for his folly. He was in Sevastopol to reconnoiter the town—in his case, for the British Secret Service. Raglan required definitive numbers on troop and battery strength, ammunition supplies, the morale of the Russian army.

He could not even consider being diverted from the task before him.

No matter how tempting the lady.

Chapter

2

On the ride to Sevastopol Hugh and Aurore had sufficient time to regain their composure. Both were fully engaged in other enterprises. Neither could afford to be distracted by frivolous pursuits. And riding separately as they were, impractical desires were more easily curtailed.

The road improved as they neared the city, allowing them to ride side by side, but they took care to speak only of prosaic matters. The weather was discussed at length—the devastating winter, the more recent thaw, the pleasant prospect of spring. The state of the war came up of course—the continuing stalemate and hindrances; they agreed a speedy peace would be most welcome. But never once on the three miles into town did either even *hint* at anything of a personal nature.

When they reached Sevastopol, Aurore asked to be deposited at the coach maker. "The hospital is near Ischenko's shop," she said. "I can walk from there. If you wouldn't mind dropping my wine at the hotel, I'd much appreciate it. Do take a bottle for yourself. It's quite good."

"Thank you, I will," Hugh replied. "The hotel is on our way; it's no imposition. We have warehouse space near the docks," he added to the query in her gaze.

"You trade in Sevastopol regularly, then."

He smiled. "We trade wherever Russian officers need our goods."

"You travel at your own peril I expect, with the armies constantly on the move."

"We're simple traders. No one views us as dangerous. And at base, there are no guarantees in this war for anyone—anywhere. Even here as you can see." He raised his gloved hand to indicate the shelled buildings.

Aurore made a small moue. "How true."

"Might I offer you something from our stores for your brother?" he quickly interposed, changing the subject. Neither of them needed more reminders of this bloody conflict. "Some sweets, chocolate, tinned pate perhaps?"

"How nice of you, although you've done quite enough already."

"Nonsense. We've done nothing but offer you a ride into town. I have English candies and marzipan from France." He grinned. "They are both much sought after by my customers, alliances be damned."

"Actually," Aurore said, returning his smile, "my brother has been craving English marmalade, and since the war"—she shrugged—"it's been almost impossible to obtain."

"We might have some; we often do. I'll check with Cafer. He supervised the unloading of our last cargo at Kerch. If we have English marmalade, I'll see that some is delivered to the hotel."

"You have been most gracious. Everything is so difficult of late, it seems," she murmured. "Although I shouldn't complain when our soldiers are suffering such awful hardships."

"Spring is near. Warmer weather will help the troops in terms of comfort at least."

She was weary to death of this war, exhausted in spirit, and whether spring mattered at all in the grand scheme of things she was not at all certain. "I'm sure you're right," she politely replied, because this man was in no position to change the course of the war or cure her afflictions. "Ah, there it is," she added, pointing ahead to Ischenko's sign.

When they came to a halt a few moments later, the marquis quickly dismounted and moved to help Aurore alight. She'd already swung her leg over the saddle when he reached her side, and lifting his arms, he smiled up at her. "Last stop, Miss Clement."

He caught her under her arms as she slid from the saddle, although he was careful to hold her well away from his body.

For which she was vastly grateful. It was simple enough to be prudent from afar, but in close proximity to her handsome Tatar, it was quite a different matter. How strong he was, she thought, as he effortlessly held her at arm's length and carried her to the pavement. No doubt he was all hard, taut muscle beneath his sheepskin capote—an image of him sans coat and shirt suddenly leaping into her mind. Which *would not* do, she sternly reprimanded her wayward senses. How could she possibly allow herself to consider such wanton behavior when the world was literally going up in flames!

The moment her feet touched the ground, she immediately took a step back, intent on putting distance between herself and this provocative stranger. Why he struck her sensibilities so profoundly was unclear. She was not normally susceptible to male virility alone. A polite, well-mannered good-bye was in order, she concluded. And that would put an end to her untoward feelings. But while she uttered all the requisite courtesies and expressions of gratitude, embarrassingly, she delivered them in a breathless tumble of words.

Under his amused gaze, her voice trailed off, her embarrassment abruptly evaporated and she said with cool affront, "You find this entertaining?"

"At the risk of offending you further, I do." He grinned. "And I sincerely thank you for the pleasure." He dipped his head. "The war affords one few opportunities to smile."

Oh dear. How reasonable he sounded while she was behaving like some juvenile maiden just out of the nursery. "I've been under enormous stress. I have no other excuse for my rudeness." She half lifted one hand in propitiation. "Forgive me. These are trying times."

He looked at her for a moment as though debating his reply. "I suppose this is where I should say things will be better soon."

"And if I were five, I might believe you," she murmured, holding his gaze.

His heavy-lidded eyes narrowed. "But neither of us is naive."

"No."

His dark lashes drifted downward, almost completely shuttering his gaze. "Perhaps under different circumstances, we might . . ." This time it was his voice that trailed off.

The fatigue in his voice was unmistakable, but then he'd come from Perekop without stopping. "Perhaps we may meet again," she politely offered, knowing it wasn't likely.

"In better times, perhaps," he said with equal mendacity, bowing faintly.

A European gesture, she thought—that bow. But before she could speculate further on his effortless courtesy, he'd turned and walked away. Since she refused to act like some green young miss infatuated by a well-favored man, she would not watch him ride off, she told herself. And she didn't. Or almost didn't. Just as she crossed the threshold of Ischenko's shop, she shot a quick look over her shoulder.

He lifted his hand in the merest wave.

Which was no reason for her heart to begin beating like a drum. No reason at all. But he'd looked back too, she thought, smiling to herself. Wasn't that somehow gratifying?

As usual, Mr. Ischenko was accommodating in all things, and thoughts of stunning men soon were displaced by affairs of more immediate import. Yes, he had a replacement wheel, the coach maker assured her. Yes, he would see that it was sent out immediately. No, she mustn't worry. Ibrahim would be back to the city with her carriage in short order.

She left for the hospital, her feelings buoyed, the problem of the carriage alleviated. But before she'd walked more than a block, she came upon a newly bombed building and brutal reality instantly dampened her spirits. The apartment block she'd passed yesterday was now in ruins—only black, smoldering debris remained. And as if she wasn't anxious enough about Etienne's safety, on nearing the hospital, she saw that the small ministry building next door had also been hit by mortar and cannon during the night.

Perhaps the time had come to move Etienne despite his condition, she nervously thought. His lodgings were becoming increasingly vulnerable to artillery attack.

A short time later, walking down the hospital corridor, Aurore stopped a Sister of Mercy to inquire whether she'd heard anything pertaining to an evacuation of the hospital.

"No, my dear. It's impossible to leave in any event," one of Grand Duchess Elena Pavlovna's ladies replied matter-of-factly. "There is nowhere to go. Simferopol is filled to overflowing with wounded, and our patients would never survive a longer journey."

Florence Nightingale was not alone in her efforts to aid injured soldiers. Both France and Russia also had charitable organizations that supplied battlefield nurses, women from all classes joining the cause. "I wish it were not so, of course," the young noblewoman added. "We are all anxious about the shelling."

"My brother is lying abed here," Aurore said, unnerved by the destruction she observed. "I'm beginning to fear for his safety."

"My brother is a patient here as well," the Sister of Mercy gently replied. "We all pray that the war will be over soon. Now, if you'll excuse me." The nurse had dealt with distrait relatives before. One was polite, but with so many wounded requiring assistance, it was impossible to allay every fear.

Standing in the hallway of what had once been the

Admiralty Palace, Aurore watched the young noble-woman hurry away, the answers she'd received disconcerting at best, and more aptly frightening. The cavernous building was filled to overflowing with maimed and dying men, the sights and sounds and smells a veritable glimpse into hell. And apparently there was no escape for them from the constant shelling—and perhaps annihilation.

What insanity drove men to engage in war, she wondered, miserable and sick at heart. To what purpose were all these young soldiers dying?

There was no rational answer, of course. The troops were fodder to what were characterized as grand and noble principles. When in fact those principles were more pertinently imperialistic aims fueled by male egos.

At least she was helping to expedite an end to this bloody conflict. Although her reasons were purely personal.

She wanted Etienne safe, well and home again.

She wanted to tend her vineyards once more and see the barren wastes surrounding Sevastopol restored to their former fruitfulness. Every tree had been cut down for firewood, every grapevine and root dug up to fuel soldiers' fires. Not even a single blade of grass remained on what once had been a lush, fertile land.

And for what, she bitterly thought.

Further reflections on the evils of war would have to wait, however. She'd reached Etienne's room. Pausing for a moment in the corridor, she drew in a small breath, forced her mouth into a credible smile and reminded herself that at least Etienne still lived. Then, exhaling softly, she pushed open the door and walked in. "How are you feeling today?" she brightly inquired, steeling herself, as usual, against the shock of her brother's paleness and emaciation.

"I am quite recovered," Etienne said, smiling faintly in return.

"He be eating right well, Excellency," one of the elderly women Aurore had hired to care for her brother declared, speaking in Russian.

"How nice to hear." She offered the woman a grateful look before turning back to her brother. "I brought you fresh foodstuffs, darling, although the carriage broke down on that awful road, so it will be a few hours until our supplies arrive. Ibrahim should be here soon, though. Has the doctor been in today?"

"Indeed, Excellency." Etienne's caretaker answered for her patient. "He was here not ten minutes ago. It was that foreign fellow—one of the Americans."

"Ah, very good. The Americans seem competent enough," Aurore remarked, slipping off her gloves. The United States while ostensibly neutral in the war was dedicated to the Russian cause. Sixty doctors had come from America to serve in the Crimea. "If you'd like to take your tea now, babushka, I'll watch over my brother."

Bowing and offering profuse thanks, the elderly woman backed from the room.

"So, the doctor looked in on you?" Aurore slid her coat down her arms and tossed it on a small table. "Tell me what he said." Pulling up a chair beside Etienne's cot, she sat down.

"Nothing much. Same old thing mostly."

She eyed him suspiciously; his tone was evasive. "Could you be more specific?"

"It's nothing, Rory, really." He tried to shrug but grimaced instead. "You know how doctors are."

"Something's wrong; now, tell me what it is." She held his gaze. "Tell me *exactly* what the doctor said." She spoke in her stern older sister voice.

Etienne exhaled softly. "The bayonet wound in my leg. He mentioned something about an infection."

"An *infection!*" Panic spiked through Aurore's brain.

"I'm sure it's nothing unusual."

That it wasn't unusual was true. That infection killed more patients than actual wounds was also true. This was the *worst* possible news! Absolutely the worst! An infection could very well mean an eventual amputation, if not a slow lingering death. Etienne *must* be removed from this fetid cell straight away. She should have insisted on it long ago, regardless of his condition. "The moment your nurse returns, I'm going to call on General Osten-Sacken. He must give you permission to leave Sevastopol."

"Even if he does, he won't let me go home. You know that."

Since Etienne was a prisoner of war, she understood that the general, amiable as he might be, could not authorize her brother's return home. "Then we'll go to Simferopol where the other prisoners are sent." Aurore spoke with deliberate cheer. "I'll make arrangements; we'll find quarters outside the hospital and you'll recover in no time."

"You make it sound simple when you know it isn't," Etienne murmured. "I'm not alone in wishing to leave this place. And you know what the roads are like. Not to mention, the facilities in Simferopol are stretched thin, lodging is impossible to find and—"

"Nonsense," Aurore interposed, dismissing her brother's reservations with a smile and a flick of her fingers, resolved to move heaven and earth to save him. "We'll leave tomorrow if not sooner—you just see."

"Somehow you almost make me think it's possible."

"Of course it's possible," she firmly declared, terrified to see tears well up in her brother's eyes. He knew, she thought, how perilous his case.

"You've been an angel in not upbraiding me for enlisting." His smile was tremulous. "Not that I don't deserve it."

"You joined with the most honorable intentions, darling. Why would I scold you?" It was useless now to say she would have locked him in his room if she'd known his plans. "Papa would have been proud," she said instead. And indeed he would have, she knew. Her parents owned a small villa in Paris, the family's roots still very much French. "Let me get you some tea or wine or something sweet," she said, wishing to change the conversation to something less grave.

"A glass of wine—and some morphine too. My leg is giving me a bit of trouble," he admitted.

Suppressing her alarm, she walked to a small cupboard that contained a minimum larder, poured a glass of wine, measured out some morphine powder and sprinkled it into the liquid. Returning to her brother's side, she helped him drink it down, then chatted inconsequentially until the drug took effect. The moment her brother's eyes closed in sleep she exhaled in relief. At least his pain had been temporarily remedied—although temporary was the operative word. Morphine would not cure his infection. Healing his wounds would require conditions more sanitary than those in Sevastopol, along with good food and vigilant care. All of which she was determined to give her brother.

While waiting for the nurse to return, Aurore paced the room and made plans. How best to plead her case to the general, she reflected, even while silently urging Ibrahim to all speed. And where were the likeliest available lodgings in Simferopol? She'd narrowed down a list of acquaintances she intended to petition for rooms to a manageable number when the nurse appeared. "My brother has just taken a draught of morphine," she immediately explained. "I shall return in the morning if not before." Quickly slipping on her coat and gloves, she thanked the nurse, took her leave and hurried toward the palace that had been appropriated by the Russian general staff for their headquarters.

Chapter
3

"I'm very sorry, mademoiselle. The general won't be back to the city until late in the day," an ADC politely explained, wishing he might be of more help to the enchanting Miss Clement. Every man on the staff was half in love with her. "If you like, I could send a note to your hotel on his return."

She debated asking to see another officer, but she knew her request required the highest authority and that meant Osten-Sacken. He was in command of Sevastopol. "Thank you. I would appreciate receiving word as soon as you may."

There was nothing more to do after that but go to her hotel room and impatiently await her summons. Putting the delay to good use, she took the opportunity to have a hot bath brought up. Readying herself for her interview with the general, she took special care with her appearance. Well aware that a woman's beauty advanced any appeal for help, she wanted to look her best.

Failure was not an option.

Once bathed, wrapped in a warm cashmere dressing gown, she curled up on a chair before the fire and waited. She not only maintained an apartment at the hotel but kept a minimum wardrobe here as well since dining with the general had become habitual. She was in no position to refuse his invitations. Nor did she actually wish to, since conversation at dinner was often of acute interest to French intelligence.

Sometime later, she woke to a sharp rapping on her door. On opening the door, she was handed a note by one of the hotel staff. Shutting the door a moment later, she immediately ripped open the envelope, scanned the bold print and smiled. Her plans were *en train*.

The general apologized for keeping her waiting and invited her to dinner. He was looking forward to seeing her again, he gallantly wrote. Dinner was at nine. They would have time for a private conversation beforehand. He would expect her at eight.

He wrote like he spoke, with the brevity and authority of a man familiar with command. She was surprised to experience a rare sense of apprehension as she set aside the note. But then why wouldn't she? Etienne's life was at stake. It was only natural to feel a certain anxiety. This was not just another dinner. And regardless how agreeable the general may have been in the past, tonight she would be asking a considerable favor of him.

With the situation crucial, she knew that she must choose her gown with care. Normally, the thought of plying her feminine wiles would have been distasteful, but this was not the night for scruples.

She had always been vastly independent, more familiar with giving orders than petitioning favors, and since her parents' death, she had taken on even more responsibility—overseeing the entire vineyard and wine-making operation while Etienne had amused himself with his friends.

Not that she had minded her brother's disinterest. In truth, she enjoyed the challenge of competing in a man's world.

But General Osten-Sacken wasn't interested in her wine business or in Etienne's health for that matter. He enjoyed her company for purely selfish reasons. In the midst of battle, a pretty woman offered forgetfulness, however brief, from the unpleasantness of war. And tonight, Aurore was more than willing to fulfill that curative role.

Her cream lace gown would best suit the occasion, she decided. The bouffant confection was innocently beguiling, while the low decolletage appealed to baser male instincts. The juxtaposition of sweet incorruptibility and a subtle invitation to ravishment was particularly apt in a war zone.

Although events tonight had nothing to do with metaphor.

Brute reality held sway instead.

And she was quite ready to do whatever was required of her to save her brother's life.

Chapter

4

She had been right about the gown.

The general was thoroughly enchanted, complimenting her at some length on how she brightened the room, the evening and in particular his spirits.

Striking while the iron was hot, perhaps attending to her nervous fears as well, she put her petition to him without delay. He immediately acquiesced to her request as though she'd asked him for the merest bagatelle.

"Of course, my dear. You have my permission to take your brother to Simferopol. Are you happy now?"

His smile was avuncular or maybe she just hoped it was. But she needed more than his promise, so she pressed on. "Would you mind signing a release order to that effect?" she prettily inquired, feeling like an actress on stage—albeit in a role of prime importance.

"Of course, of course. Sit down, my dear." He motioned to an empire settee upholstered in crimson silk. "Let me ease your mind at once."

She wasn't the first petitioner he'd dealt with, she understood. He was familiar with pleas and entreaties. What quid pro quo did he normally require, she wondered. Taking a seat on the settee, she folded her hands in her lap, sat up very straight and prepared herself for any possible demand.

He wrote the release order with dispatch, handed it to her without ceremony, then walked over to a tray set with glasses and champagne.

While his back was turned, she allowed herself to feel the smallest sense of elation before folding the paper and putting it away in her reticule. Step one accomplished, she thought, although she understood Etienne's health was still very much in jeopardy. The moment she could escape this evening's entertainment, she would fly to the hospital and relay the good news to her brother.

The general returned a moment later with two glasses of champagne. Handing one to Aurore, he sat down beside her—the settee creaking under his weight—and took her hand in his.

Her heart began beating like a drum. He was very large—a tall, blond German from Riga—a disciplined, conscientious officer loyal to the tsar. Overcome with trepidation, not sure what was about to transpire—he had never before held her hand—she smiled up at him.

He seemed not to notice either her trepidation or her tentative smile, his gaze unfocused—or inwardly focused on some cerebral scene. "Your pale lacey gown reminds me of summer nights at home," he murmured, a note of wistful longing in his voice.

"The sun never sets in midsummer; we always linger late over dinner, drinking champagne. You can hear the birch leaves rustling in the breeze, the scent of wildflowers fills the air, the Baltic waters glisten in the distance . . ." He softly sighed, and with that sigh abruptly returned to reality. His eyes were suddenly unclouded. "Unfortunately, we will be here next summer—God willing of course," he added with a grimace, smiling a second later, apparently recalling his duties as host and garrison commander. "Forgive my melancholy. I spent the day surveying our defenses." Releasing her hand, he absently patted it before lifting his glass to his mouth and draining it. "The siege is taking its toll," he bluntly declared, setting his glass aside. "The men work tirelessly, repairing the ramparts each night only to have them destroyed again the next day. They are willing and loyal to a man, but"—he shrugged—"a prolonged siege is devastating to morale. There is no glory in it."

"As a woman, I find no glory in war at all," Aurore submitted.

His smile was tolerant. "What woman does, my dear. Come now, drink your champagne. I intend to have another." Picking up his glass, he rose to his feet, the many jeweled and enameled medals gracing his white dress uniform twinkling in the light. "And by the time our guests arrive, we or at least I," he added, smiling over his shoulder as he walked away, "shall be in a more festive mood."

Was that the end of it? Had she gained the release letter she needed for nothing more than a pleasantry or two and a willing ear? Or was she expected to stay the night once dinner was over?

"Come, come, my dear. How can we forget all this misery surrounding us if we're completely sober?" he sportively noted on his return with a glance at her undrunk champagne.

In the event she would have something she wished to forget by morning, Aurore quickly lifted her glass to her mouth and drank a goodly portion.

As the general poured them more champagne a few minutes later, she covertly touched the little jeweled reticule hanging from her wrist. The rustle of paper inside her talisman.

Regardless of what the night might bring, she had what she'd come for.

Chapter

5

Dessert was being served when a servant swung open the double doors leading into the dining room and a stunning couple walked in. The man wore Circassian garb, his tunic black like his hair; the blonde clinging to his arm was splendid in a figure-hugging crimson gown—quite out of fashion but breathtaking on her shapely form.

"Gazi, my friend!" the general boomed, smiling widely. "I was beginning to despair of your company tonight. I see you've found the lovely countess." He waved them forward. "Come in, come in, my darlings!"

Aurore watched the man who had escorted her into town that morning cross the polished parquet floor, the dazzling Countess Tatischev on his arm all curvaceous pulchritude and pale beauty. That the couple had just recently risen from bed was almost palpable. Zania's adoring glances directed at her partner, the slight flush on her cheeks, the mildly di-

sheveled state of both her and Gazi's hair, all testified
to the fact.

On their approach, had anyone been unsure of
their previous activities, that uncertainty was put to
rest as the faint whiff of sex pervaded the air.

"Malekov, Oblensky, make room for our guests."
The general snapped his fingers at the officers on his
right. "Two more chairs," he ordered, waving the servants forward.

While the officers moved and servants scurried
about arranging new table settings, the general introduced Gazi and the countess to those unfamiliar
with them. It was a large dinner party, several of the
guests were nonmilitary, but even then, very few were
strangers to the pair. Several in the assembly greeted
the couple with sportive comments; most of the dinner party apparently were friends of long standing.
When the general's round of introductions reached
Aurore, Gazi simply bowed and smiled. The countess
barely glanced her way.

Aurore acknowledged Gazi as blandly. Did his reti-
cence have to do with his lover's jealousy? Certainly
understandable; Zania was possessive.

Once the servants had readied their places, Darley
seated the countess next to the general and took his
chair beside her.

Since Aurore was at the general's left, she was directly across from the countess. It was nearly impossible to ignore Zania's large breasts almost spilling
over the top of her gown—which was the point of
that extremely low decolletage, Aurore suspected.
Her own neckline seemed almost prudish in contrast.

"I shan't ask what kept you," the general remarked,
smiling knowingly at Darley. "But rest assured, we are

gratified you have finally arrived." He waved a servant over to pour them champagne. "You are looking radiant, Zania, my dear—as usual. And you, Gazi"—he winked at the marquis—"have a smugness about you, I envy."

"While I envy you your local steam baths," Darley replied, his smile bland. "After a week on the road, I am quite refreshed."

The countess smothered a giggle.

Which inexplicably irritated Aurore. When it should not, she quickly reminded herself. How Gazi and the countess spent their time was none of her concern.

"The benefits of civilization are delightful, I agree," the general returned with masculine insinuation and a wink for good measure. "Now then," he briskly added, "since you've missed most of dinner, what would you two like to eat?"

At another giggle from the countess, Aurore suppressed a thoroughly unjustified pique. For heaven's sake, she silently expostulated, appalled at her unreasonable reaction—whatever the countess liked to eat *en flagrante delicto* was absolutely of no consequence to her.

"Something substantial—meat, fish," Darley replied, then glanced at the countess. "What would you like?"

"Whatever *you* like, darling."

Good God, must she flutter her lashes like she is batting away flies, Aurore disgustedly thought. Did the woman have no restraint?

Apparently not, Aurore soon discovered. While the other guests were served dessert and Darley and the countess were provided their choice of foods, the lovely Zania occupied her time between bites by rubbing up against her lover like a cat in heat.

Making a spectacle of herself, Aurore spleenishly decided.

Not that it mattered in the least, she sensibly noted, logic coming to the fore as it should. She and Gazi were the merest acquaintances, while he and Zania were, obviously, *extremely* good friends.

And should the general insist on more than simply holding her hand tonight, she would be facing much larger problems than whether Countess Tatischev was annoying or not. With that metaphorical dash of cold water reminding her of the seriousness of her situation, she dismissed the countess's behavior as irrelevant to more thorny issues.

As the hour advanced and the general consumed more and more champagne, he became increasingly flamboyant in his pronouncements: his soldiers were saints and heroes; his enemies Satan's legions; the stalwart men under his command would fight to the death with honor and courage; with God on her side, Mother Russia would be victorious. And periodically, between his bursts of patriotic grandiloquence, he would expansively exclaim that he loved and revered all his guests.

At which point, he'd reach over, grasp Aurore's hand, bring it to his lips and kiss her fingertips with smacking gusto.

The first time he did so, Aurore went rigid, although her smile gave nothing away. The high color on her cheeks might just as well have been excitement rather than shock.

Darley's gaze narrowed when the general first snatched up Aurore's hand, but he'd almost instantly rationalized away his displeasure. Why wouldn't the two be friendly? Miss Clement was beautiful, the general was powerful. He shouldn't have been surprised at their intimacy.

As the hours progressed, the general's attentions to Aurore became more and more presumptuous, but by then, the majority of the dinner guests were well into their cups and not inclined to take undue notice.

Aurore continued playing the role required of her, smiling appropriately, responding to the general's flirtation with urbane pleasantries, hiding her increasing dismay with aplomb. It appeared likely that Etienne's release form would require compensation after all, she noted. Not that she begrudged sacrificing herself to save her brother. Whatever was required of her, she would do.

But when the general was called away shortly after midnight to attend to some urgent matter and took his leave, Aurore experienced the most enormous relief. A huge weight was suddenly lifted from her shoulders; she could breathe freely again, the foreboding tension gripping her senses disappeared like dew under a hot sun.

After the fact, she came to realize how onerous it would have been to accede to the general's demands, how horrific. No matter her dutiful intent.

Having only very narrowly escaped disaster, she wished to flee—now, this instant, in the event the general returned. Abruptly rising to her feet, she politely made her excuses. "It's been a lovely evening," she said with a smile, her gaze sweeping the table, quickly skipping over Gazi and his companion who were engaged in whispered conversation. Or rather, the countess was leaning in close and he was politely listening. "But I have early appointments, so I bid you all good night."

Several officers immediately volunteered to escort her to the hotel, their offers rising in a clamorous chorus.

There was no way to graciously refuse. Nor did she wish to show preference for any one officer. As a result, she left with a considerable entourage.

There was safety in numbers, she concluded.

And after her close call, she was not about to put herself in jeopardy again.

In a very few hours, she and Etienne would be on the road to Simferopol.

Chapter

6

Darley found himself disturbed by the fact that Miss Clement was on her way to her hotel room surrounded by six young officers.

It was a gut feeling.

Thoroughly illogical.

Much like his reaction had been to the general dancing attendance on Aurore at dinner.

He had no idea why the thought of Miss Clement's numerous admirers irked him. He was not by nature a possessive man, as evidenced by his years of wandering the globe with no itinerary and no strings attached.

So why this blind impulse to exercise some bloody suzerainty over the lovely Miss Clement?

There was no reasonable explanation other than that which prompted his wanderlust: an appetite for life and, above all, a willful proclivity to assuage his desires.

Like now.

Turning to the countess, he offered her his most winning smile. "I'm afraid duty calls, my dear. I promised my men I'd help them unload our supplies and"—his brows flickered in pointed significance—"as you know, I have been enjoying your company instead. My thanks for a most delightful evening. May I send someone to see you home?"

"You're not leaving *now?*" she hissed, her eyes snapping with affront.

"I'm sorry. I have to." Leaning over, he kissed her lightly on the cheek. "There now, my sweet, don't pout," he murmured, but rather than soothe her irritation, he rose to his feet and said to the other guests, "Much as I hate to abandon the pleasure of your company, my friends, I'm afraid I have business commitments." He smiled. "I doubt my absence will mar the festivities with the general's fully stocked cellar at your disposal. So *bonne nuit mes amis.*" Shoving his chair back, he turned and walked away.

Not unexpectedly, Zania took issue with his sudden departure and hastily followed in his wake.

Once the servants closed the doors behind them and they were alone in the hallway, he turned to face her wrath with patient forbearance. "My leaving has nothing to do with you," he explained. Which was true. "I simply have to take care of some business affairs." Which was not true. "Come, now, darling—"

"How dare you *walk out!*" she petulantly interposed, her gaze sullen. "You embarrassed me in front of everyone!"

"They were all so intoxicated no one even noticed," Darley countered. "But even if someone had, I mentioned that I had business to attend to. That's simple enough to understand."

"Well, *I* don't understand!" she snapped. "You didn't have business to attend to a few hours ago!"

"Actually I did and now I can no longer ignore it," he tactfully replied. "I'll be back in a few days, my pet. I'll stay with you longer on my return." He dropped a light kiss on her nose. "And I promise when I come back, you may order me about with impunity as long as you wish."

She gazed up at him from under her lashes for a considering moment. "Do you mean it?"

"Of course," he lied. He didn't know from day to day if he'd live, but Zania wasn't interested in larger world issues, so he chose the path of least resistance.

"You really promise?" she purred.

"Absolutely." And honestly, if he survived to return to Sevastopol, he'd be happy to entertain her. She was a passionate little minx, and since her elderly husband had died, she had been enjoying her freedom with wild abandon.

"Oh, very well," she muttered with a pretty pout. "I suppose I shall have to settle for Major Count Oblensky tonight. He's not nearly as talented as you though."

Darley didn't rise to the bait; whomever Zania slept with was no concern of his. "I sincerely apologize for having to leave. Believe me, if I didn't have my men waiting for me, I'd willingly accompany you home." He was tempted to start backing away, but this near to escape he didn't dare antagonize her afresh.

Softly sighing, Zania waved him off. "Go, then, you lovely scoundrel." She smiled. "But I will expect you to be very accommodating on your return."

"With pleasure," he gallantly replied.

She lifted her chin in a huffy little gesture. "Think

of me with Oblensky tonight, Gazi, and suffer the consequences of your actions."

"I will be desolate, my dear," he softly remarked, hoping his expression was suitably remorseful.

"You don't look desolate," she said with a little sniff, and turned away.

A shame he wasn't a better actor. In the event she had some more pithy words for him, he waited until she re-entered the dining room before leaving. As a rule, he avoided antagonizing women. And with Zania, there was even more reason for caution. She was volatile and quick tempered—more significantly, she was staying at the only serviceable hotel in town.

He would have to make certain he didn't run into her later.

With luck, she might spend the night in Oblensky's quarters.

After swiftly making his way to the hotel, he spoke briefly with the concierge and left him a quickly scribbled note he wished conveyed to Cafer. Then, moving into the ornate lobby graced with soaring malachite pillars and towering palms, he settled into a chair that afforded him a clear view of the wide, main staircase.

Glancing at his watch, he calculated the amount of time that had transpired since Aurore and her escort had left the dinner party. Not that he was *absolutely* certain of what he was going to do. He was, however, rather sure of what he *wished* to do.

Now, whether his plans prospered or not depended on six officers, one lady and her inclinations and proclivities.

At least in terms of the general, he was quite confident she'd not favored his attentions. Her smiles had been strained, the tension in her shoulders obvious to anyone less drunk than the general, while the flaring color on her cheeks when Osten-Sacken kissed her fingers was, to a discerning eye, genuine alarm.

On the other hand, the officers who'd escorted her back to the hotel were young, attractive men. Perhaps she would respond more favorably to their attentions.

Whether she would or not was the question.

Since he'd not met any of the general's staff on his brief walk from headquarters to the hotel, her plentiful escort must still be upstairs with her. A disconcerting thought, he decided, although, through force of habit, he wasn't inclined to parse the full extent of his feelings.

The impression he had of her after their ride into town might be wrong. He may have misread their mutual attraction. Also, it was possible that, attraction aside, she didn't fraternize with Tatars. Such prejudices were common enough. She may favor handsome, young Russian officers, all of whom she could be entertaining at this very moment.

He hadn't realized how unpleasant the notion was. Scowling faintly, he slid into a slouching sprawl, stretched out his legs and sullenly contemplated his options. He tried to be realistic; after all, he barely knew this woman. That he was feeling like some sulky adolescent was completely inane. Since when did it matter whom he fucked?

As he calculated the decade and more since it hadn't mattered, two of Osten-Sacken's officers suddenly appeared on the staircase.

His mood abruptly lightened.

At least it did to a marginal extent as he watched

the officers reach the bottom of the stairs and stroll away. Unfortunately, there were still four men upstairs with her.

His mind racing, he shoved himself upright in the chair. Had he judged her incorrectly? In these turbulent times, people faced more than the usual moral quandaries. Lives hung in the balance, normal conventions were cast to the winds. Was she living for the moment like so many in this city under siege?

His brows suddenly rose. *Well, well, well—look at that.* Another pair of officers were smiling and chatting with each other on their way downstairs. Apparently Miss Clement was experienced enough to dismiss her suitors without them taking umbrage. He smiled. She wasn't a tyro then. How nice. Not to mention, two more players had exited the game.

His percentages were improving.

And should all his competition fall away, he had a feeling that Miss Clement would favor his suit. Correction—he was feeling more and more confident that she would.

She had resisted temptation this morning for whatever reason.

As had he. For equally unknown reasons.

She had also avoided meeting his gaze at dinner—always a good sign. He in turn had enjoyed her presence across the table and had taken every opportunity to observe her. Which no doubt contributed to both his impetuous pursuit and his champing impatience.

His gaze narrowed. Another officer was descending the stairs.

Bloody hell.

So one lucky winner remained after all, he thought, uttering a litany of expletives under his breath. He was thoroughly pissed when he had no right to be.

When she could take whomever she wished to bed. Christ, get a grip, he silently commanded. He hardly knew her, while many of these officers might know her very well.

The thought about exactly *how* well further rankled him.

Coming to his feet in a surge of anger, he suddenly found himself at a loss. Deprived and usurped, frustratingly routed, he could go back to Zania he supposed, but the thought displeased him. He could call on any number of other women he knew despite the late hour, but he took no pleasure in that option either. If he was sensible, he would go to his apartment and get some sleep. He could use it.

Exhaling in indecision, he was reminding himself of his busy schedule tomorrow when out of the corner of his eye he caught a glimpse of a white dress uniform. Looking up, he saw Lieutenant Benkendorf standing at the top of the stairs, his mouth pursed—clearly hesitating.

Darley stood utterly still, suppressing an almost overwhelming impulse to rush up the stairs and carry Benkendorf down. *Go, go, go,* he silently urged.

A small smile slowly began to lift the corners of his mouth.

The lieutenant was moving down the stairs.

The marquis watched Benkendorf's slow descent, watched him stroll across the lobby, felt an elation out of all proportion to the mundane event as the lieutenant exited the hotel.

So the lady *was* discriminating. Or maybe just tired.

The question was which or how tired, exactly.

He was also curious to see whether he'd correctly interpreted her interest in him. He prided himself on reading nuance in a woman; maybe he wanted to prove himself right. But matters of nuance and success aside, more elemental desires were primarily at play. She excited him. Perhaps his first sight of her standing in that lush sable coat had struck some involuntary, carnal chord.

He wanted to have sex with her, no question about it.

Then and now.

Would she throw him out on his ear like all the rest, he wondered as he moved toward the stairs.

Chapter

7

Darley had almost reached the base of the staircase when Cafer caught up with him.

"I brought two different kinds," he said, handing Darley a small parcel tied with twine. "I hope the lady's brother enjoys them."

The marquis smiled. "I'll let you know."

"Kotchubey is going to take almost everything we brought in, so don't worry about getting up at dawn. He was so short of inventory he was waiting at the warehouse. Half our supplies are already on his store shelves."

"You kept our bribe materials?"

"Naturally."

"Sorry. Lack of sleep."

"You should think about getting some rest."

"Maybe later."

"She's very beautiful, I agree."

Darley shrugged faintly. "Who knows, she might not be interested. I could be back soon."

Cafer grinned. "So humble, my friend."

"There's always a first time," the marquis replied, grinning back. "Speaking of first times, the Russians have some green recruits coming down from Moscow. Osten-Sacken expects them in two weeks. Four thousand, he thought. The conversation at dinner was informative as usual. We'll get a dispatch to Raglan tomorrow. Now, if you'll excuse me, I'd like to see if Miss Clement is in a friendly mood before I fall asleep on my feet."

"You could come back to the apartment and actually sleep."

Darley's eyebrows lifted.

Cafer Giray's white teeth flashed against his bronzed skin. "You don't have to fuck them all." He could have ridden with Ghengis Khan, his dress unchanged from centuries past, his lean form taut and honed from living on horseback.

"You should talk."

"It's a busy day tomorrow—that's all."

"I know. Don't worry."

"Just a reminder—first thing in the morning, I'm taking tobacco and chocolate to the outer ramparts. I heard they're running out of canister shot. I'll see what I can find out."

"I'll be back by eight if not sooner. It all depends on Miss Clement's inclinations."

"I don't doubt you can persuade her to indulge them."

Darley held up crossed fingers, then turned and walked away.

* * *

For a small gratuity the concierge had given him directions to Aurore's suite, and short moments later Darley stood outside her door.

He lifted his hand to knock, then lowered it, Cafer's words about indiscriminate fucking suddenly giving him pause. Was he unnecessarily compromising Miss Clement? Was he so tired he was misinterpreting what he perceived as her interest?

Was this a mistake?

As he was unaccountably debating the moralities, the door suddenly opened and he came face to face with Aurore. She was holding a fur-lined velvet cape over one arm and didn't look as surprised as he.

"I thought I heard someone walk up," she said.

"And you open the door for just anyone?"

"Why wouldn't I? Only my friends know my suite number."

He understood from her sardonic tone that he did not fall under her description of a friend. "Forgive my incivility in arriving unannounced." He held out the small package. "But I found some marmalade for your brother and wished you to have it."

She gave him an assessing look. "That was fast."

He could say the same about her change of clothes; she'd had little time to discard her evening wear and don this simple gown. "One of my men brought the package to the hotel," he said instead, careful to keep his gaze well above her breasts since the soft cashmere of her gown was tantalizingly clingy.

"I see."

Her tone was unequivocally cool. Apparently, he *had* been wrong about Miss Clement's interest in him. "Please take this with my compliments," he murmured, pressing the package into her hand, well aware that the rules of chance were hit and miss. "And I apologize for calling so late. I should have left the marmalade with the concierge." He took a step back.

She held up her hand to stop him but didn't immediately speak, as though she were weighing various possibilities. When she finally spoke, she did so with a degree of hesitation. "Thank you—for your . . . thoughtfulness. I know Etienne will enjoy the marmalade." She seemed to have made some decision, for her voice took on a new certainty. "Would you like to come in for a cup of tea?"

Not really, he thought. "Thank you, I would," he said instead.

She waved him in. "Excuse my initial rudeness, but I'm very tired."

"I'm in complete sympathy," he said, walking through the door and closing it behind him. "I haven't slept in days."

"So we may be impolite together."

"Anything you wish, of course."

She looked up, about to drop her cape on a chair. "How practiced you are, Gazi. But then Zania doesn't like amateurs, does she?"

"I'm sure I wouldn't know."

"What a gentleman." She smiled for the first time. "Sit. I'll get us tea." Turning away and moving toward a samovar on a table, she said over her shoulder, "Having escaped the general's clutches, I was about to visit my brother. I have excellent news for him. Would you like to hear it?"

Her voice suddenly held a distinct buoyancy—almost a giddiness. "Tell me," he murmured, standing where he was, surveying her cautiously from under his lashes. Her moods shifted wildly—from her previous cool assessment to a polite civility to now, this patent jubilation. "Good news in these difficult times is worth hearing," he said, wondering how unstable she might turn out to be.

"The general has signed a release for my brother! Isn't that wonderful? Tomorrow I take him to Simferopol and once there he will recover completely!"

An unmistakable note of hysteria rang through her voice. "That's excellent news." Gratified there was an explanation for her mood swings, Darley suspected her brother's condition had turned grave. He also suspected she'd anticipated the general requiring something of her for his favor—her phrase *escaped his clutches* pointed. He inwardly winced; his intentions were no better. "Allow me to offer you my lodgings in Simferopol," he said, as though in atonement for his iniquitous impulses. "They are clean and fully staffed."

Setting down the teacup in her hand, she turned around in a swish of petticoats. "Truly, you have lodgings we can use?" she whispered, her eyes filling with tears. "I have been beside myself with fear that we should be forced to stay in hospital there."

"Rest assured, my home is at your disposal," he replied, all well-mannered grace. Although, the thought of Miss Clement in his home was certainly not to be discounted in terms of a further friendship.

Her bottom lip trembled. "I am so very grateful for"—her voice broke, she swallowed hard. "Etienne *must* get better—oh dear," she whispered, putting her hand over her mouth in an attempt to contain her emotions.

Fruitlessly, as it turned out.

She burst into tears.

Even discounting the general's unwanted attentions, Darley understood she'd been under a tremendous strain all evening. He also understood that he was in the wrong place at the wrong time—the seriousness of her brother's condition not conducive to a seduction. Furthermore, women's tears made him uncomfortable. "Please, Miss Clement," he restively murmured, "there is no need to cry. I am delighted to be of assistance. I'm sure your brother will soon be fine," he added, shifting on his feet with unease. "Don't agitate yourself unduly. All will be well."

"I'm—sorry." Aurore hiccuped between sobs. "I don't—mean . . . to embarrass you. I know—how men . . . dislike tears. But—I'm . . . so worried . . . about Etienne. I'd take him—away . . . right now . . . if we could . . . manage—the road . . . at night." Her breathless little sobs punctuated with erratic little gasps rhythmically lifted her lush breasts, the soft flesh rising and falling with infinitesimal quivers.

Witnessing the delectable sight at such close range was doing disastrous things to Darley's self-control. He reminded himself that the timing was inopportune. Seducing a woman in tears over her dying brother was completely improper. So he did what courtesy required. "Come, Miss Clement," he murmured, reluctantly moving toward her, "everything will look better in the morning, I assure you." No one wanted to hear the truth at a time like this. Taking one of her clenched fists in his hand on reaching her, he offered a further platitude in his effort to offer comfort. "Remember, it always seems darkest before the dawn." After which gross dishonesty he found himself at a loss. It wouldn't be proper to take her in his arms, although he was sorely tempted. Nor could he conjure up any more hollow phrases considering the possible dire state of her brother's health.

As the silence lengthened, he considered how best to extricate himself from this increasingly awkward situation. On the other hand, the longer he stood with her hand in his, with the sweet scent of Parma violet wafting into his nostrils, her vulnerability perversely nullifying whatever virtue still remained in him, the less inclined he found himself to leave.

Aurore was not immune to Gazi's discomfort. He had courteously come to her aid, offering her assistance of the most material kind both this morning and now. The least she could do was pull herself together and ease his embarrassment. "Let me . . . get you—that tea," she said with a sniffle, gazing up at him with a shaky smile.

"I'd rather have a drink, if you don't mind," he said, releasing her hand. Seriously, he needed a stiff drink with his reason and desire so sharply at odds. This was definitely *not* the seduction he'd had in mind.

With another sniffle, she pointed to a table holding decanters and glasses. "Please—help yourself . . ."

"If you think it's getting too late," he murmured, not sure if he was gallant or still looking for an excuse to flee.

"I'd like company for a few minutes"—she smiled again with a trifle more assurance—"if you don't mind."

"Not at all." What else could he say? "May I pour you a drink?" Maybe it would help her stop crying. Or maybe he wanted to stay whether she was crying or not.

"Perhaps a glass of sherry," she murmured, dropping into a chair with a small sigh. "I apologize again. I am not normally so unsteady."

Nor was he normally so selfless in overlooking his own pleasures. It must be the war. "You have every reason to be upset," he graciously replied.

"I'll have a drink and rest for a moment. Then I'll go to the hospital and give Etienne the good news."

"I'll walk with you if you wish. You shouldn't be alone at night."

The unintentional implication in Darley's last sentence brought a moment of silence—both struck by the significant phrasing at the last.

Not to mention, Darley was incredulous he'd even said what he'd said.

She should refuse his offer of an escort, Aurore thought. She was much too intrigued by him and life *did not* allow such frivolities at the moment.

While Darley was wondering if he should apologize for his slip of the tongue, Aurore was in the process of ignoring the little voice inside her head telling her to resist.

"I'd appreciate your escort," she said. "Thank you."

Darley was gratified out of all proportion for her simple reply. He didn't know why, nor did he care to question his feelings. The grim reality of war made one less prone to analyze happiness when it came your way. "In that case," he said, pouring her sherry, "I look forward to meeting your brother. I expect he'll be delighted with your news."

"Indeed he will." And for the first time all evening Aurore felt a real, true unmitigated joy. The kind that warmed her down to her toes and gave her hope. "If Etienne's awake, you must tell him of your trading routes," she cheerfully remarked. "He knows the countryside much better than I since he and his friends were forever riding off to one race or amusement."

"While you were the sensible older sister, I gather," he said, walking toward her with their drinks in hand.

"Not entirely sensible," she lightly replied.

"Under different circumstances, that would be excellent news," he drawled.

Taking her sherry from him, she dipped her head in acknowledgment. "If only things were as they once were," she murmured. Exhaling softly, she lifted her glass and smiled. "To better times, Gazi."

"To better times," he agreed, dropping into a chair opposite her. "Now tell me about your vineyard," he suggested, determined to keep the conversation innocuous. He preferred seeing her less agitated, her tears gone, her smile radiant once again.

He particularly liked that she was smiling at him.

Chapter

8

Etienne was awake when they arrived, his sleep more restless of late with his wounds festering. But he took one look at his sister and smiled. "The general must have been amenable. You're grinning from ear to ear."

"He was *most* amenable. As you can see I am quite giddy. We leave for Simferopol in the morning."

Etienne smiled widened. "So Osten-Sacken succumbed to your charm."

"He'd better. You know how many of his tedious dinner parties I have been obliged to attend." That she gathered information for the French army at those dinners was unknown to her brother. "Darling, I'd like you to meet the man who helped me this morning when the carriage broke down." She beckoned Darley forward from the doorway. "Etienne, this is Gazi Maksoud, Gazi, my brother. He was at the general's dinner party tonight and kindly offered me his escort."

"A pleasure to meet you," Darley said with a small bow, even while he wondered why he'd never seen Aurore at Osten-Sacken's parties before. Had their schedules simply been at odds or were things not as they seemed?

"Etienne, Mr. Maksoud trades over much of south Russia," Aurore went on to explain. "I told him that you were familiar with every village of the Crimea. You may also thank him for some of your favorite marmalade."

"Thank you, indeed. Breakfast will be more satisfying now. I don't suppose you know the banker Alexios Pallas from Bahcesaray?"

"We do business from time to time," Darley blandly acknowledged, when in fact Alexios was one of his informants.

"Pallas has been kind enough to cover some of my racing bets." Etienne glanced at Aurore and grinned. "Until such a time as I was able to convince my sister to release my quarterly allowance early."

Aurore smiled. "Etienne is much adored by the betting establishment."

"Aren't we all," Darley said, benignly. "Which tracks do you prefer?"

The men discovered that they were both partial to the race meets at Karasu Bazaar and had been there at the same time last summer just prior to the Allied landing at Kalamita Bay. They also agreed that their favorite horse breeds came from the Caucasus as did the best riders. The conversation noticeably enlivened Etienne's spirits, and when Darley assured him that he'd heard that the spring race in Simferopol would occur, war or no war, Etienne exuberantly declared, "I'll meet you there."

"You have yourself a deal," Darley answered with a grin.

Conscious of her brother's increasing pallor, Aurore stepped in. "It's getting late. We'll let you sleep now, darling," she said, leaning down to kiss Etienne good-bye. "I'll be back in the morning." Disturbed to find his skin frighteningly hot, she gently touched his shoulder. "Do you need anything before—"

Stifling a cry, he sucked in his breath.

Jerking away, Aurore gazed at him with dismay. "Oh God, I'm sorry, darling! So *very* sorry! I'll—"

"Morphine," Etienne whispered, rigid with pain.

As the nurse and Aurore dashed away to prepare the potion, Darley wondered if Aurore's aid had come too late. Had the infection spread beyond hope that the slightest touch was agonizing for the boy?

Should he offer his help for the journey to Simferopol? But almost as quickly as he asked the question, he dismissed it. The tasks he had before him did not allow for charitable impulses; he could not afford to be absent so long.

Quickly returning with a cup of tea infused with morphine, Aurore cautiously brought it to her brother's mouth as he lay supported by pillows. "Here, darling, drink," she murmured, her expression still clearly distrait. "And forgive me for being so careless."

"It's not your fault, Rory." His voice was barely audible.

"Just a few hours more, darling," she whispered, holding the cup as he greedily drank down the narcotic. "And you'll be away from here."

When the cup was drained, Etienne breathed, "Thanks, Rory—for taking . . . care of me." Then he shut his eyes, exhausted from his efforts.

Using the hood of her cape, Aurore wiped the tears from her eyes. Why was this happening, she thought, heart-sick and despairing. He was so young; he had his whole life before him. It wasn't fair.

But then what was in this ruinous war.

Drawing in a sustaining breath, she stood beside her brother's bed and watched the morphine slowly take effect, focusing her thoughts on the future, not the past. Come morning, she would see her brother free of this pest hole and he could begin healing. It mattered not how lengthy his recuperation; it only mattered that he survive.

Once Etienne was peacefully sleeping, Aurore turned to Darley. "Thank God the general signed that release," she said, perhaps stating the obvious in the way of a hopeful mantra.

"Thank God you asked him," Darley replied. Anyone could see the boy's wounds were alarmingly compromised. As a betting man Darley would be hard-pressed to give him decent odds. At the English hospital in Scutari the recovery rate was less than one percent for the same reasons existing here. Lack of sanitation or anything resembling hygiene. "The fresh air at Simferopol will do him a world of good," Darley kindly said, offering what comfort he could.

"I agree, although, *anywhere* but here will be an improvement." Aurore glanced at the small clock beside the bed. "Fortunately, it won't be long until morning."

Once again, the marquis was tempted to offer his help; the road to Simferopol was brutal and the lady held a rare fascination for him. Unfortunately, Raglan needed his report and realistically, should he have the good fortune to share the lady's bed tonight, a few hours of sex might very well put period to his fascination. "Are you ready to leave?" he asked, time an issue for him as well.

"Yes, I think all is in order—oh dear, the nurses," Aurore suddenly exclaimed. Quickly turning to the elderly woman hovering nearby, she asked, "Would you or any of the other nurses be willing to come to Simferopol with us? You may name your price." To find adequate nursing care in a town deluged with the wounded would have been nearly impossible.

The plump peasant woman nodded without hesitation. "Me and me sister will go." Miss Clement was a considerate employer who paid good wages, paid them on time and sent over meals from the hotel that were fit for royalty.

"Wonderful," Aurore murmured with deep satisfaction. "Absolutely wonderful!" She felt enormous relief, gratification, even a palmy hope. Which would never do with the gross uncertainties facing her. Steady now, she warned herself. Her brother's health was in her hands. This was not the time to become unglued. "Thank you *so* very much," she said, composing herself by sheer will. "The vehicles should be here at seven if that's not too early." She had sent a message to Ibrahim at the hotel.

"No, Excellency. Don't you worry none. We be ready at seven."

Aurore smiled. "Seven it is, then. Thank you again." Turning to Darley, she opened her arms in an expansive gesture. "There now, all is well," she pronounced, unable to completely restrain her good cheer. "A few hours rest at the hotel and then Etienne's true convalescence will begin."

Darley didn't think Miss Clement meant what he wished she meant. He rather thought her rest would be a solitary one. A shame. But under the circumstances, with her brother gravely ill, certainly more likely than not.

As they walked through the hospital corridors toward the exit, Aurore spoke of her brother's recovery in terms of unqualified certainty.

Politely acceding to her positive agenda, Darley didn't feel that it was his place to point out the obvious apropos ungrounded hope and wishful thinking. Or bring up the low survival rate for wounded soldiers in this war. Miracles happened. Perhaps Etienne would be one of the lucky few.

The moment they reached the street, Aurore came to a stop on the pavement and, inhaling deeply, drew the crisp, cold night air into her lungs. Exhaling, she said with a grimace, "The stench inside is intolerable. No wonder disease is rampant."

"You did well to expedite your brother's release." Darley offered her his arm. "It will likely save his life."

"I must see that it does," she declared, tucking her gloved hand into the crook of his arm. "Whatever is necessary to see him well again, I will do," she firmly added as they walked away.

"I gathered as much."

She glanced up at him. "I'm not ashamed."

"Nor should you be. We all do what we must in this senseless war."

She shot him a look. A distinct antipathy had entered his voice. "Is this war any different from any other?"

"It was unnecessary," he muttered. "Religious fanatics and overweening egos brought this disaster upon us."

"Whose side are you on?" An ambiguity had suddenly colored his tone.

"No one's," he replied, careful to rectify his fleeting candor. "I just dislike war in general and this war in particular." Which was God's own truth. He smiled, a teasing glimmer in his eyes. "Perhaps it's no more than blatant selfishness on my part. I'm finding it increasingly difficult to ignore the misery and amuse myself in my usual profligate way."

"Which is?" Gazi's provocative gaze had awakened some inexplicable, heady wildness in her.

His dark brows flickered roguishly. "Nothing conventional, I assure you."

"Is that so?" A honeyed coquetry, a lush smile.

Both irresistible. "Consider the danger in tantalizing me, Miss Clement," Darley gently warned. "I am only chivalrous under duress."

"Perhaps I'm not in the market for chivalry." Her words were quite unexpected, but once spoken, she felt no compunction to retract them.

He turned to look at her, his gray-green gaze intense. "What *are* you in the market for?"

For any number of reasons, some purely selfish, others paradoxically both whimsical and survival based, all deeply bereft of reason, Aurore said, simply, "Forgetfulness."

"With me?" He was too tired to play games.

She held his gaze, direct and unblinking. "Yes."

"In spite of your brother?"

"*Because* of my brother."

"He will soon be on the mend," Darley offered, benevolent and obliging, possibly lying as well.

"I am of the same mind," Aurore replied, unlike him, resolute in her belief. "Thank you for saying so. Now tell me, Gazi," she went on in an altogether different tone, one that threw caution to the winds without any further soul-searching, "what does Zania find so enticing about you?"

"Is this a game?" he bluntly asked. "Are you and Zania competitors?"

She shot him a sideways glance. "Does it matter?"

He didn't know why he hesitated when it *was* a game for everyone involved. "No, of course not," he finally said. "It doesn't matter in the least."

"I didn't think so. But what other than survival does at the moment?"

"Indeed," he murmured. "There's no escaping reality."

"Gazi, my sweet," she drolly murmured, "pray do not blue-devil me with such reminders, when at the moment I require only amusement from you."

"And that you shall have, darling," he said as lightly, the endearment rolling easily off his tongue. Without breaking stride, he scooped her up in his arms and moving down the street kissed her lightly, then not so lightly—and ultimately, not lightly at all. He kissed her wildly, urgently, as if there was no tomorrow—a distinct possibility for them both with the present social disorder swirling about them.

Walking swiftly toward the beckoning hospitality of Miss Clement's bed, Darley's kisses took on a burning impatience. Unlike a man who hadn't slept in days. Nor like a man who had only recently risen from Countess Tatischev's bed.

As the lights of the hotel came into view, shocked back to her senses by the imminent prospect of being seen, Aurore heatedly whispered, "Stop, stop!" She pushed against Darley's chest. "I can't do this! Put me down!"

"No." Nothing altered in his stride, not so much as a millisecond of hesitation marred his pace.

Drawing back even more, she regarded him with a hot-tempered gaze. "Put me *down* or I'll *scream!*"

"Scream away." His gait remained unchanged.

How dare he speak so calmly. "Dammit, I *will!*"

He actually looked at her then, his gaze in contrast to hers, unsullied by high emotion. "I don't know you very well," he said, gently, as though he were soothing a temperamental child, "but from what I've seen, your moods are—how do I put this—highly changeable," he diplomatically finished. "Not that you don't have reason of course." His smile was indulgent. "Why don't we talk about this upstairs?"

"Because I don't *want* to talk about this upstairs," she muttered as they entered the lobby, lowering her voice in order not to draw attention to them.

"I'm guessing you'll change your mind," he amiably replied as he moved through the lobby. Well aware that Miss Clement, only brief moments before, had been panting with desire, he rather doubted she could so easily tamp down her raging passions. "Look, darling, no one's around," he murmured, gently kissing her cheek. "We are quite alone."

Stealing a glance from under her lashes, she surveyed the deserted lobby. "That doesn't excuse you," she mulishly retorted. "You might very well have embarrassed me."

He refrained from pointing out that she had been beyond any thought of embarrassment when she'd clung to him on their trek here and feverishly returned his kisses. He only said, well mannered and polite, "I beg your pardon, of course, and hope you will forgive me."

"Hmph," she said.

But she no longer insisted on being set down, he noted, chalking up points for his side. Or rather to his years of experience with women. As they walked past a row of potted palms, he said, softly teasing, "Kiss me, darling, and I'll carry you up the stairs without complaint."

"As if you wouldn't."

He liked that the cadence of her voice was teasing too; he liked that she was appeased. "I'd go faster if you kissed me," he said with a sportive flicker of his brows.

"Hmmm . . ."

"You wouldn't have to wait, then."

"Really? Were you planning on waiting?"

He grinned. "Such assurance."

"Let's just say I can feel the evidence of your regard for me."

"But then you don't know whether I can be monkish."

"So I shouldn't take any chances."

"I wouldn't suggest it if you are inclined to impatience."

Her brows rose in mock drama, her smile candy sweet. "Blackmail, Gazi?"

"Perhaps I have a certain need for authority."

"What if I do as well?"

He chuckled softly. "Then it should be an interesting night."

"I . . . am . . . definitely intrigued," she murmured with delicate languor.

"I rather thought you were—this morning, this evening . . . and now."

"Arrogant man."

"Just observant. And the feeling was mutual, I assure you. I was hard-pressed not to seduce you on the
ride into town."

Her smile was lush with promise. "How sweet."

"*Au contraire,* Miss Clement, I am not in the least
sweet."

"Let me be the judge of that."

"You must kiss me now," he said, stopping at the
base of the staircase.

"And if I don't?"

"You have to."

His brusque, unequivocal utterance sent a piquant shimmer of lust through her body. "Perhaps
just this once," she said with a provocative smile, "I'll
obey you."

He rather thought she might do so more than
once. Not that he was fool enough to say so. He
merely inclined his head downward to make himself
more available for her kiss.

She hesitated.

He must have forgotten to mention that he wasn't
a patient man. His mouth suddenly covered hers
even more forcefully than before, and rather than
take offense, she strained upward, digging her fingers into his shoulders, welcoming him, yielding to
him, eagerly meeting his audacious assault.

For a fleeting moment she chided herself for so
slavishly falling under his spell. If she didn't feel such
blissful delight in his arms and if his kisses weren't so
wildly arousing that her body was opening in feverish
rapture, she might have. But she also needed Gazi
beyond physical pleasure, beyond carnal passion and
orgasmic release. On this night of volatile hope and
somber fear, she desperately needed him to bring

her oblivion. "Say you'll stay with me 'til morning," she whispered. "Tell me you will . . ."

He heard the faint tremor in her voice, understood her terror of the unknown, knew why she didn't want to be alone in the coming bleak hours. "Yes, of course," he whispered. "Whatever you want."

Chapter

9

As it turned out, the lobby was not deserted. A lone man sat in the far corner, slouched low in his chair, half-asleep. But he'd come fully awake when Gazi carried Aurore into the hotel, and he'd watched their progress across the breadth of the quiet room with considerable interest.

He knew them both and they, him.

So Aurore had come out of her hermitage, he mused, contemplating the couple's indiscrete display of affection. She'd not taken a lover since the Greek scholar had been lost at sea last year. But then, Gazi had a way with women. He wasn't surprised.

It was interesting though.

Had they met at some gathering of Allied commanders?

Or were they unaware of each other's civic pursuits?

* * *

Darley took the stairs two at a time with effortless strength. Hardened from an outdoor life, from living days at a time on horseback, his leg muscles were like steel.

Gazi's brute strength manifest in their swift ascent further provoked Aurore's impatient desires. It *had* been too long, she decided, when pure virility was so tantalizing it incited an overwrought, weak-with-longing neediness deep inside her. And yet, how pleasant the thought of his glorious size in terms of personal satisfaction. The exact measure was still a tantalizing unknown, but if he met Zania's criteria . . .

She smiled faintly.

Tonight for a few brief hours Gazi would serve as her antidote to fear, and sexual pleasure would be her narcotic of choice.

Not that such logic actually factored in her covetous desires. She understood that Gazi had intrigued her from the first. On the other hand, she rationalized, she didn't really want to be alone in the wee hours of the morning, and fortuitously, circumstance and opportunity had intervened. That any of her officer escort would have been more than willing to stay she conveniently ignored.

Darley's thoughts were less contemplative. They were exclusively about sex, as in when and where— particularly *when* . . . the sooner the better front and center in his brain. Miss Clement had interested him at first sight as well, and now contemplation was about to shift to consummation.

Three more doors to pass.

And here he was. He dipped his head. "Do you have a key?"

"It's unlocked."

He didn't say *You're too trusting* because it might reflect badly on him. "You must be well liked that you don't worry about theft," he said instead, leaning over enough to turn the doorknob with his fingertips and shoving open the door.

"I don't keep much here, and yes," she said with a smile, "the hotel staff does look after me rather well. Thank you for keeping me company tonight," she added, as they entered her sitting room. "I want you to know I'm very grateful."

His smile was polished. "I'm equally grateful for your company. Which door?" he asked, surveying the various possibilities.

"That one." She pointed. "Would you like a drink first?"

His gaze was stark with lust. "Maybe later."

At so conspicuous a display of raw desire, her breath caught in her throat, a hot-blooded jolt of eagerness spiked through her vagina in response and suddenly speed was of prime urgency.

He smiled. "I'll hurry," he said, as though he could read her mind.

"I'm not usually so wildy impatient," she breathed, the ravenous pulsing inside her bringing a blush to her cheeks. "Really, I'm not."

"Don't apologize." He grinned. "It's my good fortune."

"Mine as well." She held his gaze for a moment, her brief mea culpa overcome, her self-possessed assurance restored. "Although," she said with the faintest of smiles, "there *is* something powerfully aphrodisiac about you."

"The feeling's mutual, my dear Miss Clement," he said with grace and charm, pushing the bedroom door open with his shoulder. "Or maybe we're caught up in the karma of the East," he added, carrying her over the threshold.

"You believe in fate?"

He grinned. "In the current chaos and violence, I don't believe in much of anything. My goals are simple—keep breathing, stay out of the line of fire and outlast this war." Having swiftly crossed the large room, he came to rest beside the bed. "And my short-term goal is to bring us both pleasure," he said, setting her on her feet.

"We are in accord, then. My short-term goal is to make it through the night." She smiled up at him. "And I rather think you will delight and beguile me in the process."

He grinned. "I'll do my best."

"Since Zania likes versatility in bed, I have no doubt you will."

Was that sarcasm or pettishness? "I would have much preferred you," he said. "But I was resisting, or rather I thought the circumstances were inappropriate"—he smiled faintly—"among other things." Untying the ribbon closure on her cape, he lifted the ermine-lined black velvet cloak from her shoulders and tossed it in the direction of a chair with the casualness of a man familiar with boudoir encounters.

"You mean Zania was waiting for you."

Now *that* was pettishness. "I meant your brother was in hospital and gravely wounded."

"And Zania was waiting."

"For your information," he murmured, lightly brushing his index finger over the curve of her upper lip instead of answering her question, "I spent the entire evening watching you across the dinner table and thinking about taking off your dress."

"While I spent the evening concerned that Zania's breasts might actually spill from their tenuous moorings and embarrass everyone," Aurore sardonically replied.

"Really?" he said, amusement in his gaze. "When I thought you were watching me."

"I was *not*."

"I know—you were *not* watching me. Which is the very same thing."

"You think every woman is enamored of you?"

"No. But I was hoping one woman was."

"I shouldn't be."

"Why ever not?"

She had no ready answer; did Gazi's dark beauty alone prompt her powerful sexual response or was it her long celibacy? She knew the answer before she'd even completed the thought. Even darling Petros had never inspired this instant lust. "I'm sorry," she finally said. "I don't know why I'm equivocating. I've been celibate too long perhaps," she added, still struggling with her irrepressible passions.

Had he somehow known? Had he recognized her susceptibility even this morning on the road? And while he was curious about her celibacy, he wasn't curious enough to prolong their conversation when he had better things to do. "You set the pace then. I wouldn't want to frighten you."

She laughed. "I rather think the reverse might be true. So fair warning; I may go on the attack." Her brows rose. "Provided Zania hasn't sapped your energy."

"Even if she had, you're quite capable of bringing a dead man to life, my dear Miss Clement," he said with a grin. "I promise to keep up."

"What a lovely promise," she murmured, taking a step closer.

The scent of Parma violet struck him afresh as she lightly brushed against him, and suddenly he was twenty again and smelling it for the first time. "I like your perfume," he said, soft and low.

"It comes from Italy."

"I know. I once lived in Parma."

There was something in his voice. "And you're reminded of a woman," she murmured.

"No," he lied. "I was a student there." That was the summer Lucia died, the summer that had set the course for his life. "Now, where were we?" he went on, dismissing the past out of seasoned habit. "I believe you were about to attack me." His voice was smoothly urbane, his smile one of practiced charm.

"Did I say, I have a special place in my heart for Circassian men? You look splendid in your evening clothes by the way." The fine black wool of his tunic was perfectly tailored to his broad-shouldered form, his loose breeches tucked into polished black boots, the small dress dagger tucked into his wide leather belt splendidly enameled.

"I'm not sure I appreciate the plural noun, but thank you nonetheless."

"I meant it in the most platonic way."

"Unlike now."

"Very much unlike now." She glanced at the clock.

"So then," he said, taking note of her glance. "Should we move on?" Without waiting for an answer, he lightly gripped her shoulders and turned her around.

She shot him a look over her shoulder. "Would you stop if I said no?" she queried, her smile teasing.

He hesitated briefly. "I'm not sure . . . no, of course I would. But I might be sulky if I had to," he added, swiftly unhooking her dress, his fingers deft on the hidden closures.

"Hmmm," she murmured, playfully. "Would I like that?"

He laughed. "We'll have to see, won't we? Although, I *was* grateful you sent your military escort away," he noted, sliding the soft, knit fabric down her arms and over her hands. "I was waiting downstairs and becoming increasingly sullen." He turned her to face him again. "Although, maybe you'd like that as well—*very* nice," he breathed, half under his breath, her uncorseted breasts beneath her sheer chemise splendid to behold. "These haven't been touched for some time?" he whispered, trailing his fingertips over the full mounded flesh, further banter abruptly relegated to the periphery by flesh and blood reality.

She shook her head, unable to speak with his fingers gently fondling her, with her tantalized nerves on alert, with fevered anticipation swelling inside her.

Seemingly immune to her quiet frenzy, he continued to stroke the soft, showy plumpness conspicuous above the lacey undergarment, his touch measured, restrained.

Unlike Aurore's sordid cravings that had nothing of moderation in them. Clenching her thighs together, she forcibly suppressed the small quivering tremor in advance of an orgasm. "This is ridiculous," she breathed, trying to contain another trembling spasm, reminding herself that she was no untried young maid and quite capable of imposing order on her passions.

At her hushed utterance, Darley understood that however long her celibacy, it had been too long. Not that his own sensibilities were any less greedy. Quickly lifting Aurore, he seated her on the bed, eased her onto her back, brushed aside her ruffled petticoats and skirt, slipped off her silk drawers and moved between her legs. "Just a second more," he whispered, unbuttoning the few buttons necessary to free his erection.

As he spread her thighs and grasped her hips, she was noticeably panting, his cue to bestir himself before it was too late. Pulling her down to the edge of the bed for better accessibility, he leaned over, quickly guided his erection to her slick, pink cleft and slid into her welcoming vagina with direct, timely, and not entirely unselfish haste.

And fortunately he did what he did, for the exact instant he was completely submerged—she uttered a single, stifled cry and climaxed.

Snugly engulfed in her hot cunt, braced on his hands, he gazed down at her and smiled. With her unquestionable appetite for sex, the hours until morning should pass in a blissfully sybaritic blur. Questioning neither his inordinate sense of pleasure nor his curiously altruistic impulses apropos the lady lying beneath him, he gently kissed her cheek. "Next time will be better," he murmured.

Her lashes slowly lifted, and she studied him for a moment as though not quite recognizing him. Suddenly, a glimmer of understanding illuminated her eyes, and she smiled. "Thank you, my *dear* Gazi. And I must apologize. You didn't have time to come, did you?"

He generally preferred more than three seconds of foreplay, but he politely said instead, "I'm not in a rush, while you, apparently, had some catching up to do."

"And you don't." The scent of Zania's perfume still lingered on him.

If she really hadn't had sex for some time, he was *way* the hell ahead of her. But this probably wasn't the time to discuss numbers. "I was being courteous, but if you'd rather I'm not—" He shrugged faintly. "It's your call."

"No, no . . . by all means be polite." Her smile was deliciously languid. "I'm quite willing to be catered to."

He liked her cheerful tractability. It boded well for his plans. A docile, passionate lady was just what he needed tonight. Although had he said as much to Cafer, his friend would have looked at him with surprise. Darley perennially railed against docile females, finding them not only boring but much too prevalent. Nor would he ever admit to actually needing a woman. In fact, the opposite was true, his sex life notwithstanding. "Perhaps I'll be a believer in karma by morning if you and I continue in such rare accord. You wish to be indulged and I'm in an indulgent mood."

"Lucky me," she said, sultry and low. "Let me get undressed."

"Let me undress you."

"And yourself." Her gaze was amused. "Or are you shy?"

"On the contrary. I was simply at pains to accommodate your headlong rush to orgasm."

"For which I render my profound thanks again. However—"

"You want more," he finished with a grin.

She stretched lazily, her voice when she spoke both congenial and infused with a sense of entitlement. "You *said* you'd be obliging."

Chapter

10

He quickly set about undressing, a skill long since acquired. As was his competence at dressing with equal speed. Both of which had held him in good stead in countless boudoirs over the years.

Pleasantly assuaged, Aurore lay in postcoital languor, her blue eyes trained on Darley with both interest and appreciation. He wasn't shy in the least, at ease in a strange bedroom, unaffected by her scrutiny, female attention apparently entirely normal. His belt and ornate *kinjal* came off first, his tunic as swiftly discarded, both casually dropped at his feet. His skin beneath his clothes was as darkly bronzed as his face, she noted as he stripped away the black silk collarless shirt he wore under his tunic and let it fall to the floor. With his upper body fully nude, even in the flickering gaslight, a cross-hatching of scars was conspicuous. Despite the fact that dueling was commonplace in the mountain tribes, clearly Gazi had survived more than one such encounter. "You must take offense easily," she murmured, "with all those knife scars."

He looked up, a boot in his hand. "Differences of opinion come up from time to time." He dropped the heelless boot on the floor and bent over to take off his other boot.

She understood the traditions of dueling in the Caucasus; the black felt cloak universally worn in the mountains was spread on the ground and neither man could step beyond the boundaries of the burka until one was dead or mortally wounded. Knowing a woman's honor was often a precipitating factor in a duel, acutely aware of Gazi's magnetic appeal as well, Aurore said with more curiosity than tact, "I expect a woman was involved on occasion."

He shot her a sharp look. "God no."

His brusque reply gave her pause, or perhaps more correctly reminded her of the transience of this particular tryst. Like his earlier one tonight with Zania. And while his spare replies should have curbed her morbid curiosity, they did the opposite. "It was some manly disagreement, then."

He opened his mouth to speak, shut it and apparently overcoming his reservations, said, gruffly, "One time, my horse was stolen."

The warrior code of the mountains allowed swift justice for such a crime, a man's horse sacrosanct.

"And the other times?" She shouldn't be so persistent, of course; his past was his own.

"Look, my dueling days are long past," he quietly said, opening one of the buttons on his breeches still undone. "I have become more tolerant or less willing to take a life or"—he shrugged—"weary of so much killing with this war. Now if it's all the same to you, I'd prefer talking about something else."

"Or not talking at all," she replied, her inquisition having been politely curtailed.

"Better yet," he drawled, sliding his breeches down his hips.

As he stepped out of his breeches a second later and stood naked before her, any further speculation apropos Gazi's past became irrelevant, her interests having instantly shifted to the full glory of his genitalia—enormous upthrust penis, large pendent testis, his heartbeat vivid in the network of veins engorging his erection. Not that he wasn't splendidly male in every other sense as well—tall, powerful, every taut muscle honed to the inch—but her focus was solely on his intimidating but highly provocative cock. A wild throbbing had already commenced inside her, and grateful that she'd climaxed once, she was looking forward to a more leisurely appreciation of him—it—"*That* is *so* gorgeously large," she purred.

"And you have too many clothes on," he casually remarked, not unfamiliar with such compliments.

He had but to speak and her body opened in welcome. "I couldn't agree more," Aurore said with a lush smile.

"I believe it's my job to see that you're rid of them." While his voice was dispassionate and cool, his pale gaze was not.

"I like that it's your job," she murmured as he moved to stand between her legs, his towering presence reminiscent of some brute colossus. "It must be the late hour and unusual circumstances. I am not normally so willing to be compliant."

"You and I are both operating in some illusionary, highly charged universe"—he glanced around the bedroom—"this overgilded room notwithstanding." His smile was sudden and boyish. "Although, strangely—at the moment—I even find myself partial to the Russian penchant for gilding everything in sight."

"Perhaps reality is eclipsed when our brains are half-asleep."

"Just so long as the rest of us is operating, I'm content."

She grinned. "No question there."

"Perfect." Of the opinion he'd been polite long enough, conversation not particularly high on his list of priorities at the moment, he leaned over and slowly slid his palms up her inner thighs until his thumbs came to rest on the cushiony softness of her vulva. "Then again," he murmured, sliding his thumbs up and down the slick, hot flesh of her cleft, the pearly fluid oozing over his thumb pads testament to her readiness, "maybe your undressing could wait a few minutes."

"But I want to feel you everywhere," she murmured, pettishly, not an iota of compliance in her tone.

It took him a moment to respond, consumed as he was with the notion of instant gratification, although when he spoke, it was with well-mannered restraint. "Of course. Forgive me. You're just too enticing. All this sweetness," he murmured, slipping his thumbs into her slick passage, one thumb detouring to gently stroke her clitoris, "is distracting as hell."

She shut her eyes against the rush of sensation streaking through her vagina and surging upward in blissful waves to bombard her brain.

"How does that feel?" he whispered, massaging her clitoris with virtuoso gentleness. "Or do you like this better?" Slipping two fingers inside her with one hand, he shifted into a slow circular massaging of her clitoris with the thumb of the other hand.

She tried to answer; she even thought about insisting he stop and help her undress. She fleetingly considered reminding him that he *had* said he'd indulge her until she concluded that he *was* indulging her— *most* delightfully. Her resulting sigh was one of both unalloyed pleasure and assent.

"Is that a yes?" He smiled faintly, inexplicably pleased that she'd so readily and docilely yielded to him—the sensation so *outre*, he immediately tried to rationalize it away.

In these tumultuous times, with the world seemingly out of control, perhaps one exerted mastery where one could. Or perhaps his departure from past practices was due to nothing more than Miss Clement's extraordinary sexual appeal. She stirred his senses in a very different way, although it may be only that she had been initially unavailable—forbidden fruit as it were.

Not that his unusual fascination with her was even remotely based on logic. But then what was in this bloody war zone.

Fucking was, he decided. *That* was real. And with doctrinaire certainty on his side, he said in a fait accompli tone, "You'll like *this* better." Quickly adjusting her hips beneath him, he substituted his prick for his fingers with a deft, facile competence and plunged hilt deep into her delectably tight cunt.

She cried out, but before he could decide whether her cry was one of rapture or pain, she seemingly concurred with his judgment, wrapped her arms around his shoulders, her legs around his waist and whispered, sweetly, "*Everything's* better with you, my dear Gazi."

"I am gratified to hear it," he suavely replied, moving her upward on the bed with the force of his cock and a smooth, dextrous hoist of his arms.

Resting on the pillows a second later, she exhaled in a luxurious, sensual purr and, holding him close, gazed up at him with warm anticipation in her eyes. "And now that I'm crammed full of you, what now?"

"I thought I'd make you come again. Does that meet with your approval?"

"Consider my approval total and complete," she playfully murmured.

"Such unsparing largesse, Miss Clement." He grinned. "Does that mean there are no restraints?"

Her gaze was covetous, her smile ripe with temptation. "I'll let you know if there are."

His erection swelled inside her at such unqualified permission.

"He liked what he heard," she whispered, shifting her hips in a gentle side-to-side motion. "Ummm . . . you are quite wonderful, Gazi." Her eyes shut, she pulled him closer and expressing her enjoyment of his wonderfulness in soft, breathy moans, she settled into a slow delectable undulation of her lower body.

In his own definition of wonderful, Miss Clement proved to be so sensationally wet, his accommodating thrust and withdrawal was nearly frictionless. She felt like glossy hot silk around his cock—if there was such a thing. Although what was undeniably real was the fact that he was horny as hell—thin-skinned and oversensitive, frenzied beyond the norm—which may have contributed to the violence of his next downstroke.

She gasped out loud as he forcefully hit bottom.

Christ, a little restraint or she wouldn't last the night. "I'm sorry," he whispered against her cheek, although his apology didn't extend to actually moving from the gratifying location in which his nerve endings were on blissful overload. "I hope I didn't hurt you," Darley added with unimpeachable grace if not complete honesty.

"*Au contraire,*" Aurore breathed, shifting her hips ever so slightly to entice him deeper, to sharpen and provoke her own exquisite sensations. "Keep doing what you're doing. I don't want to feel anything tonight but you inside me and this prodigal, licentious sense of abandon . . ."

Who in their right mind would take issue with such unconditional magnanimity? Especially when his cock was so hard and engorged it was aching. "Let me know when you've had enough," he whispered, not sure he would be capable of determining that precise moment in his current randy mood.

"Maybe," she said, soft and low and teasing. "And maybe not."

"I'm going to fuck myself to death," he said with a grin. "So be warned."

Her blue gaze was hot as the summer sun. "How very nice . . ."

He understood that they were both there for the same thing—for the forgetfulness and escape from reality offered by wild, mindless sex. And with cultivated expertise and keen understanding Darley gave Aurore what she wanted and pleased himself in the bargain.

She in turn enthusiastically kept pace with his shifting rhythms, even as she fiercely clung to him. Tonight, he was her lifeline and safe haven, her escape from the explosive events that threatened to engulf her life.

Only a millisecond after her second orgasm, he came the first time, ejaculating on her stomach with the finesse of considerable practice and a completely unaccountable slip of the tongue—Lucia's name spilling from his lips in a low, suppressed exhalation.

"Sorry," he muttered through clenched teeth, both of them still shaking from orgasmic tumult, from skittish nerves, from a disquieting and hotspur ferment.

"What?" she breathed, her gaze half-lidded, her voice weak from the violence of her climax.

"Nothing." Grateful no explanation was required, he nonetheless grappled with his blundering faux pas. It had been years since he'd so forgotten himself, and in hindsight he didn't know whether to blame the late hour, his fatigue, an evening of overimbibing, the cloying scent of Miss Clement's perfume or none of the above.

That Aurore reminded him in some inexplicable way of Lucia was a possibility. Whether he cared to explore that dangerous territory was not.

Sex was sex was sex, he reminded himself. He'd probably been fucking too much tonight—that was all. First with Zania and now with Miss Clement.

He'd just forgotten where he was and who he was with.

It could have happened to anyone.

Chapter

11

"Don't move. I'll get a towel," Darley said, easing away from Aurore and sliding off the bed.

"Don't worry. I have no intention of moving. Who's Lucia?"

He'd not taken more than two steps from the bed and for a fraction of a second he froze. "Did I say that?" he asked, his long stride uninterrupted to all but the most discerning eye.

"Yes, you did." So she was curious. Why shouldn't she be? It wasn't often she was called by some other woman's name in the throes of an orgasm. Actually, this was a first.

"What if I said I didn't want to talk about it?" Taking a towel from a shelf near a small corner sink, he wet it, wiped himself off and discarded it.

"What if I said I didn't want any more sex tonight?"

He turned from the sink, a fresh towel in hand, a smile on his face. "As if you could."

"Don't be so sure."

His smile widened. "Oh, I'm sure."

She smiled back. "Let me put it another way, then. If you tell me who Lucia is, I might be much more willing to, say—be experimental."

He walked toward her, his gaze amused. "I expect you'll be willing to be *experimental* whether I tell you or not. I can be very persuasive."

"Nevertheless I will be sulky if you don't."

"My cock doesn't give a damn whether you're sulky or not."

"You would have your way with me even if I were disinclined?"

"Sweetheart, look," he said, sitting on the side of the bed and beginning to wipe his semen from her belly, "you and I both know you are very much inclined."

"You're much too assured, Gazi," she petulantly said.

"While you're much too beautiful; I find myself obsessed."

"Only because I remind you of Lucia," she retorted, meeting his gaze with unflinching directness. "So tell me about her and then we can proceed with our pleasure."

He frowned. "Why be difficult?"

"And she wasn't, I suppose."

He didn't immediately answer. Outside of physical similarities, Lucia had been as different from the lady pinning him with her gaze as night from day. Wiping Aurore's belly dry, he tossed the towel across the room into the basket beside the sink before looking at Aurore again. He wanted to say, *You ask too many questions,* but understanding such a reply would be counterproductive, he blandly said instead, "There's not much to tell."

"I won't be jealous if that's what you're thinking. You and I are quite unattached."

"Not completely unattached," Darley replied drily.

"You know what I mean." Her voice, too, was sardonic.

"I know very well what you mean since I have remained determinedly unattached all these many years."

"How many years?"

He shrugged. "Lots."

"Good God, Gazi, you're secretive."

"I don't know you." A mildly put but nevertheless blunt reply.

"Tell me anyway." Her smile, in contrast, was sunshine bright.

Perhaps he was being unduly evasive, perhaps nothing in his past mattered when he might be dead in a few hours. Or more to the point, when he was unlikely to ever see Miss Clement again. "It's been almost eighteen years," he submitted, deductive reasoning having come to the fore.

"*That's* why you're so good," Aurore murmured. "You needn't look at me like that. I mean it sincerely. You are quite the best I have ever had."

He tried to suppress a smile and didn't quite succeed. "I might say the same of you."

"Pshaw. If you expect me to believe that, you must have been sleeping with the wrong women all those eighteen years."

"Maybe I was." He found the thought less depressing than it might have been had not Miss Clement been smiling at him so appealingly.

"The sooner you tell me of this paragon of womanhood," Aurore prompted, Gazi's reluctance intriguing, "the sooner we can return to our sexual pleasures."

He hesitated still, having suppressed his feelings about Lucia for so long. On the other hand, this fleeting encounter was by definition ephemeral as a bubble in the wind.

Dilemma solved.

"I was in love with Lucia a very long time ago," he said, his voice expressionless, the bare facts no longer able to elicit the sharp pain they once had. "She died unexpectedly. Until tonight I had never been reminded of her so forcefully; I apologize for speaking her name aloud."

"Did she live in Parma?" Somehow Aurore knew that she had before he answered.

"Yes," he said in the same tempered way.

"How did she die?"

"Cholera," he lied. "There was an epidemic that summer."

"I'm sorry."

"Thank you, but it was years ago and memories fade." Another lie, but in amorous situations like this, prevarication was taken for granted. Words of love were never actually about love, while saccharine compliments were only a means to an end. Not that Miss Clement appeared to be a novice at the game. "Now then," he said, his smile lightly teasing, "are you over your pet?"

"Was I pettish?" She had been, of course, but to confess as much caused her a degree of unease inappropriate to their unattached relationship.

"So it seemed."

"I apologize."

His gaze flicked to her enticing nudity, her white

petticoats and green cashmere skirt framing her bare legs, smooth belly and golden-haired mons. "I accept your apology, and if you're in the mood for more, perhaps—"

"I am so *very much* in the mood," Aurore interposed, a beguiling pink flush warming her cheeks, "I feel as though I have drunk some powerful aphrodisiac. When you leave in the morning, you must tell me if you have plans to return."

"I rather think I do," he murmured, when until that second he had not. "The war allowing, of course," he added, running his fingertip lightly over her silky mons.

She lifted her hips into his touch.

Taking his cue, he slid two fingers inside her honeyed cunt and stroked the hot, slippery tissue.

Sucking in her breath as a shockingly violent, flame-hot desire hurtled through her senses, she clenched her vaginal muscles around his deft, gratifying fingers and basked in the stupefying pleasure. When at last she found the breath to speak, when, in fact, Darley had paused in his masterful massage, she looked up at him and whispered, "Where . . . have you—been . . . all my life?"

"Waiting for you," Darley answered without hesitation. He might even have meant it. Not that his current rapacious mood inclined him to analyze or examine nuances of meaning. "Although, I'm done waiting now," he brusquely added, withdrawing his fingers and pulling her up by the arms. "Let's get these clothes off. You're not the only one who wants to feel the full skin-to-skin impact of this lustful wave."

Wanting what he wanted, perhaps wanting it even more since she'd not spent the early evening in bed with anyone, Aurore quickly obliged, twisting around so he could finish unhooking the back of her gown. As he lifted the soft garment over her head a few moments later, she swiveled back, flung her arms around his neck and kissed him with giddy delight. "I am so very, very glad you chanced to come my way today," she whispered. "You have dispelled all my demons tonight and brought in their stead halcyon delight."

If he had been poetically inclined he would have said she'd brought back the sun in what had been a sunless world for much too long. But he wasn't the poetical kind, nor would he so forget himself that he'd actually say as much, no matter how appealing the lady. But he smiled and kissed her in return and obliquely acknowledged his feelings by saying, "You delight me as well, my little Miss Sunshine."

Her blue eyes were very close and affectionate. "Serendipity is in play, Gazi. There is no doubt."

He grinned. "Indeed—if not for that pothole in the road . . ."

"I would not be sitting here insatiable and filled with longing."

"You should be filled with more than longing," he roguishly murmured, reaching for the ties on her petticoat.

"Posthaste if you please."

"Imperious little puss."

"I gather you don't mind though," she purred.

"Not at the moment," he said with a smile. "Although I do mind these many impediments to seduction," he murmured, untangling a knot on one of her numerous petticoats. Fashion called for a multitude of petticoats under the voluminous skirts. "Did you actually dress yourself in all these layers?"

"I had to. My maid wouldn't think of leaving the house with this war raging."

"Your brother is fortunate you're willing to brave the roads in these dangerous times. There, finally." Untying the last ribbon, he slid the froth of petticoats down her hips and tossed them aside. Lifting her into a seated position again, he began to unbutton her chemise. "Although, I am fortunate as well," he said with a flashing smile.

"We both are," she softly replied.

"Love amid the ruins," he whispered, dropping a light kiss on her nose. "Or as Virgil said—love overcomes all obstacles . . . even on occasion"—his brows rose—"grim reality."

"And we are living proof. Although," Aurore added, with a measured gaze, "I wouldn't expect such poetry from a Tatar. They are generally not so romantic."

"You know that, do you?"

"Not personally, but through association."

"For your information, many of my friends are romantic. They love like any other man."

"And yet, you seem different somehow . . ."

His defenses immediately went up. "I spent time in Europe," he pointed out, hoping to allay her suspicions. "Education is a requirement if we wish to survive the modern age."

"Ah, yes, Parma."

"And Italian poetry, if you please. Now, raise your arms."

"Did Lucia like poetry?"

"Do you?" He had no intention of discussing Lucia again. "Hafiz isn't precisely Tatar, but close enough. What do you think of him?" Stripping away her chemise, he dropped it on the bed and turned his focus on more pertinent issues like sex. Whether Aurore was suspicious of his Tatar background, curious about Lucia, even actually interested in poetry, was irrelevant at the moment.

Only sex and more sex was relevant.

Until morning.

At which point, he'd get on with his life.

"I do like Hafiz, in—"

His kiss effectively curtailed Aurore's utterance, and very soon she was as focused as he. He saw that she came twice more in quick succession before he allowed himself to climax. After quickly wiping them off with the sheet, he rolled onto his back, pulled her up on his chest and said, slightly breathless, "Give me a minute."

"Take—two," she panted. "I have—to catch . . . my breath."

He liked that she was ready for more; it matched his own plans. Not that he hadn't recognized a woman of urgent passions in their recent carnal romp. She was not what you'd call the passive type; she liked to fuck.

"You feel—delicious," she whispered, shifting slightly as she lay atop him, the slick skin-to-skin contact inexplicably gratifying as if their heated bodies were uniquely attuned, in perfect pitch, sexually at least. Wrapping her arms around his neck, she rested her head on his shoulder. "Don't go away . . ."

"I'm not going anywhere," he murmured, responding to the hint of winsomeness in her voice. "I promise." In fact, just as soon as his breathing was restored, he was going to fuck her again. Not that it wasn't strangely satisfying as well, just holding her in his arms. A rare occurrence for him—that earnestness in regard to the finer feelings. Perhaps the lovely Miss Clement's misfortunes were to blame.

Whatever the reason, touch him she did—a considerable accomplishment when he'd thought his emotions numbed by both his past and the continuous tragedies of this war. At the moment, she was blanketing him in an outrageously snug content— her breath warm on his throat, her golden curls soft against his jaw, her breast cushioned against his arm giving rise to a bedeviling sense of delight.

For a man who had lived—by choice—aloof from feeling for a very long time, that she so profoundly moved him required a new intellectual construct— or barring that—more realistically . . . evasion.

Considering his history, his choice was inevitable.

He reverted to form, tender sentiments jettisoned.

With libertine ambitions comfortably restored, he gently caressed the naked woman in his arms, rousing her from her drowsy repose by slow degrees, kissing her softly, whispering in her ear—telling her what he was going to do to her. How he would give her pleasure.

Darley was very persuasive or perhaps Aurore was easily persuaded, her body rapidly warming to his touch, her senses quickening at his erotic words, the hot glow of arousal beginning to pulse deep inside her. Raising herself on her elbows after a time, she met his gaze—more gray than green in the shadowed light—and said with a seductress's smile, "You have a real talent with words, my dear Gazi. I am *wide* awake."

"Then I haven't lost my touch."

"No, you haven't," she purred, and rolling off him, she lay on her back like the enchantress she was, her legs gracefully disposed in open invitation, her smile tantalizing. "So what will it be first?"

Propping himself up in a lounging pose beside her, he gave her a considering look. "I could say it's up to you, but I'm not feeling chivalrous. I feel like exerting my authority."

"Just so long as we take turns being authoritative, exert away," Aurore replied, her tone as softly assertive as his.

"We'll see."

"No, we won't."

"You're right, of course," he agreed, suddenly affable. "We'll take turns." He didn't care to fight over something so ridiculous. He dominated her in size and strength; whether she took control was entirely up to him.

"Excellent choice."

"Do all your lovers so readily comply?" he murmured, amusement in his gaze.

"Do yours?"

There was the merest pause and then he said, "I retract my question."

"I rather thought you might."

"We *do* have more interesting avenues to explore," he said with an urbane smile.

"I couldn't agree more."

"So then," he said, "let's start with these." Reaching out, he lightly traced the plump mounds of her breasts with his fingertips. "If that's all right with you, of course," he added, his voice velvet soft.

It took her a fraction of a second to answer, her exaggerated response to his touch momentarily focusing her concentration on the most exquisite internal stimuli. "Do what you will," she finally said, occupied by the wild throbbing in her vagina.

"Such gratifying hospitality," he murmured.

Transiently meeting his gaze, she arched her back into his skimming fingertips. "I have expectations of gratification in return."

He didn't often find a lady so inclined to arrogance. "Does this please you then?" Dipping his head, he lightly nibbled on one nipple. "Or do you prefer this?" Her challenging presumption brought his blood up, and when he drew her taut nipple into his mouth he sucked several degrees more forcefully than he ordinarily might.

Aurore moaned deep in her throat as a sharp frisson swept downward from her compressed nipple and settled with a fierce, quivering jolt in her heated sex.

At her suppressed pleasure sound, Darley lifted his head marginally and surveyed her face—flushed pink with passion. "You like it hard, I see," he gruffly said. "How hard exactly?" Operating in some reckless no-man's-land, feeling both a rare tenderness toward this lush beauty and an audacious disregard for anything but brute sensation, there was a possibility he might be guided by her answer—but only barely.

"You decide," she whispered.

They were both in a foolhardy mood tonight.

But perhaps, feeling *anything at all* meant you were still alive.

He decided, she screamed, and lunging upward slapped him viciously. "You bite me again," she hissed, "and I'll take a piece out of your cock."

"As if you could," he mildly said.

She slapped him again, even harder.

He could have stopped her; his reflexes were superb. "You're strong." His gaze was amused, his lounging pose unaltered.

"And you don't flinch."

"You're not *that* strong."

"You hurt me," she muttered.

"I'm sorry. Lack of sleep or something."

Her eyes flared wide at his indifference. "I should call you out, you rude man. I can shoot as well as you."

Predictable though she was, Zania might have been less trouble, he thought, not sure he was in the mood for hostility with his sex. On the other hand, Miss Clement was within reach, nude, at least formerly receptive and he had a hard-on. An easy decision. "Since I didn't bring a weapon," he drawled, "let's fuck instead."

"I'm *no longer* in the mood," Aurore snapped, coming to her knees, her spine rigid, her pose combative.

"You don't mean that." Bland words, an even blander gaze.

"I most certainly do," she hotly retorted.

Aware of her swift glance at his crotch, however, as well as the rising blush on her cheeks, he suavely said, "You're right, of course. I *was* rude. I apologize most profusely for hurting you. Do you suppose we could be friends again?" Adept at reading women, he understood a modicum of groveling was called for. Other than that, the lady was more than willing.

"You must do as I say then." Balky, imperious words.

"Willingly," he smoothly replied; she was clearly unable to resist her sexual urges. "May I touch you?"

He was much too assured, and if she wasn't caught up in a tumult of emotions—all inexplicable save for her frenzied need to make it through the night—she might have answered differently. "You may touch me gently," she said, with the merest temper in her voice, submitting with bad grace to her predicament.

"Like this?" He slipped his hand between her

thighs and pressed his palm upward until her pubic bone came in contact with the heel of his hand. Since her eyes had gone shut and she wasn't moving, he took the liberty of running his middle finger down her slippery cleft and was gratified to feel her shudder. "I'll be particularly gentle from now on," he whispered, smoothly rising into a seated position in a graceful flex of abdominal muscles.

Picking her up with ease, he placed her on his lap. "If I'm hurting you, tell me to stop and I will." It might be difficult, but he was capable of controlling himself, and in the interests of politesse he would. "Up on your knees, darling," he murmured, guiding his erection to her sleek cunt and slipping the crest of his cock between her pouty flesh. "There, now, come down," he prompted, and with exquisite restraint, he slowly eased her down his engorged cock, practically counting to ten between each measured gradation in her descent.

As the sheer size of Gazi stretched her taut, as she was forced to accept his huge penis, as every and all of her megalomanic, selfish, carnal cravings were exquisitely indulged, the phrase *die of pleasure* took on a whole new meaning.

Insensible to all but the intoxicating pressure, her every quivering nerve ending inflamed and seething, nothing mattered—not discretion or options, not motive or cause—only stark, ravenous need.

She was whimpering softly as he penetrated her lush cunt that last small distance, and fully submerged, engulfed by her hot, honeyed flesh, he decided that if heaven on earth existed, this particular bed in this particular hotel was the spectacular location. "Am I hurting you?" he whispered with the doting affection of a man inexorably caught in the throes of over-powering voluptuary sensation.

She shook her head in the barest of movements, unable to force her brain to send the signals necessary for speech.

"Good," he said approvingly, as though praising her for a deed well done. "Is it all right if I move?" Overwhelmed by an exceptional solicitude, he carefully watched for her response.

"Please." Desperately needing what he alone could give her, she managed the single, almost inaudible word.

Feeling as though he'd been offered a glorious gift, he whispered with unprecedented fervor, "Thank you."

That they'd met in this star-crossed world by a fortuitous accident of fate was as inexplicable as their explosive passion. Although, perhaps it wasn't fate at all but the happenstance of Aurore's hair color and scent that had prompted Darley's offer of a ride. Not that either were inclined to debate why they were together with wild, impatient lust swamping their reason.

"I'm going to lift you now," he whispered, politely giving her warning.

She didn't reply.

But her fingers tightened on his shoulders and he knew he'd been given license. Nearly circling her slender waist with his large hands, he slowly raised her up the rigid length of his erection with an effortless strength.

She whimpered at the last, fearful of losing contact with the tantalizing source of her pleasure.

"Here, here," he quickly acceded, kissing her gently as he began to lower her once again. "You can have it back."

Her small sigh was one of voluptuous satisfaction, and when she came to rest on his thighs brief moments later, when she was fully impaled on his stiff, pulsing cock, she languidly opened her eyes and offered him the sweetest of smiles. "When I feel this heady rapture, how can I possibly stay angry with you?"

"I'm glad you're not angry," he said, his tone uncommonly grave.

Both instantly uneasy, they spoke in unison.

"You first," Darley said, gruffly, chagrined by his momentary lapse.

"I was just going to say I very much appreciate your company tonight," Aurore offered blandly.

"A benign interpretation for this," he murmured with a polished smile, and flexing his hips, he deliberately terminated the conversation.

She gasped as he thrust upward with unchecked power, and a hot flood of pleasure washed over her. A moment later, when the shimmering glory had passed, she slowly came up on her knees, triggering another breath-held moment for them both. The world righted itself brief seconds later, her lashes lifted and meeting his gaze, she said, sweetly, "You are *most* obliging, darling Gazi."

"I promise to be obliging as long as you can stand it," he replied with a faint grin.

"A contest I look forward to." She smiled. "Perhaps you'd care to place a wager on what—our endurance?"

It was amazing how long his adrenalin could keep pumping when the perfect enticement was at hand.

It was even more amazing how many times Miss Clement could come, Darley decided after losing count. Then again, she said she'd been celibate for some time. While he didn't have that excuse, he acquitted himself well. Practice *did* make perfect.

But in time, even Miss Clement called quits.

"I can't," she gasped, swiveling a look over her shoulder. "No more."

"What do I win?" he teased, his hands hard on her hips, his cock buried deep in her creamy cunt.

"How about—my eternal gratitude?"

"Whatever you say, darling."

"As if what I say—has mattered . . . a whit tonight," she panted.

"Au contraire. I have been more gentlemanly than usual."

She glanced back again. "Meaning—no whips . . . like Zania prefers?"

Darley's eyes widened marginally.

"Surely you don't think—gossip like that . . . can be suppressed?"

Darley shrugged, indifferent to gossip. "I'm not sure I'm capable of thinking at all anymore," he murmured. "Although I do need another few seconds if you can stand it."

"Don't expect me to move," she warned.

"That won't be necessary." His continuous erection in close proximity to the captivating Miss Clement required little stimulation, and gentleman that he was tonight, he quickly finished. "There now," he said with a grin, wiping her back with one of the towels he'd brought to the bed, "no further duties are required of you."

"Good," she whispered, falling back against the

pillows and offering him a dazzling smile. "Then I don't have to apologize for having been demanding."

"Not really," he drawled, wiping himself off.

"You're vastly accommodating, Gazi," Aurore purred, slowly stretching like a cat in the sun. "I like that no thought was required tonight, only feeling."

He shot her a look from under his lashes. "Anything *but* thinking was on my agenda tonight." And Miss Clement was unrivaled in offering him mindless pleasure, he decided, dropping into a sprawl beside her. "In fact, thinking is much overrated at the moment, if you ask me. To whit—the respective commanders in this damnable war who are incapable of rational thought. What we shared tonight is probably the only sanity in a world gone mad."

Realizing that his harangue was falling on deaf ears, he turned to find his companion had fallen asleep.

Rising on one elbow, he took the opportunity to contemplate her at leisure, her fair, blushing beauty a delight to the eye. An intangible familiarity about her may have factored in his appreciation as well— that sense of recall therapeutic rather than burdensome, the unalloyed pleasure she'd brought him tonight, singular.

Nor was it exclusively about sex. He'd stayed when normally he would have made his excuses after a decent interval and left. Granted, he'd promised her that he'd stay, but who wouldn't have prior to consummation?

His continuing fascination with her despite a surfeit of sex, however, *was* unusual. Sexual *surfeit* generally prompted him to a swift departure.

And yet here he was like some besotted fool when he should have been long gone.

Which word, besotted, abruptly curtailed his musing.

He wouldn't say he'd *never* been besotted, but he was no longer a green youth like he'd been with Lucia. Nor was he about to contemplate so bizarre an emotion after only a few hours in Miss Clement's bed.

Good God, he *must* be exhausted to even consider such a notion.

Quickly sliding from the bed, he covered Aurore with the quilt and began gathering up his clothes. Just as he was stepping into his breeches, Aurore softly moaned in her sleep and he made the mistake of looking.

Standing motionless near the bed, his breeches halfway up his hips, he stared at the glorious sleeping woman. She'd shoved a portion of the quilt aside and one of her breasts was exposed—a pink, soft, little hillock with a jewel-hard nipple, tempting as hell, tantalizing as food to a starving man.

He softly swore and attempted to tamp down the surge of lust swelling his cock.

He told himself he'd damn near worn himself out tonight.

He told himself he should sleep for at least an hour before morning.

He told himself he was getting in too deep.

Then she abruptly rolled over in her sleep, turning her back to him, and the covers twisted away, exposing her lush, shapely bottom.

There was only so much temptation a man could take. Dropping his breeches, he stepped over them and climbed in beside her.

He had no explanation other than lust.

Or not one he wished to acknowledge.

Sliding into her welcoming sex from behind, he pulled her close, their bodies fitting together as perfectly as ever, the peerless merging instantly inflaming every overwrought nerve and cell and fervid sensibility to fever pitch.

Aurore woke enough to die away with a whisper of thanks at the end and flooded with sumptuous well-being, Darley held her close, sated and content.

He hadn't planned on sleeping, but exhausted after days without rest, he too succumbed his weariness.

They slept like the dead.

Or rather, considering their recent sexual transports, their sleep might be better characterized as one of Arcadian bliss.

Whatever the designation, in those brief hours before dawn, they escaped the beleaguered world and found peace in each other's arms.

Chapter

12

A hard pounding on the door woke them.

"*Merde,*" Darley muttered, glancing at the clock on the mantel.

Shaking herself awake, Aurore sat up and, raising her voice enough to be heard by the hotel servant sent to wake her, called out, "I hear you! Thank you! And thank *you,*" she softly added, turning to Darley with a smile as she slipped from the bed.

"It was definitely my pleasure." He didn't ask her to stay. She only had a half hour to ready herself before her seven o'clock appointment at the hospital.

"If you don't mind," she said, moving toward the armoire, "I'd like to go downstairs first. You could follow at a decent interval."

"Understood." Although he would have preferred pulling her succulent nude body back into bed.

"And just for the record," she added, turning back to him, one hand on the armoire door, "I am not in the habit of doing what I did last night."

She was frowning slightly, so he answered with well-mannered grace. "I never thought you did. I was merely hopeful."

"If my brother wasn't so ill," she said with a sigh. "Not that I feel the need to make excuses," she added, a new briskness in her voice. "I don't." Turning away, she reached for her gown.

"I understand. I'm completely discreet if you're worried."

Swinging back, a blue gabardine traveling dress over her arm, she met his gaze. "You weren't discreet with Zania."

"I could have been. Discretion is not Zania's strong suit, however, as you may have noticed."

"Point taken," Aurore noted drily, tossing her gown on a chair. "She was practically eating you alive."

He had no intention of discussing Zania's sexual appetites. "Will you be traveling in your carriage?" he asked, deliberately changing the subject.

"I'll bring my carriage along, but Ibrahim was to hire a suitable vehicle in which Etienne can lie down. I talked to him after dinner last night; he stays down the hall. Now, if you'll excuse me." Retreating behind a screen in the corner that shielded the newly installed water closet added to the palatial hotel built in the previous century, she took advantage of the facilities. Reappearing some moments later, she moved to the sink in the corner.

"You should be safe in Simferopol," Darley offered, making polite conversation. "I'll send a message so my staff will expect you. Since you have to travel slowly with your brother, everything should be in readiness on your arrival."

"I am so very grateful." She spoke over the sound of running water. "Naturally, I will repay you for your kindness."

"You already have," Darley said.

She smiled at him over her shoulder. "Nevertheless, I am beholden."

He smiled back. "In that case, I shan't refuse your gratitude in whatever form it takes."

"Libertine." But her tone was teasing.

"Vixen." His tone was bordering on affectionate.

So much so that she looked up from wiping her hands.

"We were well matched, darling," he drawled, one dark brow lifted.

How smoothly he reverted to type, she thought. How tempting he looked, lounging in her bed, brute male with his scars and provocative virility. "Truly a night to remember," she said in the same sardonic tone as she moved toward a chest of drawers. Selecting serviceable undergarments for travel, she began to dress.

They spoke of mundane matters as she put on her clothes—the weather, the distance to Simferopol, the state of the roads—and they'd smile at each other from time to time, but neither made a move to do more.

Darley didn't trust himself and he knew her time was limited.

Aurore almost said a dozen times, *Will you be in Simferopol anytime soon?* But she curbed her impulse. A man like Gazi regarded trysts like theirs in purely physical terms. It would have embarrassed them both had she asked.

Darley helped with the hooks on the back of her

gown when she asked, although he found it difficult
to resist undressing her instead.

But they were both adults.

Once all the hooks were fastened, he casually said,
"There you go now," and lay back down.

It took considerable effort to let her go.

Aurore concealed her shaking hands as she
moved away. Crossing to the armoire, she quickly
pulled out her sable coat and slipped it on. After surveying herself in the cheval glass, she picked up her
gloves and turned to Darley with a polite smile.
"Good-bye now," she said, her voice composed by
sheer will. "I wish you pleasant travels."

"And I you as well—along with good health for
your brother." Politesse echoed in every bland sylla-
ble.

"Thank you." She hesitated for a fraction of a second, then turned and walked from the bedroom.

Darley heard the outside door open and close a
few moments later.

And only then did he dare leave the bed.

After taking care of his swollen cock, he set about
washing and dressing. He wasn't exactly late yet, but
later than he had planned. Once he was fully attired,
however, he sat down and watched the gilded clock,
wanting to give Aurore sufficient time to exit the
hotel before leaving the suite.

He didn't wish any scandal accruing to her on his
account.

Arriving downstairs a full fifteen minutes later,
Darley walked through the bustling lobby and out
the door of the hotel. Standing on the pavement, he

inhaled the cool morning air and ran through his schedule for the day.

It was not yet seven.

He would first write his report for Raglan.

"Did you have an entertaining night?"

The familiar voice came from behind and Darley turned with a smile. "Don't I always," he replied. "How was your evening, Hausmann?"

"Not as interesting as yours, I expect. How long have you and Miss Clement been friends?"

"Meaning?" A hint of challenge reverberated in the marquis's voice.

"I am discreet, my friend. About many things as you well know," the middle-aged man murmured. "I happened to be in the lobby last night when you walked in carrying your *inamorata*—quite oblivious, I might add, of prying eyes."

"On the contrary, I looked and saw no one. You must have been well hidden."

"Perhaps." The German smiled. "More likely your attentions were otherwise engaged."

"Apparently. Now, if your catechism is over, I'll bid you good morning. I have a busy day." He would not give Hausmann the satisfaction of knowing he was annoyed. The old roue would only press him.

"Have you heard," Hausmann said, lowering his voice, "there is talk of attacking Eupatoria."

Darley nodded, gratified to change the subject. "Wrangel is already there with his Russian cavalry," he said, speaking as softly. "Raglan knows, not that it will do much good. Our commander-in-chief couldn't contrive a battle plan if he had a gun to his head."

"Canrobert isn't much better. The French have a bureaucrat when they need a commander."

"If only you and I were in charge," Darley noted drily.

"It couldn't be any worse, believe me. The incompetence at headquarters makes our work of little use. By the way, why is Miss Clement on her way so early in the morning?"

Darley debated answering but decided a casual reply would better serve Aurore than taking issue with the question. Hausmann would only want more detail if he suspected Darley was keeping something from him. "Thanks to Miss Clement's intervention with Osten-Sacken," Darley said, "her brother is being sent to Simferopol. He has taken a turn for the worse and she is naturally hoping he will recover once he is free of the putrid hospital air."

Was something about to occur in Simferopol? Some change of plans in the war he was unaware of? "Aurore is a most dutiful sister." Hausmann watched Darley's face for some possible clue.

"Indeed. Etienne is very fortunate."

Nothing, not a flicker of mendacity or evasion. The Englishman must not know of Aurore's undertakings for the French. "I see my man bringing up my horse." Hausmann nodded, his schedule requiring an early morning ride to Balaclava where an informant was waiting to be paid. "Stay alive, my friend."

"I intend to. You as well."

"Should you see Miss Clement again, give her my regards."

"I doubt we'll meet again," Darley replied with a shrug. "We go in different directions."

But as Darley walked to his apartment in the warehouse district near the docks, he found himself thinking that he would not be averse to a renewal of their friendship. In fact, he would be willing to ride a considerable distance to see Aurore again. An unlikely occurrence, however, with the state of the war. The Russian attack on Eupatoria was imminent and since Raglan would need some eyes and ears on the ground, no doubt he and his men would be riding west by nightfall.

Chapter

13

An official of middling rank in the Third Section watched from a doorway across the street as Darley and Hausmann took leave of each other and went their separate ways.

The tsar's secret police kept records on non-Russians with what could only be characterized as a German efficiency. The movements of foreigners in the Russian empire came under scrutiny from a vast army of informers, some voluntary, others working for the secret police out of fear. And Captain Nikolay Nikolaevitch Kubitovitch was certain that both Hausmann and Gazi Maksoud were not what they seemed. Hausmann was no more a scholar researching Crimean history than Kubitovitch was the Pope in Rome. Nor was Maksoud the simple trader he professed to be.

Perhaps it was time to bring both men in for questioning.

A spy's confession—and the secret police *always*

obtained a confession—would be sure to win him laurels from his superiors.

An hour later, Kubitovitch was cooling his heels in Osten-Sacken's anteroom. His temper rose as he watched several officers go in and out of the general's office while he was ignored. Did Osten-Sacken not realize the consequence that an affiliation with the Third Section entailed? He could have the general charged with treason if he chose. It was simple enough; any informant would willingly attest to some fabrication about the general to save his own skin. In Kubitovitch's world, with truth elastic or fictitious, anything was possible.

He would apprise the general in no uncertain terms of his power to make men disappear. It was one of the gratifying components of his job—the authority to intimidate. A capital resource to a man as unprepossessing as Kubitovitch. Of medium height and weight, with the bland countenance inherited from his peasant ancestors, he was nondescript save for his fierce competitiveness and ability to survive. Both attributes had lifted him from his parents' hovel into the meritocracy of the Russian educational system where he had caught the notice of the secret police in Odessa.

Men who came from nothing had nothing to lose.

A prime asset in espionage.

Osten-Sacken on the other hand detested the Third Section. He saw it as a disreputable blot on the nation. As a military man, he preferred engaging his adversaries honorably—in the open, man to man. Furthermore, as a nobleman, he subscribed to certain principles of justice and fair play.

As a result, Kubitovitch was left waiting.

When at last he was ushered into the general's office, Osten-Sacken's antipathy showed. "State your business quickly," he muttered, continuing to write as he spoke. He glanced up briefly, his gaze cool, dismissive. "Have I seen you before?"

Six times. But Kubitovitch kept the anger from his voice as he said, "Yes, Your Excellency. We have spoken before." The general did not offer him a chair. Kubitovitch mentally recorded the slur.

"Your employers would do well to stay out of my business," the general bluntly declared. "I have a war to run. There are no anarchists here, I assure you." The Third Section harshly repressed any form of political dissent. While Osten-Sacken's family had faithfully served the tsar for centuries, he abhorred the kind of wholesale repression practiced by the Third Section. He disliked the greasy little men who victimized and persecuted the innocent and guilty alike for what they might say or think—for reading the wrong book or newspaper.

Kubitovitch knew better than most that there were anarchists everywhere, but he chose not to argue. He said instead, "I wish to discuss two possible spies with you."

"Only two? This place is teeming with spies. Why are you bothering me with your nonsense?"

"One was at your dinner last night."

Osten-Sacken set down his pen with a sigh, leaned back in his chair and directed an exasperated look at his unwanted caller. "Since you seem to be intent on telling me who it was, do so with dispatch and be on your way. For all I know, there could have been ten spies at dinner with me last night. You don't actually think it matters a jot when the only way the Allies can win this war is by throwing their men at our ramparts until they're all dead or we are. There is nothing subtle about a siege."

"Nevertheless, Excellency," Kibitovitch returned doggedly, "my superiors are trusting me to protect the government from those who would do it harm."

"Yes, yes . . . very well—the name if you please."

"Gazi Maksoud."

Osten-Sacken threw back his head and laughed until tears came to his eyes, his guffaws trailing off into chuckles that only slowly subsided. "My good man," the general finally said, deliberately enunciating each word as if he were addressing some mental incompetent, "Gazi is first and foremost a cunt-hound, and a very accomplished one I might add. If he's doing any spying it's up some woman's skirts. I suggest you direct your attentions elsewhere."

"And what of Hausmann?"

Why did these little men always look as though they'd crawled out from some dung heap? Although to Kubitovitch's credit, everyone looked small to Osten-Sacken who was larger than most. Viking blood in the Baltic region still ran true. "Hausmann is harmless," the general declared.

"So you don't deny he's a spy?"

"I repeat. He's harmless. He is given the information we wish the Germans to have. Now, if you've finished, my schedule is demanding."

"I'm having the two men brought in for questioning."

The general's jaw tightened. Was the man completely witless? Had he not just made it plain that he had vetted both Gazi and Hausmann? "I suggest you alter your plans," Osten-Sacken said coldly.

Kubitovitch drew himself up to his unimpressive height, squared his jaw, tamped down the impulse to clear his throat under Osten-Sacken's chill gaze and said into a room that had become ominously silent, "My orders come from St. Petersburg, Excellency. They are quite precise. I doubt you would care to lock swords with my superiors." He rallied behind the matchless power of the Third Section. "I assure you," he added ominously, "the consequences would not be to your liking."

The malicious little man was trying to threaten him. Osten-Sacken found his audacity astonishing. "You realize, I presume, that I command an army of fifty thousand men. If that, however, has escaped your notice, let me point out to you that the Grand Duke—*your employer,*" Osten-Sacken added with silken emphasis, "is a personal friend of mine. As a matter of fact, he stood best man at my wedding. If either Gazi or Hausmann is brought in for questioning I will see that you spend the remainder of what will no doubt be a very short life at hard labor in Siberia. Is that clear?" The tsar's brother held the courtesy title of Commander of the Third Section and while he took no part in day-to-day affairs, Osten-Sacken would have no compunction asking him for a favor.

Kubitovitch could feel the heat of anger rise to his face. This nobleman, however, could have him sent into exile without inconveniencing himself in the least. "Perfectly clear, Excellency," the police agent replied. Another black mark against the general was added to Kubitovitch's ledger.

Osten-Sacken went back to his writing.

Summarily dismissed as though he were no more than a servant, Kubitovitch tamped down his fury and walked from the room.

Osten-Sacken gave no further thought to the secret police agent. His kind were wearisomely prevalent—like mold. At the moment, the general's concerns were centered on the powder magazine near the Mamelon that had sustained a direct hit last night. A quarter of their munitions would have to be speedily replaced. Looking up, he shouted for his ADC.

Temporarily checkmated, convulsed with rage, Captain Kubitovitch stalked from the headquarters building, a new enemy added to his lengthening list of adversaries. He was a patient man, though; how else had he climbed from the abysmal depths of his peasant birth to his present position? *All in good time—he would have his revenge.*

At the same hour, several miles away, Darley was seated across from Lord Raglan and his intelligence chief, Charles Cattley. The men were discussing Darley's recent report, or rather Raglan was listening while his operatives talked.

"Russian supplies and troops keep coming in unencumbered," Darley said. "Unless the road can be closed between Sevastopol and the interior, the city can hold out indefinitely." Why the Allied forces hadn't cut the supply route in the last five months was beyond comprehension. The Russians could and *were* increasing their forces and replacing losses with impunity.

Raglan, recently chastised for his handling of the war by Queen Victoria's new Prime Minister Palmerston and the secretary for war, Lord Panmure, was paying more attention to the intelligence reports of late. Unlike Wellington who had had a hands-on approach to intelligence, interrogating prisoners himself, reading several foreign newspapers a day, even accompanying irregular scouts on patrols, Raglan rarely left his cozy farmhouse. Plodding and conventional, too old to have taken on the role of commander, he relied exclusively on Cattley's reports.

Not that Cattley wasn't familiar with the area, having been born and raised nearby at Kerch where he had served as British consul before the war. But he wasn't an aristocrat, nor did he hold military rank, both obstacles only recently overcome by the British command. With the general staff in the Crimea having so seriously bungled the operation in the early months, they were now forced to accept a more inclusive view apropos advisors. Family connections or quarterings mattered less; experience and knowledge were acknowledged as meaningful assets. With the new protocols in place, Cattley had become one of Raglan's inner circle. Young Cattley and his local coterie provided accurate information on enemy forces and tracked the movements of Russian forces. Darley and his men aided in those missions as well.

For the past half hour Cattley and Darley had been detailing the extent of Russian preparations outside Eupatoria. Since both men had agents in the field, they knew that Menshikov's concentration of troops near the town meant an imminent attack.

"From what I've heard, all should be in readiness for an assault by mid-month," Darley noted. "Menshikov has over twenty battalions of infantry in place as we speak."

"Both the marquis and I have heard that Wrangel has been ousted as cavalry commander in favor of Khrulev," Cattley said. "Wrangel disagreed with Menshikov's plan to attack. He's right of course. It's too late for a successful assault with the town fully garrisoned. But Menshikov's hand has been forced; St. Petersberg is becoming disenchanted with him."

"At risk of losing his command, under pressure from the tsar, Menshikov is finally acting. Had he attacked sooner rather than sitting with his army at Balbec all winter, he might have taken the town. Omar Pasha's troops only landed a week ago," Darley pointed out, uncertain whether Raglan was still awake with his eyes half-shut. "His delay will cost him dearly," he went on, hoping for the best. "The conditions around Eupatoria are appalling with the spring thaws—deep mud has rendered the roads nearly impassable. Menshikov won't be able to bring up his artillery."

"Omar Pasha, on the other hand, has thirty-four guns inside the town, while our ships lying offshore also will be able to lay down fire." Cattley turned to Darley, his sideways glance indicating their slumbering companion. "Can you get a message through to our garrison?"

Darley nodded. "Of course."

"One of my informants tells me that the Russian attack from the west will be only a diversion. Such information would be useful to Omar Pasha."

"Consider it done."

Rising quietly, the two men left the English commander in chief asleep in his chair and walked outside to continue their conversation.

Soon, Darley and his men were riding cross-country to bring Cattley's message to the garrison at Eupatoria. At the same time, Aurore and her party were slowly traveling toward Simferopol. She'd seen that her report of both Ibrahim's surveys and her information gleaned at Osten-Sacken's had been relayed to the French command by one of her Tatar servants. She'd also promised to forward any useful information she might discover while in Simferopol. A further message had been sent to her staff at home, informing them of her coming absence.

They were traveling at a snail's pace for Etienne's sake. Even sedated as he was, the rough roads were an agony for him.

The forty-mile journey took them three days.

Arriving in the Crimean capital at last, they were warmly welcomed by Gazi's staff. But the trip had taken its toll on Etienne; he'd been carried into the house unconscious and desperately weak. That first night, Aurore sat beside her brother's bed, watching his every breath, the almost imperceptible rise and fall of his chest, the occasional flutter of his eyelids. Try as she might to convince herself that he would survive, she found herself in deep despair. Particularly in the pre-dawn hours when Etienne's breathing became more labored. She was terrified that he was slipping away.

Watching the clock with the vigilance of a sentinel, prey to an increasing dread, she waited for morning—persuading herself that if her brother survived the night, a new day would offer renewed hope. At the break of dawn, with Etienne still alive, Aurore sent up whispered prayers of gratitude and thanksgiving to every god she could recall. Having propitiated the spirits and the intangible mysteries of faith, she rose from her chair, walked to the glass-paned doors overlooking the garden and threw back the curtains.

The morning sun was dazzling bright—dare she hope, auspicious?

But even more heartening, as the golden light filled the room, Etienne's eyes fluttered open and he whispered, "Where are we?"

Dashing back, Aurore dropped to her knees beside the bed. "We're in Simferopol, darling. You made the journey in excellent form," she lied. "In no time, you'll be feeling your old self—just wait and see," she cheerfully added. "Gazi's cook is busy even now preparing nourishing food for you. If you're hungry of course," she quickly went on, not wishing to pressure him when he needed calm and serenity above all else.

"I—am . . . hungry."

While her brother's voice faltered, the fact that food appealed to him was enormously reassuring. He'd scarcely eaten during their journey. "Let me call in a nurse to sit with you," she murmured, rising to her feet, "while I fetch you something to eat."

"Coffee—with milk . . . first."

She smiled, thrilled that he wanted coffee. It had always been a ritual with Etienne—that first cup of coffee in the morning. "One or two sugars?"

"Two."

"Excellent." It was a sign, she thought.

It was a beautiful, hopeful sign.

In the following days as Etienne slowly regained his appetite and his recuperation continued apace, Aurore concentrated exclusively on catering to her brother's wishes. At first, he could do little more than eat and sleep, but before long, he felt strong enough to sit out in the garden for brief intervals. As his health improved, he enjoyed the sunshine and fresh air for lengthier periods of time.

The courtyard was protected from breezes, the warmth of the sun contained within the stone walls, the scent of spring blossoms fragrant in the air. An ancient apricot tree heavy with blossoms graced the center of the courtyard. Hyacinth, scilla and wild tulips bordered the meandering paths in waves of color. A fountain constructed from Greek architectural relics ran the length of one wall, the water dancing prettily in the sunshine, splashing and gurgling, entrancing the senses.

And so a fortnight passed, with Aurore's every waking minute defined by invalid duties—until . . . Etienne began sleeping through the night. Welcoming her evening respite, Aurore often would take advantage of the quiet garden at night, and resting under the stars, she would collect her thoughts and plan the events of the coming day. She'd stayed in touch with her staff, so a certain amount of contemplation centered on activities concerning the vineyard and her household at Alupka. And of course, the ongoing intelligence that Ibrahim was collecting even during Etienne's convalescence had to be dealt with and relayed to the appropriate parties. But after the necessary utilitarian issues had been discharged, her thoughts often wandered to pleasantries, and inevitably, tantalizing images of Gazi would float into her mind.

She cautioned herself against dwelling on that which was improbable, impractical and unlikely—on roseate dreams. With the world in flux, neither he nor she knew from day to day what life had in store. Gazi might be dead by now for all she knew. But even

if he wasn't, their romantic tryst had been, by definition, transient.

It was futile to expect more.

She was not blind to social custom.

Affaires were what they were.

But as the days progressed and her brother's
health continued to improve by leaps and bounds,
she found herself with increasing time on her hands.
Etienne didn't require much of her assistance anymore, while reminders of Gazi struck her more profoundly each day as she became more familiar with
his house.

Nor did it help her intemperate desires when his
servants spoke of him in clearly adoring terms. Not
that she took issue with their assessment. Gazi was
definitely a man to be adored. But when she began
actually dreaming of him on a nightly basis, she decided that she had too much free time on her hands.

In the interest not only of her peace of mind but
of France's ultimate success in the Crimea, she set
about paying calls on the local gentry. Attended by
Ibrahim, she reacquainted herself with local society,
and together, she in the drawing rooms and he in the
servants' quarters, they collected information for
their spy masters.

Once Etienne's health was completely restored,
he could have accompanied her to the provincial entertainments, but sitting through teas or musicales
was not his idea of pleasant diversions. Furthermore,
wealthy prisoners were allowed considerable freedom within the city in this civilized war for those with
family and fortune, so he chose amusements that
better suited him.

With Russian society an amalgam from the empire's satellite nations, along with prisoners residing in the capital city of the Crimea, the resulting mix of nationalities in Simferopol was considerable. Over tea one met English, French, Greeks, Turks, Tatars, Poles, Germans, Italians, those from the Baltic and a variety of other nations. It wasn't long before Aurore dispatched her first comprehensive report to the French Secret Service. Nor was it long before Etienne was involved with an international cadre of young officers who spent their leisure time much as they had before the war—with wine, women and song.

"The young master is back in form," Ibrahim noted with a smile one morning. "He sleeps 'til noon and thinks of nothing but the ladies."

Etienne was tall, fair and as handsome as his sister was beautiful. "If only he doesn't succumb to the governor's daughter," Aurore noted drily. "Miss Adlberg has a cool assessing gaze behind her brittle smile. Although I doubt Etienne has noticed with her other— ah . . . assets." The young girl's bosom was large and rather prominently on display in her corseted gowns.

"Rest easy, miss, the young master has no favorites," Ibrahim replied with a reassuring certitude.

"Thankfully." Etienne was barely twenty-one. "Now if only Miss Adlberg doesn't seduce him or compromise him in some way. She is looking for a husband— without a doubt—and the wealth of the Clement estates is well known."

"Are you talking about me?" Etienne strode into the small office near the kitchen where Aurore and Ibrahim were collating their reports.

"Yes. I am hoping Miss Adlberg does not lure you into marriage," Aurore said bluntly. "You could do better."

"Acquit me, sister. I am decades away from marriage. Tell her, Ibrahim. You know."

"I have done so, and yet she worries."

"Don't worry." Etienne smiled. "I'm not about to marry anyone."

"Then we agree."

"When haven't we," Etienne expansively remarked.

"When indeed," Aurore pleasantly replied. That she allowed her younger brother carte blanche accounted for their happy accord. But Aurore wasn't so unkind as to point that out to him. He was all she had now that their parents were dead; *he* had almost died. She would permit him anything.

"There's a race this afternoon outside town," Etienne declared. "Would you like to go with me?"

Aurore glanced at the clock. It was almost one and she'd promised Ibrahim she'd finish her report for his messenger. "I'd better not."

"Why not? It's a gorgeous day. Sunny, no wind, it's warm as summer and it's only March."

"I could finish what you're doing," Ibrahim murmured.

Etienne glanced from Ibrahim to Aurore and then to the papers before her on the desk. "Who are you writing to?"

"I'm just sending a message back to the house." Quickly coming to her feet before Etienne asked more, Aurore turned to Ibrahim. "You can give instructions for the vineyard as well as I," she mendaciously said. "Thank you, Ibrahim. I appreciate your help."

"My pleasure, miss."

"So, are you coming with me then?" Etienne's smile was brilliant. "If you say no, I'll pout."

"I doubt you need my company with all your friends about."

"I don't *need* your company, Rory. But *you'll* enjoy the races. A dozen horses from the Caucasus were brought in earlier in the week. The betting is fierce. I have five hundred roubles on a glorious black racer from Daghestan."

Chapter

14

Provincial society was less formal, and the bustle at the racetrack had the look of a country fair. Children were everywhere, running and playing, their parents and governesses having lost the battle for control. Hawkers were crying out their wares, and everything was for sale from tack to jam tarts; the rough stands were jammed with viewers, the verge of the track crowded with those of lesser rank. And in the festival atmosphere, one could forget for a time that there was a war going on.

Aurore had found a seat with some ladies in the stands, Etienne having disappeared moments after their arrival, as had most men. Male camaraderie apparently required a position nearer the track. Not that Aurore needed her brother's company; she knew most everyone.

In the relaxed fairground milieu, Aurore had loosened her bonnet and let it hang down her back, and her gloves were tucked into her reticule. She'd even pushed her sleeves up to her elbows to better enjoy the warmth of the day. It was absolute heaven to bask in the sun after such a bitter cold winter.

"Your brother is in fine fiddle once again," the governer's wife murmured, her gaze on Etienne and his friends in a huddle near the starting post.

"Thankfully," Aurore replied, ever grateful for his recovery. "He would not have survived in Sevastopol."

Countess Adlberg grimaced. "Nor do many as I understand."

"I have General Osten-Sacken to thank for Etienne's release. He was most gracious."

"He is a good friend of yours, is he not?"

The insinuation in the countess's words was measured. "We have known each other for some time," Aurore said, her voice as tempered as the countess's. "His daughter and I were friends growing up." The two women sat a little apart from the female group in the area designated for the governor's use.

"Ah, yes . . . Ingrid. How does she?"

"She is in Moscow and well. She's concerned for her husband's safety, of course. He is with Menshikov."

"Who is not long in command, I hear."

"Indeed? I know nothing of the military, I'm afraid," Aurore lied, when she'd known of Menshikov's weakened position for months.

"My goodness—look!" Countess Adlberg cried, leaping to her feet. "It's Gazi!" Ignoring propriety completely, waving frantically, she shrieked, "Gazi! Over here! Over HERE!"

If it was possible for her heart to skip a beat, Aurore felt as though it might have. And when she followed the direction of the countess's shamelessly come-hither gesticulations and saw him, there was no doubt her heart stopped.

Drawing in a quick breath as if to remind her body to continue functioning, Aurore took in the sight of the man who had been too much on her mind.

He wore utilitarian Tatar dress—black leather breeches and boots, dun-colored tunic half-open at the neck, the only embellishment to his attire, small silver studs on his belt. His dark hair gleamed in the sun—like his sudden smile.

He was waving back—a man's wave . . . unfrenzied and calm.

And then he began walking toward the stands.

"Isn't he just the most *beautiful* man you have ever *seen*!" the governor's wife exclaimed as she sat down. "But then the Caucasus tribes are known for their beauty. I swear, if he asked me to ride away with him, I would without a second's delay. They think nothing of it, you know—abduction." She glanced sideways at Aurore. "They consider it a form of courtship."

"I daresay your abduction would still cause a bit of a scandal *here*," Aurore remarked.

"Wouldn't it just!" The countess sighed. "Not that any such thing will ever happen, but"—she shot Aurore a smile—"he is most, most glorious in every way—don't you think?"

"Indeed. I first saw him with Zania at the general's dinner party in Sevastopol."

"So you know him! Of course—I forgot. You are staying at his farm."

"I only know him casually," Aurore lied. "He offered his farmhouse in the most offhand way when he heard of my plight. He and Zania were thoroughly engrossed in each other at the time." Another lie, but she wasn't inclined to offer Helena gossip for her rumor mill; the woman was a notorious busybody.

"Zania is nothing but a little tart!" Countess Adlberg sniffed. "She is quite disreputable."

"Consider though, she was married to an old man for many years. Perhaps she should be allowed some pleasures now."

"You are much too kind. Zania would not be so lenient toward you."

"Perhaps," Aurore replied, wondering if her benevolence was simply a means of protecting herself from disappointment, her sympathy for Zania in the way of self-pity. Gazi hadn't even bothered stopping by his own house to say hello and yet here he was. With equal disregard, he'd divested himself of Zania that night in Sevastopol.

As he approached, Aurore purposefully schooled her expression, refusing to display any interest. No doubt he was aware that every woman who saw him wanted him—the governor's middle-aged wife included. She would not be so gauche.

Particularly since he'd chosen *not* to pay her a call on his return.

As he stopped before the governor's dais, Countess Adlberg held out her hand with a majestic flourish. "Gazi, my dear boy," she said with an ingratiating smile. "Promise me you have only just arrived so I shan't feel slighted."

"Rest easy, my dear Helena. I rode in an hour ago and have to leave in the morning." Taking her hand, he bowed over it with punctilious grace. "My apologies for not calling, but as you see, my time is limited."

Was he apologizing? Aurore thought. *Might that be an apology?*

"You know Aurore," the countess said with a cursory nod to good manners, her gaze still unerringly on Gazi.

"I told Helena that we met at Osten-Sacken's dinner party," Aurore quickly noted to allay the sudden uncertainty in Gazi's eyes, "where you were gracious enough to offer us the use of your house."

"How nice to see you again, Miss Clement," he smoothly answered, having been cued. "I hope the accommodations are to your liking."

"Indeed they are. Thank you again."

"It's of no consequence," he carelessly replied. His feelings however were less nonchalant. While he had sensibly decided not to renew their acquaintance when he'd arrived in Simferopol, he could not curtail the immense joy he felt on seeing Aurore again. Perhaps after so many years in the mountains, his pagan sensibilities were more acute or maybe logic was at a disadvantage when Aurore was near. Whatever the reason, rational thought had apparently debouched, for against his better judgment he gave utterance to a personal remark. "I'm pleased to hear that your brother has recovered his health."

He'd spoken to someone in his household, Aurore thought, charmed by his concern. "Thank you, he is quite his old self again."

"You must come to dinner tonight," the countess interrupted, her tone one of regal command. "And I forbid you to refuse."

"Alas, I fear I must," Darley replied with a disarming smile even as his plans were rapidly changing— resisting temptation no longer a priority. "My men have family in town and I'm promised to Cafer's sister's for dinner tonight."

"You will be in my black books if you don't at least make an appearance, you bad boy," the countess scolded. "Come later. Unlike the natives," she said with a sneer, "we dine at a more civilized hour."

"If possible, I will. Tell me now, do you have any favorites in the races today?" Gazi inquired, preferring to change the subject with the governor's wife displeased at his refusal. "Two of my horses are running." Well aware of Helena's penchant for gambling, he said, "You might care to wager on them. I can guarantee they'll win."

"Tell me their names at once!" The countess's resentment was instantly replaced by a piquant excitement.

When Gazi did, Countess Adlberg leaped to her feet, pushed past Aurore and dashed off to place her wager without so much as a good-bye.

Aurore's brows rose faintly. "Apparently, she likes to gamble more than I thought."

"She does like to gamble, but she likes a sure winner even more."

Aurore's gaze narrowed. "Don't say you deliberately baited her?"

"I like to think I made her a nice profit." Darley's voice was teasing. "She'll be extremely happy at the end of the day."

"I see."

"Meaning?"

"Nothing."

He smiled. "You think I'm manipulative."

"Yes."

"I had good reason." His voice was no longer teasing, his smile replaced by a patent solemnity. "I'd like to get away from here—with you."

Aurore drew in a small breath, myriad possible answers racing through her mind. Yet when she spoke, her response was completely divorced from all myriad possibilities. "Would you have *ever* come to see me?" she asked.

He didn't immediately reply. Glancing at the press of people around them, he said with soft restraint, "It's a long story. Could we talk about it somewhere else?"

"I should be angry with you."

"That would be better discussed somewhere else as well. Please," he murmured, his gaze earnest.

It took every ounce of willpower she possessed to keep from throwing her arms around his neck and crying out, *Take me anywhere at all.* "I have to tell Etienne where I'm going," she said instead with deliberate calm.

He immediately smiled and held out his hand. "Lead the way."

As they descended the few stairs from the viewing stand to the ground and stepped onto the grass bordering the track, they did so in an awkward silence.

Speaking first, Darley muttered, "You've been on my mind."

"And you are displeased by the fact?" His disgruntled tone was unmistakable.

"I was in Eupatoria where distractions were perilous." He'd been in the thick of battle.

"I'm sorry." But she couldn't help feeling pleased that he'd been thinking of her.

He shrugged. "I shouldn't have mentioned it."

"Once Etienne was on the mend, I confess you were in my thoughts as well."

He shot her a look, opened his mouth to speak and, apparently thinking better of it, shut his mouth again.

"You leave in the morning?"

His sudden smile was brilliant. "You read my mind."

"Are you going to Helena's tonight?"

"Will you be there?"

She nodded.

"Perhaps I'll come later should politesse allow." Or perhaps his vaulting desires would be sated by then. "Cafer's sister is an old friend."

"Indeed."

He smiled. "Not that kind of friend. There's your brother. Tell him I'll drive you home."

Even as she understood his familiarity with command, she bristled at the absolutism in his tone. "Would you care to rephrase that?" she said, over-sweet.

With the prospect of soon having Aurore to himself, Darley was willing to do most anything. "Forgive my abruptness. I would be extremely gratified if you would allow me to drive you home, Miss Clement." He dipped his head deferentially. "Or should I ask your brother for permission?"

She winked. "Very nice, Gazi. You have expectations, I gather."

"Only if you approve, Miss Clement," he replied with an answering wink.

She laughed. "I'm very glad I came to the races today."

"Not as glad as I," he murmured, careful to keep his voice low as they closed in on Etienne and his friends.

Greetings were exchanged, the civilities observed apropos Etienne's recovery, introductions made to various of the men unknown to Gazi before Aurore informed her brother that she was leaving. "I'll see you after the races," she said.

"I have other plans, Rory. I'll be back in the morning. Would you care to join us tonight?" he inquired, glancing at Darley. "We plan on taking our track winnings to the gaming tables."

"I leave early tomorrow, so I'll decline. But thank you for the invitation."

"Will you be back soon?" Etienne smiled. "I'm here for the duration, not that I'm complaining when I might have been in my grave instead."

"You were fortunate indeed," Darley noted. "As for my return, one never knows from day to day. My schedule is erratic with the war."

"They're lining up," one of Etienne's friends cried, and all eyes turned to the horses being brought up by the jockeys.

Remembering his manners, Etienne turned back and put his hand out to Darley. "Thank you for the use of your home," he said. "I recuperated in great comfort thanks to you."

"My pleasure," Darley said, shaking his hand. "Stay healthy."

"This far behind the lines, how can I not? You, on the other hand, are in constant danger."

"I have good men with me. It's quite safe," Darley lied. "If you want to make a profitable wager, bet on Bashi and Pera in the fourth and fifth races. They're my horses and winners both."

Etienne grinned. "Done." And turning to his friends he repeated Darley's offer.

As the young men ran off to place their wagers, Aurore and Darley were left forgotten.

One brow raised, Aurore glanced at Darley. "Do I

succumb to your manipulation as easily as everyone else?"

"On the contrary, you are highly suspicious of my designs."

She smiled. "And yet intrigued."

"We both are. I believe we came to an understanding on that point our first night in Sevastopol. Now, if you'll allow me, I'll endeavor to intrigue you further just as soon as we return to town."

"To your house?"

"If it's a problem, we could go somewhere else."

"You have alternate sites for your amorous activities?"

"Tut, tut—that suspicious tone again. I only meant, I would *find* another location should you be uncomfortable with your servants in place."

"Or yours."

"My servants are completely amenable."

Her gaze narrowed slightly at the intrinsic authority in his voice. "Why do I get this feeling that you are more than a trader?"

"I have no idea." He grinned. "Dare I say, women are more imaginative?"

"Only if you mean it in both a singular and laudable way," she retorted drolly.

"Naturally," he murmured. "I applaud *your* imagination specifically. In fact, your very imaginative accomplishments filled my dreams in my absence from you."

"Even in Eupatoria?" she waggishly queried.

He dipped his head. "Admittedly, even at times in Eupatoria. Discounting the obvious dangers in being distracted, the images of you were not only gratifying but cherished."

She made a moue. "You are much too suave. I shouldn't succumb to your flattery."

"It's not flattery, darling. It's the truth." Terrifying thought, but there it was when he'd not previously acknowledged the sobering fact that she had become more than a passing fancy. "Come now," he added, determined not to travel down the path of candid revelations. He crooked his arm. "What time do you have to be at Helena's?"

"Nine-ish. Dinner is at ten." She twined her arm in his. "And you? When do you have to be at your dinner?"

"I confess I lied."

"Why am I not surprised?"

He looked pained. "You don't really think I was going to spend my only night in Simferopol at Helena's dinner party." He grinned. "After you sit through sixteen boring courses, perhaps I'll join you then."

"She might have an opera singer for entertainment afterward. Helena professes an interest in culture."

"In that case, I might indeed come. When all eyes are on the fat lady, it will give us an opportunity to slip away."

"You'd risk incurring Helena's wrath?"

"I can handle her."

"I do hope you meant that rhetorically. Otherwise I find the image highly disturbing."

"Jealous?" he drawled.

"Of Helena—no. Of your facile and probably much used sexual skills, perhaps yes. Although I have no right, nor in truth any previous tendency to be so inclined."

It unaccountably pleased him that she might be jealous in however small a way. It pleased him even more that he was the reason for her possible volte face. He had no idea why. He had less idea why he was beginning to think of her as his—an incredible notion from any number of aspects. "I'm going to have to steal a carriage somewhere," he said, abruptly curtailing any further contemplation of so outre a concept. "Or did you bring yours?"

"I did. You are saved from criminal activities."

If only she knew, he thought. "Perhaps I can think of some way to thank you," he murmured.

"I'm sure you can," she purred.

Chapter

15

When they reached Aurore's carriage, her driver was nowhere to be seen.

"I expect Safa is at the races." Surveying the numerous parked carriages, Aurore took note of a servant lying on the seat of an open landau. With a wave, she called out to him, "Tell Safa I took the carriage!" She glanced at Darley. "Like my brother, Safa has a multitude of friends here. He won't have any trouble finding a ride back into town."

"Would you like me to drive?"

"If you wish. I'm quite competent though; you needn't worry."

"I was just being polite."

"In that case," she said with a smile, "be my guest."

Reminded how fiercely she guarded her independence, Darley warned himself to not offend those sensibilities. "My compliments on your many talents," he said with polished grace. "There are few women who can handle a team," he added as he handed her up onto the driver's bench.

"My parents were of the mind that a woman was capable of doing whatever a man could—obvious physical differences aside, of course," she answered, taking in Gazi's obvious and delightful differences as he walked around the horses' heads to the off side of the carriage. "Etienne and I were raised very much alike—with the same tutors and lessons and responsibilities."

"A commendable policy." Repressing an impulse to say, *I have sisters who were raised very much like you,* Darley swung up onto the seat beside her. "I expect your parents were pleased with the result," he said instead, unlooping the reins and urging the matched pair of grays forward with a soft command rather than with the reins. Horses were highly prized in the mountain tribes, a warrior's bond with his horse often crucial in battle.

"I don't know about that, but my parents wanted us to be self-sufficient. Those tendencies were fostered in part by my grandfather's involvement in political dissident at one time." She smiled faintly. "Grandpere escaped France just ahead of a lettre de cachet, Empress Catherine's offer of land coming at an opportune time."

"Your decided opinions are a family tradition then, and I mean that in the most flattering context," he added with a grin.

"You'd better smile when you say that." Her voice was sportive.

"Have I mentioned how much I like strong-willed women?"

"Lucky for you then that I was raised to believe in liberty, equality, fraternity," she lightly replied, "concepts that put my family at odds occasionally with the local administrators. Justice frequently is dispensed with a heavy hand around here as you may know."

"Particularly with the Tatars."

She shot him a look. "You and your men have been unfavorably treated?" Although she still wasn't sure whether he was Circassian or Tatar, their time together having been given over more to amorous sport than conversation.

"Some have tried," he said quietly.

"And no one threatens your troop, I presume."

"Not with impunity."

"Dear me, should I take alarm?" Her blue eyes sparkled.

He laughed. "On the contrary. I am at great pains to please you."

"How very nice," she softly replied.

"Not as nice as your fresh-as-the-dew allure. Your tousled curls and freckled nose make you look eighteen. Although I hope like hell you aren't." The sudden thought was alarming.

"You needn't frown like that. I am twenty-six; you are quite safe."

She didn't say from what and he didn't ask, although his relief was obvious.

She smiled. "I gather you are not enamored of young misses?"

"Definitely not."

"I don't know if I should be resentful or flattered by your reply. Are you saying I'm old?"

"No, no . . . not in the least."

"Tell me—what is it that you don't like about young misses?" A woman's question—personal and probing.

"Honestly?"

"If you please."

How to answer when honesty was always a liability in the game of amour? "I'd say it's the giggling." Not the whole truth, but a legitimate complaint nonetheless.

"You prefer serious women."

"I prefer *women*. Tell me, do you like young men?" The topic was too fraught with complications; he chose to turn the tables.

"Some."

The casualness of her remark offended him. Without reason. Or at least not for any reason that bore close inspection. "How many might that be?" he unaccountably asked.

She looked up, took note of the twitch over his cheekbone, his clenched jaw and deliberately said, "Surely it doesn't matter."

It took him a moment to reply, but when he did he had regained his composure. More important, he was fully cognizant of the practicalities. "Forgive me for asking."

"Certainly."

You had to give her credit, he thought. She didn't give anything away—an unusual trait in a woman. In his experience females were inclined to talk too much. "In any case, young women and men aside, may I say that I was hard-pressed not to toss you over my shoulder and carry you off the moment I saw you today. You have an extraordinary effect on me."

"My heart stopped when *I* saw *you*."

Both the sentiment and her frankness pleased him. "You don't flirt," he said, a note of appreciation in his voice.

"Cajole and simper you mean?"

He smiled. "Or cling and wheedle."

"Perhaps I could do so if it would get me what I wanted," she said waggishly.

"No, don't. I like your candor."

She smiled. "Even when I say, *More,* for the tenth time?"

He grinned. "Particularly when you say it for the tenth time."

"We did rather get along."

He laughed. "A vast understatement, darling."

"With this sudden talk of orgasms, perhaps you could set my horses to a quicker pace. They are excellent in the traces."

He immediately urged the horses to more speed, and soon the carriage was bowling down the road.

Aurore clung to the seat with both hands, enjoying the warm spring air rushing by her face, tossing her golden curls, the high speed and Gazi's closeness making her pulse race from sheer exhilaration. Or perhaps anticipation.

"Feel free to hang on to my arm!" Darley shouted over the wind and the sound of galloping hoofs. "I won't accuse you of being clingy!"

"I wouldn't want to ruin my image!" Aurore shouted back, grinning.

"I would consider it an honor!"

She seized his arm in a fierce grip and they both felt a spine-tingling jolt.

No longer caring whether her freedom was being subverted, she leaned into his hard muscled arm and felt an unalloyed pleasure.

Less poetically inclined, but equally moved, Darley considered only how much longer it would be until he was buried deep inside the lovely Miss Clement.

It was anticipation at its finest.

It was blinding desire.

The ardent intensity of either sentiment unusual for them both.

Very shortly, but *too* long for the two involved, the gateway to Darley's house hove into view. The small estate, once a working farm, sat apart from the town on the rolling steppes.

"Hang on," he shouted, approaching the driveway at high speed. Both horses performed beautifully, careening sure-footed on the turn. He flashed Aurore a smile as they raced down the drive. "Great team!"

She could have said, *Expert driving,* but she only smiled. It couldn't have been a more perfect day.

As it turned out, there were various degrees of perfection to come.

He carried her into his house with both an effortless strength and a noblesse oblige indifference to their surroundings, his servants melting away before them. He carried her to his bedroom on the second floor, a room she'd seen only once before, having slept downstairs near Etienne.

Kicking the door shut behind them, he said with an instinctive courtesy, "Do you need anything?"

"Yes, I do."

As if startled by the sound of her voice, he met her gaze and smiled—in recognition perhaps. "We both do. You don't know how many times I've thought of this since last I saw you."

She grinned. "We could compare numbers."

"Or we could add up some other numbers," he murmured, gently setting her on her feet. "Like say—orgasms."

"Yes, yes, yes," she cheerfully murmured, feeling as though she were suddenly alive again, feeling as though he had but to smile her way and she was lost to all reason. "Immediately, if you don't mind," she whispered, tossing a smile over her shoulder as she moved toward the bed.

He only smiled, the question not actually requiring an answer. "You have to be at Helena's at nine?" Unbuckling his belt, he glanced at the clock on the wall as he followed in her wake.

"You have to come with me." She was unbuttoning her bodice as she walked.

He groaned. "What if I don't?" But even as he spoke, he knew he was willing to please her even in that miserable endeavor.

She turned to him as she reached the rustic bed. "I want you near me every minute until you have to leave. There, I have become as insufferably clingy as all the rest."

"I don't mind." A stunning admission for a man who had spent years avoiding intimacy.

"Then you'll come with me?" She slipped her dress down her arms.

"Don't worry," he murmured, taking pleasure in the sight of her bare shoulders as he kicked off his boots. "I'll come with you as often as you wish."

"Libertine. I mean to Helena's." Shoving the frothy muslin of her skirt upward, she pulled on the tie of her petticoat.

He shrugged. "Why not."

She glanced up at him, her eyes alight. "Thank you, you darling man. I am absolutely giddy with happiness about that and everything else. Don't ask me why. You do that to me. By the way, you are not allowed to look at another woman at Helena's party." As her petticoats fell to the floor, she kicked them aside.

"Why would I want to," he said, his answer unthinkable until today.

"Would you have come to see me if I hadn't met you at the races?" A blunt question, bluntly put. She reached for the tie on her drawers.

He was stripping off his tunic and paused. "I was trying not to," he finally said. "This is not the time to think about caring for someone—with a war raging. That was my thought"—another shrug—"but as you see I changed my mind."

The word *caring* strummed through her senses in a heavenly chorus, only adding to her joy. "For my part," she said, a note of seriousness unmistakable in her voice, "I would rather have these few hours today than nothing at all. With war and death all around, I am deeply conscious of how fleeting is life, how pleasure and the very air we breathe can vanish. I want to take with both hands while I can," she whispered.

"Yes," he said, although he had gamely fought the impulse.

"Life is uncertain, Gazi," she softly noted, aware of the minute reluctance in his voice.

"I know."

"You needn't fear I'll make demands." Nor could she if she wished with her diverse duties and responsibilities. "This is a brief holiday, no more."

He took issue with her casualness even as he understood that the perimeters of his life didn't allow him more than these few short hours. "Carpe diem it is," he agreed with an obligatory practicality. Sliding off his riding pants, he stepped out of them and dropped a light kiss on her cheek. "I'm really pleased we found each other today—even more pleased to be here with you," he murmured. Then reverting to a more comfortable stance that ignored intense emotion, he said in an altogether different tone, a teasing, playful one, "Now, do you need some help?"

"Yes, indeed"—her smile was coquettish—"you are exactly the kind of help I need. He," she added, glancing downward at his erection standing hard against his stomach, "in particular. I am quite enamored of your talented cock."

He grinned. "My cock thanks you. We thank you." He dipped his head. "You've made a mess of that knot. Let me undo it."

The silk tie on her drawers was hopelessly tangled. "Such fumbling," she murmured with a little moue. "Zania would never be so gauche."

Zania didn't wear drawers, but he decided against saying so. "But then making love is less about dexterity and more about feeling," he softly replied, his slender fingers unloosening the tangled cord with delicacy and competence while she held her skirts out of the way. "And you inspire rather strong emotions in me. So don't worry about any gaucherie. There," he murmured, pulling the knot free, watching the swift descent of her white silk drawers with a smile of appreciation. "Now, lift your arms," he said, shifting his attention to removing her dress, "and soon I will have you naked in my bed. A constant dream of mine of late," he added with a small smile.

She raised her arms, and he lifted her muslin gown over her head, dropped it on the floor and removed her chemise with the same swift dispatch.

"There—just as I remembered," he said, husky and low, gazing at her intently. So she had looked in his dreams—shapely and nude, ripe with desire, a small impatience in her eyes. He traced the curve of her upper lip with a brushing fingertip, an intemperate territorial gesture. "You don't know how many times I thought of you like this." *When he shouldn't have. When he should have been concentrating on staying alive.*

She would have gone to him at the races today, she knew, whether he had come to her or not. She should thank Helena for saving her from the embarrassment of seeking him out. "It's the war," she whispered, perhaps needing an explanation for her own intemperance as well. "We are more alive to pleasure with life so uncertain." Guarding against emotional involvement—highly impractical with a man like Gazi—she said, playfully, "For instance"—glancing down, she lightly touched the swollen crest of his erection—"he and I are equally impatient." She looked up and smiled. "If you don't mind."

He laughed, sensibly reminded of why they were both here. "So I have my marching orders."

"Nothing you can't handle, I'm sure." She must not consider this rendezvous as anything more than it was—delectable sport.

"It would be my pleasure," he said, suave and polished. "Now, if I lose control at any time"—picking her up, he lifted her up onto the bed—"hit me hard and there's a chance I might notice. I haven't had time for sex since last I saw you." His brows flickered sportively. "There's little opportunity in the trenches."

It shouldn't matter that he hadn't had sex. It shouldn't matter in the least when they barely knew each other, when one night in Sevastopol was the extent of their familiarity. "Don't worry, I'll find some way to get your attention." Her tone was as flippant as his. "By the way," she added, lying back on the pillows, "my opportunities for sex have been equally limited with nursing duties consuming my time." *Was*

*she some infatuated young miss that she felt the need to offer
him her celibacy? There was no earthly reason why she
should.* "Not that it matters in the least," she casually
noted.

"It matters to me, darling. I like that you're impatient for this," he said, his gaze flicking to his erection as he joined her in bed.

Such a splendid sight. A little shiver raced up her
spine.

He noticed and more gratified than he would
have thought, he rested on one elbow beside her and
spread her legs with a delicacy that was both mannered and prurient. He tried not to dwell on her recent celibacy; it made no difference, he told himself,
whether she had been chaste or not. But his cock was
less circumspect in separating sex and emotion, and
in anticipation of a beautiful, eager woman his erection swelled to new heights.

"Really, Gazi," Aurore whispered, her gaze on his
turgid penis, her voice pleading. "You can't expect
me to look at that and actually wait."

For a brute moment, he considered exerting his
authority. She was so temptingly vulnerable it brought
out the rare impulse in him. Quickly overcome.
"We've both waited too long," he murmured, moving
over her with a lithe grace and settling between her
legs. "So the first time will tamp the fire," he whispered, guiding his rigid erection to her sleek cleft,
pleasure washing over him as he began to slide inside
her slippery warmth. "And after that we'll play."

The phrase *die of pleasure* suddenly took on a tangi-
ble presence in Aurore's mind and body, in every
ripe, quivering nerve and cell and hidden recess. He
filled her slowly, slowly, so she could feel the exquis-

ite pressure, so anticipation shimmered through her senses, so she waited breath-held for that raw intense moment when he was fully, completely submerged.

There. Now for the precise degree of ravishment.

It was up to her to decide.

He waited.

She whispered, "More, more, more."

And he complied, driving in that small combustible distance to the ravenous center of desire where intellect gave way to something inexpressible. For an explosive, tenuous time, they were heedless to all but raw sensation.

Reason ultimately prevailed, or Darley's professionalism in amour came to the fore, and sensibly curtailing his forward momentum, he allowed them an opportunity to breathe. Drawing in deep shuddering breaths as though they'd broken the surface of a lake from thirty feet down, they basked in a gluttonous, unspeakable, rarely granted pleasure that rippled up his penis and down her vagina in spendthrift profusion.

How could she live without this, she thought, dazed.

Was it possible to forget the war and stay in this bed forever, he wondered, not dazed so much as champing at the bit for more.

"Don't leave me," she breathed.

"No, never." And he kissed her hard, hard in an ungentle kiss that marked her as his.

Nothing mattered to the reunited couple that fine spring afternoon in Simferopol but the blinding need for sensation and orgasmic release, and the sweet anaesthesia of tangled limbs and hot-blooded passion. She came, then he, then she and she and he once again in an endless insatiable sybaritic give-and-take that ultimately made them uncomfortably aware of a new pitch and range of personal compulsion.

Each in turn attempted to rationalize the inexplicable hysteria, the wildness and violence of their feelings. The war, the war—it had to be the war. Why else were they so unstrung, so fevered, so frantic for more and more and more? Why else was the pleasure so extraordinary, each climax bewitchingly excessive, the merest touch heart-stirring and vivid?

But almost instantly, a new wave of ravenous lust swamped puny, intellectual conundrums, and hotheaded and impatient, they yielded to the rough and tumble ferocity of their vaulting desires.

"I need a drink," Darley finally said, an hour later, two hours later—who knew. His nerves were strumming at lightning speed, his heart was pounding, his judgment had run amuck. He'd almost hurt Aurore a second ago with the brute force of his downstroke. Rolling off her, he left the bed without waiting for an answer.

What he needed more than a drink was a few minutes to talk himself into a slightly more rational frame of mind.

He wasn't alone. Aurore lay panting, eyes shut, on the bed, her arms at her sides, her hands closed into tight fists, trying to compose herself. She'd turned into some wild, frenzied wanton so outrageously demanding the poor man had to flee. And yet, she wanted him still. Probably even more than Zania, who everyone knew was insatiable.

"Would you like a drink?"

Turning her head, she opened her eyes. "Yes," she said, thinking he was the most gracious man she'd ever known. "And I apologize for"—she sighed—"for being so completely obsessed. I have no explanation." She grimaced faintly. "And it's not as though I'm sated."

He turned and smiled. "Nor me." He nodded at the clock. "There's time yet—we'll try."

"I think you must have drugged me. Why else am I still ravenous after how many orgasms?"

"Your guess is as good as mine. I lost count a long time ago." He turned with two glasses in his hands and walked toward her. The animal inside had been tamed; he could look at her now without wanting to ravage her. *Moderation in all things. Remember that.*

"You're too beautiful, that's all," Aurore said, struggling to achieve her own measure of sanity. "I am dazzled by your magnificence." He was male perfection, flawless and superb. Classic features such as his had been portrayed by every artist of note through the centuries, his powerful form the standard for perfection—broad shoulders, lean torso rippling with muscle, long legs toned and strong. And yet over and above the paragon of manhood, it was the sensual fire within him that lured and enticed.

"Or," he said, waiting for her to sit up, "you've been celibate too long," he replied, indifferent to his looks. Handing over her drink, he sat beside her on the bed and raised his glass. "To pleasure. It has taken on new meaning today."

"I couldn't agree more." Although she was struggling mightily to control her muddled, adoring sensibilities.

"Tell me how Etienne is doing," Darley said, gratified to feel his pulse rate diminishing. He preferred his sex without undue emotion. A drink, a moment or two to relax, a little conversation—everything would return to normal, he decided.

"As you saw, he's in fine shape and quite content

to return to his former activities. I don't see much of him between his friends and his paramours. And you? How are Cafer and Sahin?" Was she not capable of nonchalance, too?

"Good. Excellent. They're with friends tonight." And then Darley couldn't think of a single thing to say. Unless it had to do with sex and Aurore or her and sex or any combination thereof. As he searched his brain for a more appropriate topic—to no avail— the silence lengthened. He lifted his glass to his mouth, drained the remainder of his drink and set aside the glass. "What the hell," he muttered, glancing at Aurore. "It's not as though we have unlimited time."

"Or that there's some reason we *have* to talk."

He laughed. "I can't think of one." He nodded at her drink. "Finished?"

She quickly drank her brandy. "I am now," she said, and handed him her glass.

Setting the glass on the bedside table, he turned back to her. "I just want you to know, out-of-control sex is not the norm for me." What he meant was that it wasn't the norm with a woman he actually cared for.

"I understand. I am not usually such an insatiable wanton—let me correct that . . . a wanton of any kind. I am astonished at my appetite for sex with you."

"Are we done justifying this"—he grinned—"aberrant behavior?"

"Done," she said.

And in the remaining hours before dinner they capriciously and willfully ate at the smorgasbord of sensation. He would say, "Do this now," and she would. And she would say, "You have to give me this," and he would. Ultimately, they found themselves on the floor, although gentleman that he was he lay on the bottom. The carpet, while silk, could still scratch the skin. Aurore, seated astride him as the clock struck half past eight, said with a little pout, "We have to stop now, don't we?"

"We probably should. Helena's dinner starts at ten and we might want to consider a bath."

"I don't *have* to go," Aurore murmured, bouncing lightly on his rigid erection. "Really I can see her anytime."

He gently stroked her nipples, the delicacy of his touch testament to a certain virtuosity. "Perhaps we should, darling," he mildly noted, "although it's up to you, of course."

"Ummm . . . let me think about it." She raised herself up his indefatigable penis and, hovering on the crest, smiled at him. "Maybe after another orgasm . . ."

Chapter

16

Darley and Aurore purposely avoided the before-dinner assembly in the drawing room. Neither cared to exchange tepid small talk with Helena's guests. But provincial society being what it was—gossip the only excitement in an otherwise dull company—they were not able to avoid the numerous raised brows as they entered the dining room . . . slightly late.

"Forgive our tardiness," Darley mendaciously offered. "Since Miss Clement and her brother are staying at my house, we drove over together," he went on, feeling the many rapt and inquisitive expressions required some explanation.

"I see," Countess Adlberg said, her tone gelid, her narrowed gaze on Aurore hard and assessing. The little baggage knew him better than she'd let on this afternoon. "Come sit by me, Gazi. Aurore, do keep the governor company," she added with a sly smile, exiling her competition to the far end of the table beside her boring husband. With a negligent wave, the countess called servants forward to arrange two more places at the table.

The dinner party was a large affair: retired military men like the governor; their plump wives with hair in tight sausage curls; the occasional businessman whose bribes for government contracts nicely supplemented Count Adlberg's government salary; country gentlemen and their wives with suitably large estates or titles; several young officers on leave or unassigned for the moment; an equal number of young ladies whom Helena had carefully screened to not outshine her daughter. It was the usual blend of what passed for society a thousand miles from St. Petersburg.

Seated at opposite ends of the long table, under Helena's ever-watchful eye, Aurore and Darley could only exchange surreptitious glances from time to time.

Helena was obviously jealous. Not that she blamed her, Aurore thought. On the other hand, the governor's wife was far from her first bloom or even her second. Which only confirmed how age was irrelevant to infatuation. In fact, the older the *less* irrelevant was often the rule—elderly men in the company of their *nieces,* May/December liaisons between older women and handsome young men. Helena's pleasant flight of fancy, no doubt.

Although, as it turned out, Helena was not alone in her infatuation. Gazi, apparently, was universally adored by *all* the female guests tonight—young, old and in-between.

Bombarded with flirtatious remarks and invitations, he responded to his admirers with unfailing graciousness, acknowledging their blandishments with that perfect balance of warmth and civility. And while the ladies did their very best to be noticed, Gazi was not without his male admirers as well. Those were more restrained in their flattery, but it was clear as male eyes followed him that many a young buck aspired to Gazi's cool competence and charismatic charm.

In the midst of all the flattering cajolery and dinner conversation that inevitably centered on the war, Gazi marked out Aurore for the odd stolen glance on occasion.

She found herself unaccountably touched. She was not so naive as to be unrealistically sentimental over a few sweet glances. But clearly, she was no more immune to his captivating appeal—sexual and otherwise—than the other ladies.

That she had recently enjoyed his undivided attention, however, did give rise to a sense of smug satisfaction.

As if she had won the prize and these women had not.

Or at least not yet.

A likelihood she would do well to keep in mind. Gazi's interest in her was no more than what he might feel for any other woman. Although her interest in him was equally conventional—was it not? Outside the force majeure of her physical desires, of course.

Which must be contained. Particularly under Helena's watchful gaze. Reminded of the social necessities required of a guest, she set about responding to her own many admirers at table tonight. To that purpose, she particularly recognized the governor, two elderly generals and a newly arrived guardsman from St. Petersburg in her immediate vicinity, all of whom were doing their best to attract her attention.

Looking up from her veal cutlet, she smiled and with practiced grace offered them her undivided attention. An easy-enough task—Count Adlberg was a bureaucrat who liked nothing better than the sound of his own voice. The two retired generals were content to drink their dinner and send clumsy compliments her way. As for the young guardsman with slick-backed hair and immaculate dress uniform, his favorite topic was *himself*—his idea of flirtation apparently an immediate disclosure of his title and financial assets.

While she ate with a healthy appetite generated by hours of sex with Gazi, the governor held forth on Menshikov's various missteps and errors in the battle for Eupatoria, arguing point by tedious point how he would have made a better, more decisive and ultimately more successful commander if the military had but listened to his advice.

"Such a shame the general staff is so insular," Aurore commiserated when he briefly ceased his harangue to take a sip of wine. "Anyone knows, a man such as yourself who has lived in the area would have the necessary background so crucial to battle planning."

"Here, here," one of the retired generals barked, drained his wine glass and snapped his fingers for a refill. "Have to know the terrain, damned right!"

"Did I not mention exactly that to Menshikov and his staff on more than one occasion; did they take notice?" The governor snorted. "You saw what happened—defeat in every sense of the word."

"Stupid asses—the lot of them," the other old general muttered with a sympathetic nod for the governor.

"Are you concerned for Simferopol now that the Allies have won the day in Eupatoria?" Aurore asked, her voice tremulous by design, hoping to unearth some pertinent information. "Might they march on the city?"

"No, no. There is nothing to fear, my dear," the count said with an indulgent smile. "The Turks will not move from the garrison. Omar Pasha is content to rest on his laurels." He leaned forward slightly and lowered his voice. "We have well-placed spies inside. Our information is completely accurate."

"Vicious fighters, those Turks," the elderly general on Aurore's left grumbled. "Fought them twice and bloody tough they were."

"With a top-rate cavalry too," his companion grunted. "Still have the saber cuts to prove it."

Tossing a dismissive glance at the elderly men who had turned to each other and were reminiscing about their prowess in the Turkish wars, the governor offered Aurore a kindly smile. "You must not worry, my dear. We are quite safe here."

"You don't know how reassuring it is to hear you say so, Your Excellency. One worries, naturally, that the Allies might march northward."

"The roads are impassable," he noted brusquely. "Even if they wished to invade our town, they couldn't transport their artillery. We are out of harm's way. Furthermore, it's just a matter of time until Menshikov is removed. Our security will soon be in much more competent hands." He leaned very close this time and whispered, "Only today I received a dispatch informing me that old Gorchakov is to be installed in Menshikov's place." He sat back again and smiled. "We'll see how the Allies do against General Gorchakov who single-handedly broke Napoleon's army."

He was referring to the winter campaign of 1812. Forty-some years ago.

"Good God, how old is the man!" the guardsman exclaimed, having appeared bored with the conversation until the governor's last comment. Like so many young officers, he felt far superior to the military relics from the past.

"Experience will tell in the end, not some wet-behind-the-ears upstart," the governor snapped, the man in the immaculate uniform patently untested in battle.

The lieutenant flushed red and looked away.

"You're right, of course, Your Excellency," Aurore murmured, affable and gracious, when in truth she agreed with the young subaltern's assessment.

Both the Russian and British command relied on generals who hadn't been to war in more than two decades. Unlike France, Russia and England had refused to take advantage of the young commanders who had fought recent colonial campaigns. Instead, they used men long past their prime who were ignorant of the new techniques of warfare and—most telling—were physically unable to meet the daily demands of battlefield operations. Both Menshikov and Raglan had spent the winter in their snug farmhouses instead of waging war.

"Was your message from the tsar or from the war office?" Aurore inquired, pressing for more information. "Not that I know anything about such important subjects," she added with a sweet smile, "but you know how ladies like to gossip, and rumor has it that the tsar follows the campaign closely. They say he even occasionally takes a hand in strategy," she finished with a look of wide-eyed innocence.

"Just so, my dear," Count Adlberg murmured. "He does indeed. My dispatch came directly from the tsar by the hand of his son, Alexander. I hold a very important post, as you well know. The royal family relies on me in significant ways."

That the count was as vain as his wife was well known. "Everyone is aware of that, Your Excellency," Aurore noted with an ingratiating smile. "That the tsar depends on your good judgment is no surprise. He is intelligent enough to understand that you are here in the midst of the campaign. Who better to relay the true nature of the situation."

"Exactly." Count Adlberg puffed out his chest so his medals glittered, Menshikov's disinterest quite forgotten. "A Horse Guard is always a Horse Guard," he pronounced, his cavalry mustache twitching as he shot a withering glance at the lieutenant who was from a less exalted regiment. "We are honor bound to do our duty to God and country, and we will!"

The young officer was sulking, his gaze on his wineglass, the governor's blunt insult to his corps falling on deaf ears.

Offering the governor a warm smile to divert him from pressing the young officer with some male unpleasantness having to do with so-called *principles of honor,* Aurore said, admiration in her gaze, "We are all most fortunate to have men of your stature leading us to victory."

"And victory *will* come, my dear, never fear." Leaning forward again, the count spoke in an undertone. "Today's dispatch also stated that five more divisions are marching south. Those together with Gorchakov's new command will assure us victory within the month. Everyone knows the English ranks are seriously depleted. The French still have a considerable force, but their emperor is a trial for General Pelissier. The fool wants to command by telegraph from Paris." The count snorted. "Napoleon's nephew is no general—mark my words."

Mark his words in more ways than one, Aurore thought, determined to see Adlberg's recent dispatch for herself. Smiling prettily at the governor as he rattled on about how intimate his relationship was with the tsar, she wondered whether music would follow dinner. If not, the usual dancing would allow her the opportunity to slip away for a few minutes. Concentrating on the governor's face, she gave every appearance of absorbed attention while she planned how best to accomplish her mission.

At that point, she refused more wine—feigning a ladylike gentility. She would need all her wits about her to get to the dispatch undetected. With the task before her occupying her mind, she impatiently waited for the tedious dinner to end.

At long last, dessert concluded, Helena rose to her feet, her diamonds sparkling on her ears and plump bosom. Smiling at her guests, she announced with her usual commanding air, "We have an epic performance for you tonight. Madame Vicoli, fresh from her recent triumph in Venice, will entertain us with her most successful role as Violetta in *La Traviata*."

The men inwardly groaned, as did a good number of the ladies who were either impatient for their whist game or the more pleasant game of dalliance.

Aurore almost crowed with delight. With what might very well be a lengthy program, with what would at least be a *noisy* program, she would have an excellent opportunity to slip away—ostensibly to the ladies' retiring room.

She could even plead a headache if necessary.

Taking advantage of the governor's momentary inattention as another guest spoke to him, Aurore quickly rose to her feet and moved away from the table. She had no wish to be escorted into the music room by Adlberg; she particularly didn't want to be seated at the front of the room near her host and hostess.

Darley was unable to leave the dining room with equal ease. Claimed by Helena as her partner for the evening, he was obliged to conduct her into the music room, with good grace if not his full attention. Like Aurore, he had other things on his mind.

After seating the countess, Darley stood behind her chair, playing the gallant. A captive one. Turning to survey the assembly at one point, he caught Aurore's eye and grimaced.

She understood. He was being forced to play cicisbeo to Helena.

Having deliberately seated herself near the back of the room, Aurore bided her time, waiting for the opportune moment when she could leave with the least notice. After Madame Vicoli took her first bows and embarked on her second solo, "Ah, fors e lui," Aurore considered the time appropriate. Everyone was still nominally focused on the stout singer from Milan, boredom not having set in yet.

Just as she was about to rise, she saw Gazi lean over and whisper into Helena's ear. A moment later, he stood upright, turned and walked from the room.

Swearing under her breath, Aurore considered

her options. If she left now, she risked running into Gazi. Should that happen, she would likely have to abort her mission. On the other hand, *if* she left now and *didn't* see Gazi, her absence was less apt to be noticed with everyone's attention still on Madame Vicoli. Gripping the arms of her chair, she hesitated. Should she or shouldn't she? Ultimately, time constraints determined her course of action. It was now or never. Coming to her feet, she smiled at those guests who had also chosen to sit at the back of the room and moved past them with a studied casualness.

Once out in the hall, she allowed herself a small sigh of relief.

Step one accomplished.

Glancing up and down the empty corridor, she quickly moved toward the main staircase. Having visited the governor's house often, she was familiar with the floor plan. That the ladies' retiring room was on the same floor as the reception rooms was a slight problem, but she would claim ignorance should she be stopped by anyone of consequence as she made her way downstairs.

Understanding time *was* of the essence, she cautioned herself to remain calm. Instead, as though defying rational thought, a cold chill gripped her senses and it took all her will to tamp down the rush of fear. That spies were summarily executed if captured was not helpful to recall. *Concentrate,* she silently urged herself. *Concentrate on the task at hand.*

She was breathing hard—from both nerves and her speedy trek down the stairs and ground floor corridors—when she reached the count's study. The room was distant from the main reception rooms, tucked away at the back of the house. Not exactly in close proximity to the music room. Which was both good and bad.

Placing her hand on the door lever, she rehearsed her lie should someone be inside the study. She would give the appearance of being tipsy and say, *So very sorry, I'm looking for the ladies' retiring room.*

So then . . .

Taking a deep breath, she pressed down on the door handle, heard the soft click of the latch give way and, pushing open the door, slipped inside the dimly lit chamber.

"You!" she gasped.

Gazi was standing at the desk. "Get out," he said, his voice knife sharp.

She shut the door instead and locked it.

"Don't be foolish," he muttered, his face half in shadow with only the desk lamp lit. "Leave."

"If someone knocks we can be lovers looking for privacy."

"They won't believe it." From the moment she'd locked the door there had been no question in his mind what she was here for.

"I'm surprised," she said, moving toward him.

"We both are," he said drily. "But this isn't a game."

"I'm aware of that. Was Helena as revealing as her husband? You needn't answer. It appears she was. Who do you work for?"

"I might ask the same of you."

"The French."

"The English."

"Are you English?"

He hesitated a fraction of a second, having lived with his disguise for some time. "Yes," he finally said. There was no longer any point in subterfuge.

"That explains the mannerisms that didn't quite fit a man called Gazi."

"How perceptive," he muttered, his gaze flipping back to the documents he was reading. "Now, go. I'll share this with you later."

"Why should I believe you?" She'd reached the desk although he gave no notice, his attention on the dispatches before him.

"You have to know this is fucking dangerous," he growled, turning over a page. "Let *me* take the risks."

"You didn't answer my question."

"What difference does it make? Either you believe me or you don't."

"Considering the circumstances, I'm not in a particularly trusting mood. You're not who you said you were, you're not a legitimate trader. Who knows, you may not even be English."

Darley looked up once more, gave her a disgusted look and said, "Fine. Stay. But don't expect me to save your hide if something goes wrong."

"I can take care of myself."

"Sure you can. Here, help yourself." He shoved some sheets of paper her way.

Darley was reading the last page of the dispatch when he lifted his head. He quickly shut off the gas lamp. "Did you hear that?" His nostrils flared like a wolf on the scent, his face washed in silver moonlight.

Aurore hadn't heard a thing.

"Now listen and don't argue." His voice was pitched low. "There's someone outside the window—maybe more than one. I'm guessing we have guests outside in the corridor as well." He was shoving the papers down the front of his tunic. "How good a shot are you?"

Aurore's heart was beating so loudly, she had to strain her ears to hear him. But her voice was steady when she said, "I'm good."

"Here." He pulled a small revolver from his trouser pocket and handed it to her. "You have four shots. Use them wisely. I'm going to throw a chair through that window to give us a moment of surprise. Then I'm going through; you're to follow on my heels. It's only a foot or so to the ground, but don't stumble. You understand?" he murmured, slipping a second larger handgun from under his tunic.

She nodded, then said, "Yes," because he wasn't looking at her, his gaze was on the windows.

"You know what will happen to us if we're caught."

"Yes."

"Good." He swung back. "Then you won't be queasy about using your weapon."

"No."

Quickly checking the rounds in his revolver, he tucked it in his belt and lifted the desk chair. "On the count of three—the chair, me behind it, you behind me. With luck we'll only have some house guards to deal with. With *real* luck the rest of the party is unaware of our activities. But those footsteps in the corridor could mean I'm wrong. The door's locked though"—his smile flashed—"thanks to you. We won't have to immediately deal with that threat. Ready? Here we go—one, two, three."

The crash of breaking glass was followed by a series of gunshots. From the garden outside, through the locked door. From Darley's Lefaucheux Francotte revolver as he leaped through the smashed window, gun blazing.

A man screamed, the sound echoing in the still, black night.

Two more quick rounds from Darley's pistol and a second anguished cry.

"Are you there?" he grunted, shoving his hand backward as he ran.

Aurore caught his hand.

His fingers closed on hers, and an instant later she was swung off her feet and swept up into his arms. A hard-as-nails Hercules to her rescue.

As Darley raced through the silent garden, the sounds of pursuit were left behind.

"We're lucky that was a good solid door," he muttered.

While Aurore wasn't precisely in shock, having experienced violence directed at her for the first time left her breathless. Or perhaps leaping through the window and keeping up with Gazi was the cause.

He glanced down. "Are you all right?"

She forced air into her lungs. "Fine," she whispered.

He laughed as if this was some lark. As if he regularly fought his way out of deadly ambushes. "You'll be even better soon, my fearless little lioness," he said, still smiling, scarcely breathing hard. "We're almost there."

She thought about asking where there was but couldn't quite put words in order with her nerves still quivering and her heart beating like a drum.

After leaping over a low stone wall bordering the garden, Darley tossed her through the open door of his waiting carriage. "Go!" he ordered, slamming the door shut and leaping up beside Cafer.

In seconds, the horses were galloping full-out, the black coach careening down the narrow lane toward town. Braced to remain upright in the luxurious interior, bobbing like a cork in the sea with the continuous crack of the whip urging on the team, Aurore understood now why they'd taken Gazi's—or whatever his name's—carriage and driver tonight. She also understood why the carriage was not where they'd left it.

She should have known something was in the air when Gazi had had a change of heart and insisted they go to dinner while she had changed her mind as well and was coaxing him to stay in bed.

She should have known when he'd said, "Be a dear and come along with me. I'll see that you are suitably rewarded when we get back home." His smile had been deliciously wicked. "Whatever you want, as long as you want," he'd whispered against her ear.

How could she have refused *that?*

He had known as much.

She was grateful at least that the self-styled Gazi had been cautious enough to plan for all the eventualities. Not that she didn't doubt he would have preferred their activities had gone unnoticed.

But now that their conspicuous departure exposed them to unaccountable dangers, her first order of business was to find Etienne and warn him. Their pursuers would soon be in full cry.

When the carriage came to a stop and Gazi opened the door, she said exactly that in a frantic, blurted-out exclamation of consternation and fear.

"Don't worry. My men will find your brother," Darley said, much too calmly she resentfully thought as he lifted her out of the carriage and set her on her feet. "Come," he said, brusque and peremptory now. "You have to change into riding clothes. Adlberg's troops will be here shortly."

"I can't just leave Etienne behind!" she cried, racing after Darley as he turned and strode toward the house. Stumbling over her shredded skirt and petticoats, she quickly grabbed up fistfuls of silk fabric ripped by the jagged glass from the smashed window and rushed to follow his swift unremitting pace.

"He won't be left behind. I have a number of informants in town. They'll find him and take him to safety." He shot her a hard look over his shoulder. "Don't argue with me."

"Take him to safety *where?*" Accelerating, she tried to keep up with him as he entered the house.

"To Eupatoria. He'll be safe in the garrison. Omar Pasha is a friend of mine."

"I don't even know your name!" she shouted. He was halfway up the stairs and moving fast.

"Darley," he shouted back. "You can ask me anything you want once we're in the saddle! My staff will see that your servants are safely away. Cafer is sending men to track down your brother as we speak. Now fucking hurry. I'm not in the mood to be hung tonight!"

Chapter

17

An hour later, they stopped to rest their horses in a ravine carved deep into the treeless steppe. Cafer and Sahin led their mounts to a bubbling rivulet that had been pooled up long ago for just such a purpose.

There had been no opportunity to talk as they'd ridden hard to outdistance pursuit. Seizing the moment now, Aurore peppered Darley with questions. She wanted to know who he was, what his plans were, how she would be impacted by them.

He answered her with reluctant yesses and noes. When those weren't possible, he chose opaque, ambiguous responses. He was civil but evasive.

"I'm not asking you to hand over your soul," she finally said, her voice fretful, exasperated, pugnacious challenge in her scowl. "I would just appreciate a general idea of who you are and where we're going."

He wanted to say, *You know me already,* but understood that a man's knowing and a woman's weren't

the same. She was not likely to accept his male interpretation. "My name is Hugh D'Abernon, Marquis of
Darley," he said. "I'm English as I already mentioned.
I've been living in the mountains of Circassia for almost five years. Before that I lived all over."

"All over? What does that mean? And where in the
mountains? I know the mountain tribes."

Not so well that she'd known for certain he wasn't
Tatar, he thought. But he answered as politely as possible, even as he realized that she was about to become a bloody lot of trouble for the immediate
future. "I've lived in North Africa, Istanbul, Sicily"—
he paused, going back through his history—"San
Francisco during the first months of the gold fever.
From there, India"—he paused again. "Not so long in
India. Too hot," he said, clearly not meaning it, meaning something else. "After that I crossed over the
Caucasus and settled in Circassia."

"Don't forget Italy," she said with stiletto-like finesse.

Bitch, he thought. "Yes, and Italy," he said, reining
in his temper. "As for where we're going, we have to
leave the Crimea. At least until the war is over."

"Don't be ridiculous." Outraged and resentful,
she glared at him. "I'm not leaving the Crimea. How
can you even suggest it? This is my home!"

Her reaction was predictable. Which was precisely
why he hadn't wanted to have this discussion. He
knew she'd be quarrelsome and difficult. "Our exile
may be only temporary," he explained, striving for a
degree of patience he was far from feeling with a
mutinous female on his hands and forty miles of
Russian territory yet to cross before they reached
safety. "And admit, if you return home, even if your

estate currently lies within Allied lines, Russian agents could reach you. The Third Section—*the secret police*—is relentless as you well know."

"I could tell them that I had been coerced by you—forced to accompany you to dinner in order to dupe the Adlbergs," she argued. "I could make it clear that my life would have been forfeit had I not submitted to you. Surely if I explained that I had been compelled to do your bidding, I would be believed. I've lived here my entire life. My father was born here. Why wouldn't I be considered trustworthy?"

"Probably because your brother enlisted in the French army. You have to admit, that rather flagrant transgression sends up a warning flag or two."

"I could explain that he was young and misguided."

"Perhaps a compassionate judge might believe you," he said, with forced courtesy, glancing at his men, gauging their readiness, wanting this useless conversation over. "Or maybe a judge would be willing to negotiate some kind of—ah—settlement, shall we say, with you," he added, softly sardonic. "But you wouldn't go free. Not with Russia losing this war."

"So, that's it? Don't argue with me," she snapped, glowering at him, her voice hot with affront. "I'm right, you're wrong. Just do as you're *TOLD?*"

Oh fuck. "I would rather you thought of my solution as mutually beneficial," he said in a carefully controlled tone of voice.

"Easy for you to say," she churlishly retorted. "You're not leaving a prosperous estate behind."

"I will personally see to it that Raglan understands your property requires security." He was mentally counting to ten.

"Don't bother," she shot back. "Our French forces are much superior to yours. General Pelissier will see that my property is kept safe."

Feeling victory within his grasp, he resisted the impulse to smile. At least she was no longer refusing to leave the Crimea. With luck—who knew—by the time they reached Balaclava, she might be reconciled to the inevitable. As he saw it, her choices were severely limited—not that he intended to be so brutally frank with her. But if she stayed, she would be tracked down and hung. Both of them would be if caught.

With Russia's recent disastrous defeat at Eupatoria—the battle lost in only three brief hours—the government needed scapegoats. Rather than take the blame, the incompetent Russian command would willingly sacrifice someone like Aurore.

What better excuse than that a spy had delivered the Allies their victories?

What better excuse for the gross mismanagement by the Russian general staff?

"Tell me where my brother is or I'm not going anywhere," she muttered, willful and mulish, not yet ready to cede complete victory to Darley. "Is Etienne safe? Has he been taken from Simferopol? I have a right to know that at least, damn you!"

She was working herself into a frenzy. "Cafer," Darley called out softly, motioning him over.

Leaving the horses with Sahin, Cafer strolled toward them with the rolling gait of a lifelong horseman.

"Miss Clement was inquiring about her brother," Darley said, a note of warning in his voice as Cafer approached.

"The youth should be halfway to Eupatoria by now." Cafer smiled faintly, understanding that his friend had his hands full from the look of Miss Clement's scowl. "I believe he's riding his favorite horse. That high-spirited black with white markings."

"Thank you." Aurore smiled at Cafer. "Thank you very much. I'm very relieved." Darley received neither thanks nor a smile.

"Are we about ready?" Darley briskly inquired, meeting Cafer's gaze with a significant look.

Cafer understood that look—long-suffering, asking for mercy. "Anytime," he said, knowing Darley always made it a point to give wide berth to contentious women. "The horses are ready."

"Then we'll ride for another hour before stopping again," Darley noted, his voice crisp.

Either Darley had reason to stop or he was doing it for the lady. Their Karabagh mounts were bred to run for days without rest. Cafer dipped his head in acknowledgment, the silver ornaments on his hat glittering with the movement. "Are you thinking Bahcesaray?"

Darley nodded. "At Alexios's."

Question answered, Cafer turned and went to bring up the horses.

A few moments later, Darley offered his hand to Aurore, then lifted her up onto her saddle.

Having chosen boy's clothing for their escape—part of her contingency wardrobe kept at the hotel in Sevastopol and transferred to Simferopol—she rode astride. Taking time to double-check her cinch and stirrups, Darley slid his fingers over the smooth leather straps with a practiced touch.

Such a courteous man, she thought, when she would have preferred not thinking of him with kindness. When she would have preferred continuing to stoke her anger. But he suddenly touched her thigh, a gentle brushing stroke, and her body—immune to umbrage or resentments—automatically quickened.

"You can rest at Alexios's," he said. "We'll stay long enough to have tea."

He was adjusting his schedule for her, she knew. He didn't drink tea and she doubted he needed rest. "I'd appreciate that," she said, as a pleasurable warmth spread through her senses. And when he smiled up at her, she couldn't resist smiling back.

That she had favored him with a smile shouldn't have meant so much. This was not the time to yield to tender sentiment. They were still at risk. Bahcesaray had spies everywhere. Not to mention the countryside was swarming with deserters riding in brigand troops, living by rape and plunder. And deserters had nothing to lose, their lives already forfeit.

Regardless all the hazards and perils facing them, Darley nevertheless experienced a gratifying sense of happiness as he swung back into the saddle.

For the next hour, they pounded east under the light of the moon, avoiding roads and villages, riding cross-country to save time and evade notice, alert to any sign of life on the vast, open steppe.

As they entered the outskirts of the old capital city of Bahcesaray, a church bell somewhere tolled the hour of two. Traveling through the narrow streets, on watch for any individuals out in the wee hours of the night, they traveled for some time before reaching Alexios's neighborhood. The horses lifted their heads and picked up their pace, the smell of a familiar stable in the air.

A few minutes later, they rode past the two guards at Alexios's gate and brought their mounts to rest in a large courtyard. A number of grooms and servants immediately appeared to offer their assistance, fol-

lowed shortly by their host knotting the tie on his
crimson silk dressing gown. "Come in, come in,"
Alexios exclaimed, greeting them warmly. "I will
have tea brought up." He knew better than to ask
why they had arrived in the dead of night.

After introducing Aurore, Darley added, "We won't
stay long. But if you could see that a telegram is sent,
I would be grateful."

Aurore pinned Darley with her gaze. "A telegram?"

"I'll send one for you as well."

Not knowing their host, she didn't question Darley further. "Thank you," she simply said.

"Is all well then?" Pallas pleasantly inquired, meeting Darley's gaze.

"As well as can be expected," Darley said, his brows
lifting expressively, "with the country at war."

"Ah, yes, the continuing machinations of govern-
mental forces," Alexios murmured, knowing he'd
have an explanation from Darley later. "Come
now"—he waved them toward his mansion. "Have
some refreshments while I see that your messages are
sent."

Cafer and Sahin opted for the servants' hall, familiar with both the establishment and most of the
inhabitants since the banker was a close friend of
Darley's.

Pallas, in turn, escorted Aurore and Darley upstairs to a large room overlooking a moonlit garden.
Servants had preceded them. The room was lit by
two magnificent chandeliers, the candlelight warm
and welcoming. Exquisite carpets lay haphazardly on
the floor, one atop the other in luxurious, colorful
excess. Silk-covered divans in brilliant colors lined
the walls. Antique sculpture, so prevalent in a region
populated for two millennium, adorned the room,

while the walls were embellished with ancient fres-
coes depicting frolicking gods and goddesses.

"If you'd like to freshen up first, Miss Clement,"
Pallas murmured, beckoning a servant forward.

Grateful to have an opportunity to wash away the
dirt of the road, Aurore willingly followed the servant. She was tired, her life was in disarray, her future
unknown. To wash her face and hands and have a
cup of hot tea was sufficient at the moment. She didn't
want to think of anything beyond those basic needs.

In Aurore's absence Darley quickly explained
their situation to Alexios while his host escorted him
to a small office. Shown to a large desk set in the center of the room, Darley sat down and swiftly encrypted
a message, detailing Governor Adlberg's dispatch.
He readied one message for Raglan and another for
Pelissier. Although Pelissier would have to have his
telegram translated by Cattley's staff since Darley was
unfamiliar with the French code.

Once finished, Darley handed the two sheets of
paper to Pallas, who, in turn, handed them to his
waiting native factotum.

"I own the telegraph office," the banker said with
a slight smile as his steward exited the room. "Not of-
ficially, of course. The French ostensibly do. But who
will guard their lines if not for me. Rest assured, your
messages will go through. My men patrol the entire
telegraph line east of Varna." He rose from his lounging pose in a beautifully carved armchair. "Now, let
us join your lovely lady friend, who by the way is a
pleasure to behold in her leather breeches. And I expect you'd like something stronger than tea."

Darley debated explaining the state of his and Aurore's friendship, but transient as it was, decided
against any disclosure. "If we didn't have two more

hours to ride," he said, instead, "I'd say give me the whole bottle."

"With the exception of deserters, the Allies control the country from here to the coast. I'll send some of my men with you as well. So have your bottle if you wish."

Darley grimaced as he came to his feet. "I'd better not. I don't want to risk losing my temper."

Alexios grinned. "I rather thought I detected a bit of trouble in paradise." He and Darley had done their share of carousing together. "The lady looked slightly disgruntled." With Darley, there were always women and, from time to time, the inevitable difficulties as well.

Darley shrugged and moved toward the door. "We're arguing about leaving the Crimea. Aurore doesn't want to leave; I don't blame her. This is her home."

"But we don't want her to hang," Pallas pointed out softly.

"You tell her that," Darley muttered. "I've tried."

"She runs their estate, according to her brother." Pallas bowed Darley through the door before him. "And now I find out that she's a competent secret agent as well." He kept pace with Darley as they moved down the hall. "Miss Clement is a woman of parts, my friend. You can't expect her to be docile."

"At this particular time, I prefer she was," Darley grumbled. "In her current mood, I don't relish being in close quarters with her on my yacht."

"Are you sailing home?"

"Yes. My work here is over for the moment. As is Aurore's. So before the assassins get us, I thought I'd escort her to Paris on my way to England. With luck, her brother might be in residence when we arrive.

He left for Eupatoria while we rode east." Darley smiled. "Or at least such are my plans. To convince her is another matter."

"You don't think she'll eventually understand?"

Darley shrugged. "She would prefer returning to her estate. She would also like to ignore the fact that the Third Section will come and exact their revenge on her."

"As they surely will," Alexios agreed.

"Now, if only she will see the light," Darley drawled.

Alexios smiled. "You have an interesting conundrum on your hands, my friend. You who rail against the boredom of overly obliging women have found your match in this lovely lady. Perhaps you should simply sit back and enjoy the fireworks."

"You have a point. She *is* damned interesting."

"I presume you are not speaking of her conversational skills," Pallas murmured.

Darley grinned. "No. But she is well read."

"Then make sure you bring along plenty of books for your journey home," Pallas suggested drolly. "For those times when you're too tired to fuck."

"I have not yet reached that stage," Darley replied, considering their sea voyage with slightly more optimism.

"Lucky man," Pallas quipped.

"Perhaps." Darley still wasn't convinced, but he had to admit, there were definitely compensations.

As the men approached the door to the salon, Pallas's factotum came racing toward them down the hall, frantically waving a sheet of paper.

Pallas touched Darley's arm. "Wait. Kosmas is not easily excited."

"The tsar is dead!" Kosmas gasped. "I waited for—a

reply—as you instructed," he panted, stopping before them. He handed the telegram to Pallas. "The French speak openly of his death."

Lips pursed, Pallas digested the shocking news before handing the telegram to Darley.

"Nicholas died March 2," Darley murmured. He looked up. "The information arrived in France and England via Berlin the very day he died."

"Yet seven days later, no one here has heard the news." Pallas shrugged. "No wonder Russia is losing this war. Thank you, Kosmas. I won't need you again tonight." He glanced at Darley. "Will I?"

"No, we're leaving soon. Thank you, Kosmas," Darley added, smiling at the factotum before turning back to Pallas. "Nicholas's death should help bring the war to an end."

"One can only hope," Pallas noted, waving Darley before him into the salon.

The two men found Aurore seated on a pink silk divan, a teacup in hand. She'd loosened her hair from the pigtail she'd worn for riding, her golden tresses pale against the blackness of her jacket.

Leather became her, Darley reflected, but then what didn't? She would have been equally enticing in sackcloth or—nothing at all, he luridly thought. Curtailing his carnal impulses—this was hardly a practical time—he said, "We have unexpected news." At the sudden panic in her eyes, he quickly added, "It's of a political nature, not about your brother. Tsar Nicholas died last week." He bowed faintly. "We are obliged to your countrymen for the information—the news was relayed by French telegraph."

"You may thank the French for their greater troop strength as well." In Darley's absence, Aurore had continued to augment her laundry list of his short-comings and misdemeanors. "Or you'd be losing this war."

A muscle twitched along his jaw. "Agreed."

The look passing between Darley and Miss Clement was definitely acrimonious, Alexios decided. "Vodka?" he blandly inquired, glancing at Darley. "Or would you prefer brandy?"

"Brandy. Bring the bottle," Darley muttered, dropping down on a vividly patterned divan a room's width from Aurore. His temper barely in check, he thought it prudent to keep his distance.

Pallas left to find a servant, and a heavy silence fell.

Lengthened. Poisonously.

"How's your tea?" Darley asked at last, clipped and indifferent.

"Excellent." Aurore offered him a frozen smile. "Are we staying long?"

"Perhaps." Lounging back against the pillows, he put up his booted feet and leisurely crossed his ankles. Making it plain who was in charge of their schedule. Taking pleasure in her scowl.

"Is pursuit no longer an issue?" An icy voice to go with her frozen smile.

"Not much of an issue."

"Meaning?"

"We'll take some of Alexios's troopers with us when we leave. And this is more or less Allied territory now."

"Thank you for the information." Malice in every word.

"You're welcome," he replied with equal spite, unsure why he felt the need to win this fight. Just knowing he did.

As it happened, they stayed longer than Darley had planned.

The brandy was to blame. It helped blur the sharp edges of his anger, or he felt as though it did. Or perhaps it no longer mattered when they left since Raglan and Pelissier were in possession of the pertinent facts. Not to mention, they'd be safe against pursuit with Alexios's troopers guarding them.

Why not drink when he was in a drinking mood?

As the brandy bottle was emptied, the men discussed the war, the state of readiness of the opposing armies, the ineffectiveness of the siege. They both knew to a farthing the quality of the officers in charge, the good ones, the bad ones, the ones like Cardigan who only played at war until it was no longer amusing. Contriving some flimsy excuse about his health, Cardigan had already sailed home on his private yacht with the comforts of a French chef and cases of champagne to ease his journey.

The two men compared notes on the rising number of cholera cases, a fact of life with the winter cold dissipating and the water supplies contaminated. They bet large sums on when the war would be over, whether typhus and cholera would ultimately prevail or the huge new artillery guns pounding Sevastopol would eventually win the day.

Darley bet on August for an end to the gore.

Pallas was of the mind that the Russians would fight to the last man. He put his wager on December.

Their examination of the war came to an end once the bottle was empty.

Darley slowly rose from the sofa, not unsteadily, but with the exactitude of a man who had had considerable drink. He bowed to his host. "We thank you for your splendid hospitality. It's time to bid you and the Crimea adieu. We have become personas non grata."

"I understand." Pallas smiled. "It was inevitable was it not in your trade?"

Darley's white teeth flashed in a grin. "I suppose."

Turning to Aurore who had immediately stood when Darley had, the Greek banker bowed. "It was a pleasure to meet you, Miss Clement. Give my regards to your brother."

"Thank you. I shall."

Her smile was quite dazzling, Pallas decided. He expected Darley would soon find a way to assuage her anger. Leading his guests downstairs, he escorted them outside to the courtyard where their mounts waited. "I wish you good journey," he said. "You should be safe with my troopers."

Their leave-taking was exquisitely polite. The tension between Darley and Aurore went unmentioned, all the requisite courtesies performed with a cultivated civility. Darley helped Aurore into her saddle, she thanked him, Darley mounted, thanked his host and wheeled his mighty Karabagh with perhaps only slightly more force than necessary.

His charger was well trained and generally treated with affection; Aristo forgave his master's display of temper. And once out in the country, Darley bent low over the massive, golden neck, patted the silky coat and whispered an apology in his horse's ear. Then he murmured something more.

Aristo blew down his nose and pricked his ears; a second later he dug in his heels in a great surge of power, responding to Darley's quiet words. His hindquarters sank away as he prepared to spring into his stride, and in a great bound he leaped forward. He was galloping full out in seconds.

The Karabagh were a competitive breed, so the other horses took up the charge and followed of their own accord.

How pleasant it was to forgot all else with a racing horse beneath you running wild and strong, Aurore thought, in the mood for speed. With the wind in her face, the grassy steppe rushing up toward her between her horse's ears, powerful frame and limbs moving under her with the rhythm and force of a freight train, the contentious world blissfully disappeared.

They galloped for miles hell-bent for leather over the moonlit steppes, Darley remaining well in the lead. Everyone rode superbly. This was a country of horsemen, their mounts all hard and lean and trained to the inch. They raced through light fog banks in the valleys, flew full tilt over the moonlit high ground, rode through fields of spring flowers and waves of grass, inhaled the sweet scents washing up over them in fragrant clouds.

Until—at last, Darley closed his fingers around the reins, squeezed lightly, slowly fed out the leathers again, and Aristo slowed to a canter.

And so they traveled the remainder of the night, rocking softly in their padded saddles, dozing at times—leisurely advancing on Balaclava.

His temper dispelled, Darley no longer felt the need to ride like a man possessed.

They were well within Allied lines as well.

And reaching their destination only meant a renewal of the struggle between Aurore and himself.

Chapter

18

When they reached Raglan's farmhouse on a hill above Balaclava, it was almost dawn, a faint golden glow streaking the horizon.

"This shouldn't take long," Darley said, dismounting, Aurore and the men remaining in the saddle. "Raglan's still abed, I expect, but Cattley will be up." Raglan's intelligence chief occupied a room in the farmhouse to expedite the transmission of critical information. "We'll ride over to French headquarters after this."

True to his word, he returned shortly, his report to Cattley quickly done.

"Your brother reached Eupatoria safely," he mentioned as he remounted. "A messenger recently arrived with that and other news." What he didn't say was that Etienne was aboard ship bound for Marseille. He wasn't yet ready for the argument about who was going where, when and with whom. "Now, we're off to see Pelissier, right?" His tone was bland as was his query. He wanted her aboard his yacht before any contentious issues came up.

Aurore's report to Pelissier took considerable time. Seated on a makeshift bench constructed from packing crates that had been set beside what had once been a garden fountain—now bereft of Neptune's head—Darley checked his watch again.

"Maybe she went out the back," Cafer murmured, lounging in his saddle, rolling himself another cigarette.

"I'd like to think not, but—"

"I'll check." Slipping his unlit cigarette in his shirt cuff, Cafer nudged his mount with the merest touch of his heels and rode away.

He was back five minutes later, a satisfied smile on his face. "No back door—or rather, it's nailed shut. So much for French trust."

Darley smiled tightly. "A sensible people."

"Like your darling?" Cafer teased.

"She's not my darling." Darley grimaced. "As for her being sensible, I have no such illusions."

"Tie her up and carry her aboard."

"It might come to that." *He wasn't joking.*

When Aurore reappeared nearly an hour later she had a sullen look on her face. Unconsciously bracing himself, Darley came to his feet. The next few hours could prove difficult.

"The general agrees with you," Aurore said, her nose curled in distaste, her chin lifted defiantly. "I hope you're happy."

Understanding that she didn't appreciate having

been overruled by both Pelissier and him, Darley carefully refrained from saying he was. "It's only a temporary retreat," he said, in an effort to mollify.

"Pelissier said as much," she replied with a sniff of displeasure.

As would any reasonable man. "You should pack a few things," he suggested, following her to her horse. "Will your staff stay or go do you think?" He wanted to talk about mundane things in order to avoid the more divisive issues. "Should I send Alexios's men home or would you like them to stay?"

"Send them home." She turned on him as she reached her horse. "And you needn't speak to me as though I were a child. I won't embarrass you and make a scene." She was tired, tired of fighting the black and white certainties.

She wouldn't have liked him to say thank you, so he didn't. But he thought it. "Here," he said instead, cupping his hands. "Let me help you up."

As she stepped into his cupped palms, he threw her up on her horse.

She sat a horse with ease, she rode well, she was an accomplished woman in any number of ways. He couldn't expect her to be a pattern card for submission, now could he? "I'll let Alexios's men know our plans and see Cafer and Sahin off, then I'll follow you."

With the briefest of nods she turned her horse toward home. Pelissier had promised her the war would be over by the end of the summer. She hoped he was right. She hoped even more that she could return to her vineyards and when she did everything would be as it once was.

But she wasn't delusional.

There were always winners and losers in conflicts like this.

Countries' borders were often redrawn after a war.

Even local authorities might covet valuable property such as hers once she left. The taint of Etienne's defection would be a reasonable enough excuse to confiscate the land. She sighed. If crying helped she'd cry an ocean of tears.

Not likely that however.

Squaring her shoulders, she faced the sobering truth.

Leave she must.

And after that—who knew?

She could only hope for the best.

The Third Section's agent in Sevastopol had been wakened with very important news from Simferopol. Gazi Maksoud and Miss Clement had been exposed as spies.

In his nightshirt and slippers, Kubitovitch snapped at the breathless rider who had ridden forty miles in less than four hours. "Are they captured?" He could practically taste his triumph as he marched the pair into Osten-Sacken's office.

The messenger visibly quailed.

"Well?" A voice cold as the grave.

"They escaped, sir."

The captain swore. "Wait outside," he ordered curtly, then turned and walked to a desk in the corner of the small apartment.

As the door closed on the messenger, Kubitovitch smoothed out a map and studied it for a moment, lips pursed, one finger tapping the desktop. One made one's own decisions this far from Petersburg and while he didn't precisely have carte blanche in his operations, if he could capture these two, it was worth the risk of taking responsibility into his own hands.

His superiors had been exceptionally free with operational funds since the war had taken a turn for the worse. They were willing to pay any price for victory. He would send a message to his informants; they were to notify him immediately if either Gazi or Miss Clement were sighted. After walking to the door, he pulled it open and beckoned the messenger in.

"Tell Shuvkin I need him now." He gave directions to his adjunct's lodgings. "Then come back for further orders."

Kubitovitch shut the door, then poured himself a fine brandy. He had aspirations beyond his present rank. Once he had been gazetted captain, he had availed himself of a fashionable tailor, given up vodka for the more fashionable brandy, and had on occasion now been known to peruse etiquette books. There would come a time when people like Osten-Sacken would rue the day they'd crossed him. The Grand Duke might hold the title of commander of the Third Section, but affairs could be handled outside protocols if one was careful.

Taking a sip of the aged brandy, he rolled the liquid around on his tongue, savoring the subtleties of the grape for a brief moment. Then he set about putting his orders for the coming pursuit in writing.

The two culprits would be leaving the Crimea.

The only question was where they would go to ground.

* * *

With the exception of the vineyard, Aurore was pleased to note that nothing had changed at her estate in the weeks she had been away. The house was the same, her staff as warm and familiar, the vineyards beginning to leaf out in the warmth of spring. After gathering everyone in the large drawing room, she explained what had occurred in her absence, editing her account in order not to either implicate or alarm her staff unnecessarily. She offered them all the choice of staying or being paid a generous stipend and returning to their home villages.

"The outcome of the war is still uncertain. Nor can I promise our vineyards will continue to be secure. Although, I have every faith they will," she finished with slightly more hope than confidence.

Her steward and housekeeper were determined to stay and she thanked them for their loyalty and courage.

"The men are all armed, miss," her steward, Kalgay, said. "And word has it Sevastopol will fall before long. Peotr was there the other day and the bombardment of the town is emptying entire neighborhoods."

Her staff, from housemaids to field workers, all agreed to stay.

She hadn't realized it mattered so much; she'd thought she could deal with their decision whatever it might be. But she found her eyes welling with tears, and swallowing hard, she said, "I thank you all. Papa, Maman and Etienne would thank you as well if they were here. Rest assured, I shall return just as soon as the war is over." And in that moment she realized she would pay whatever price she must to come back home.

Darley had overtaken Aurore before she reached

home and now watching Aurore speak to her staff, he was touched with a sense of nostalgia. How many years had it been since he'd been home? How many years had it been since he'd felt as though he *had* a home? While he'd visited his family from time to time, he'd not spent more than a fortnight in England in years.

As Aurore hugged every one of her servants goodbye, he felt a sudden pang of loneliness. He once had a home and family. He once had a wife and son.

So long ago now . . .

Case-hardened against useless regret, he quickly repressed his mournful thoughts and focused instead on the here and now—more pertinently on their time constraints. He glanced at the clock. Dare he say he'd like to sail with the tide?

"Do you need any help with anything?" he said instead.

Aurore turned around. She knew what he meant. "I suppose we should leave."

"I *would* like to catch the tide if possible."

He had said his yacht was in the harbor at Balaclava. "How much time do I have?"

"Three hours."

It would take them forty minutes to cover the distance. "I'll be ready soon," she said.

"If you don't need me, I'll go outside and wait."

"Please do. I won't be long."

Moving through the enfilade of elegant rooms, he reached the entrance hall and walked outside. Sitting down on the steps, he leaned back on his elbows and gazed out to sea. Catherine the Great had offered her foreign businessmen some of the most valuable coastal property in the Crimea. Aurore's estate bordered the sea for miles, her house built on the crest of a rise that fell away to spectacular cliffs and sandy beaches below. The house was a French chateau design, constructed from local white limestone, the parkland surrounding it lush with vegetation, flower beds and the occasional palm tree.

The climate was generally temperate except for those few winter months when the winds brought the arctic air down from the north. Unfortunately, last winter had been even more brutal than usual.

A shame Raglan and his staff had been relying on English travel reports from misleading sources when they'd planned the campaign. That mistake had proved fatal for thousands of troops. No one had thought to order warm clothing for the soldiers or proper tents or fodder for the horses.

The Duke of Newcastle, secretary of war at the time, had assured the dissenters, including Charles Cattley who had lived his entire life in Kerch, that according to Dr. Lee, winter in the Crimea was *entirely open to the warm breezes that blow across the southern sea. It enjoys consequently an exceedingly mild climate*. Refusing to listen to Cattley who had argued that the Crimean winter was bleak and cold, Newcastle instead promised to send a copy of Dr. Lee's account to General Raglan.

If Newcastle hadn't been titled and wealthy, he would have been hung from the nearest tree for the many thousand lives that had been needlessly sacrificed to his stupidity. Parliament had since voted for a Commission of Enquiry to review the mismanagement of the war, but no one of consequence would ever likely be punished.

The general staff and war office would go unscathed. Not so the English army that was down to less than thirteen thousand troop strength from the original twenty-one thousand soldiers who had landed at Kalamita Bay in September. Aurore was right when she'd said that England would lose the war if not for the French.

The French army was one hundred twenty thousand strong, well equipped, well fed, well housed. Famous chefs had organized the menu and camp kitchens, recruited the cooks and ordered the food stuffs for the army. The uniforms had been designed for the cold and ordered in vast quantities, French arms were equally abundant, their tents as well superior to anything the English had.

The French army never went without food, nor had they slept in summer-weight, ragged uniforms in muddy trenches without blankets like the poor, suffering English troops.

The sheer horror of the English soldiers' living conditions was the main reason Darley had volunteered his time and expertise. The English army needed all the help they could get. And for months, he and his men had supplied Cattley and Raglan with a steady supply of critical intelligence.

Until now.

He felt as though he'd come to some inexplicable crossroad in his life.

It was a thoroughly illogical feeling.

Or at least one he'd not felt for a very long time.

The last time he'd stood at a crossroad was in Parma eighteen years ago.

Softly swearing, he shut his eyes and willed himself to think less painful thoughts. He'd soon see his family; that would be agreeable. And tonight, he'd be sleeping in his own bed on his yacht. There was the prospect of Aurore's company as well—a not unpleasant consideration.

Then spring was in the air as well—an added plea-sure.

He could feel his tension ease in some small mea-sure.

Perhaps fate had taken a hand in all that had be-fallen them.

Or maybe it was simply time to move on.

Exhausted in body and spirit, largely sleepless since he couldn't remember when, the warm sun and gentle breezes tranquilizing, he dozed off.

When Aurore walked out on the front portico, she stood for a moment, watching him. He lay sprawled on his back on the warm marble—the scratched, worn leather of his breeches and boots, his dark linen shirt, his weapons tucked under his belt, pistols fastidiously oiled, kinjal large and lethal, all pro-claimed him a Caucasus mountain man—a warrior.

She noticed that some woman had lovingly em-broidered red stylized horsemen within the frame of entwined initials on the yoke of his shirt, and Aurore was surprised at the pang of jealousy she felt thinking of it. How foolish that would be, she decided, with a man like Gazi—she smiled . . . Darley. An English lord. She wasn't used to it yet.

He slept with his arms over his head like a child at peace.

Not that he had anything of the child in his beau-tiful, stark visage.

Nor in his strong, virile body.

But she liked that he felt at ease on her porch.

She liked a great deal about him—when she shouldn't.

No sensible woman should. That first night in Sevastopol, he'd said that he'd been wandering the world for eighteen years—remained unattached for eighteen years. A man like that wasn't likely to change.

Although why she was even thinking such thoughts was ludicrous.

She would find Etienne in Eupatoria and bid this English lord adieu.

There. Reality.

She thought she and Etienne might settle in Istanbul for now. It was a compromise; far enough away to possibly thwart the Third Section, yet close enough to quickly return home should the war end well for them.

She had also forgiven Gazi . . . Darley—really she must get that right—for his part in her flight. He couldn't have helped what happened at Adlberg's, no more than he could help that the war still presented risks for them all. She would have gone to find Count Adlberg's dispatch regardless. In truth, he'd probably saved her life.

Or at least partially saved her. She liked to think she could have talked her way out of the predicament if she'd been discovered in Adlberg's study. She had lied convincingly many times before in her role as spy for Pelissier. It helped to be a woman—a hapless, flighty woman who wandered into places she shouldn't.

"A penny for your thoughts."

She looked down and found him smiling up at her.

"I was thinking how much I'm looking forward to sleeping tonight."

"You're ready then." He came to his feet, all grace and supple muscle.

"Yes, ready."

A small silence fell, only the sound of the waves washing against the shore faintly heard.

"You haven't changed clothes."

"It doesn't matter." She'd been tired and he was in a hurry.

"No, of course not. Are the horses in back?"

She nodded, and he offered her his arm with the casual charm she knew now wasn't part of his role but intrinsic to the man. With equal urbanity, he engaged her in conversation of the most banal nature as they made their way down the stairs and around the side of the house to the back.

He helped her mount like he had so many times before, sprang in his saddle with his usual ease and with her carriage and luggage following in their wake, they rode to Balaclava.

They could very well be under scrutiny on their journey to the harbor, but the area was awash with Allied military. He wasn't concerned for their safety.

But he understood that the Third Section's reach was long.

He wasn't fool enough to think they would be forgotten.

Chapter

19

Darley and Aurore were observed from the shore as they were rowed out to Darley's yacht. Kubitovitch's deputies were efficient—or more to the point, numerous. The harbor was only one of many sites being watched.

As their launch pulled alongside the yacht, Aurore saw that Darley had named his vessel *Argo*, the name painted in Greek letters on the prow. Had it been named before or after Parma, she wondered? After, he would have said had she asked, the sleek 120-foot corvette constructed in 1838—although it had been retrofitted several times since. The latest refinement was a recent conversion to screw-propulsion. With their schedule no longer tied to the winds, the run time from Balaclava to Istanbul had been much improved.

An asset considering the yacht's recent missions.

As the launch came to rest at the base of the gangway, Darley lifted Aurore onto the stairs. The sea was becalmed, making it possible to ascend the stairway with ease. Was this an omen, she reflected. Did placid seas auger a tranquil voyage and possibly a tolerable exile?

On nearing the top of the gangway, however, any notions of tranquility were dispelled as an increasing clamor reached her ears. And stepping onto the gunwale a moment later, she stood transfixed.

No tranquility here. Chaos and tumult instead.

The deck was a mass of cots and makeshift awnings from fore to aft, starboard to port, the cots filled with wounded soldiers, while scores of doctors and nurses ministered to their needs. The sight of so many mangled, ravaged bodies brought back memories of Etienne's ordeal in the hospital at Sevastopol, the soft anguished cries beneath the din of activity all too familiar.

"Welcome aboard, my lady."

Jolted from her reverie she saw a wiry, red-haired man in a plain blue jacket devoid of embellishment or insignia offering her his hand. As she stepped down to the deck, she heard Darley say behind her, "Good afternoon, Harris. It's a pleasure to see you again."

"Aye, my lord. And you as well." The two men shook hands a moment later, a smile creasing the captain's leathery cheeks. "Still have all your limbs intact, I see."

"Just barely. We've recently outrun the gallows. Allow me to introduce Miss Clement. Miss Clement, Captain Harris."

"Pleased to meet ye, my dear. I heard things were heating up for spy folk inland. We're locked up right and tight here. No Russkies aboard. Those blackguards—and there be a right passel o' them ashore"—

he indicated the docks with a jerk of his head—"can just cool their heels, eh, my lord?"

Darley grinned. "That's the current plan." He shot a glance at the crowded deck. "We're full up I see."

"To the gunwales, sir. We were about to sail when I received your message."

"Excellent timing then. Miss Clement will be using my cabin. Have her things carried there."

"Beg pardon, sir. But there's ten men in your cabin. The worst of them, sir," the captain added under his breath. "Lost legs, the lot of 'em."

"Then we'll find some other quarters for Miss Clement."

"Anywhere, really," Aurore said, surveying the multitude before her. "I'll be quite comfortable in any corner at all."

Darley had other plans, but he only said, "Harris will manage something, won't you, Harris."

"Yes, sir, not a problem, sir. I'll put Tait on it."

While his crew brought aboard Aurore's luggage, Darley escorted Aurore to the officer's wardroom and offered her a chair. "Let me have the cook bring you tea while I go and pay my respects to the medical staff."

"I'll go with you. We'll have tea later."

He found he liked the thought of having tea with her later. This from a man who didn't drink tea. But *she* would be keeping him company, which made all the difference. And no doubt cook had some brandy on hand.

Since Darley hadn't answered, Aurore quirked one brow. "Is it my clothes? I could change."

"No, no . . . no one stands on ceremony here. I was thinking about the tide," he lied. "Come, I'll introduce you. I have a marvelous medical staff. Scottish." He smiled. "They're the best. Exemplary education, no nonsense, scrupulously clean in their surgeries. Their recovery rate is outstanding."

"How did you happen to involve yourself in this?" she asked as they walked down the passageway.

"How could I not? When Cardigan slept on his yacht every night while his soldiers died in the cold and mud, I felt like throttling him—vile beast. But I was helping Cattley and didn't want any repercussions. So I had the *Argo* brought up from Kerch instead and hired a medical staff. Harris shuttles the wounded to Mary Stanley's hospital at Kulali. Mary and her twenty nurses lasted a week at Scutari with Nightingale—egotistical bitch that she is—before leaving and opening her own hospital. It's excellent. She's already saved four hundred of the men we've brought her. Here's my cabin."

Darley introduced Aurore, then talked with each doctor, nurse and wounded man. He was cordial and warm to one and all, speaking to them of their families and friends, encouraging the injured who most needed heartening, joking with others, asking each one what they needed. A clerk had materialized behind him as though familiar with the drill and, pencil and pad in hand, registered each requested item.

Darley repeated the process in each cabin in turn, speaking to everyone. He did the same on deck, moving between the cots and men with a sympathetic word or a benevolent smile, promising them that they would soon be safe in Istanbul and ultimately home in England.

If it was possible to fall in love with someone because of their compassion alone, Aurore was very much inclined to do so as she watched Darley minister to all those less fortunate. Deeply moved by his generosity and kindness, she found him even more captivating. He offered comfort with touching tenderness, personalized every conversation with ease, never resorting to a litany of conventional phrases. He listened with genuine sincerity and responded in kind.

She had always considered herself a benevolent estate manager, but Darley put her to shame with his goodness.

As if she needed another reason to fall under his spell.

As if she wasn't already much too infatuated.

Which *would not* do. After the painful loss of her parents, she'd managed by sheer will and single-minded purpose to surmount her sorrow and take charge of the estate and her life.

She would not allow herself to succumb to some indefensible, ultimately futile desire.

She would not become mired in some romantic, fanciful illusion.

By the time Darley finished his rounds and they returned to the officer's wardroom, Aurore had brought her unruly emotions to heel. She could not afford to yield to unrealistic sentiments with not only her world but the greater world in such desperate straits. Good judgment and sound decision making were called for—indeed required—at times like these.

Tea was awaiting them, the china service prettily flowered and made for a lady's table. "How lovely." Aurore smiled, admiring the display—dainty sandwiches, scones, brandy for Darley. Once again in command of her passions, she said, sweetly cordial, "You have a very clever cook."

"He did it for you." Darley pulled out a chair for her.

She knew he hadn't. He had done it on Darley's orders. But she liked that Darley had wished to please her. "I must admit I am becoming increasingly enamored of you," she said in a deliberately coquettish tone as she sat down. There was safety in flirtation and none at all in sincerity. "You were just wonderful with everyone—staff and wounded alike. You made them laugh and smile; you truly brought them comfort. Is there anything you can't do, my darling Gazi?" She'd used the name deliberately; he seemed more hers when he was Gazi. When he wasn't an English lord who would sail away. When he might instead live in the mountains for another five years.

"Later tonight we'll see what I can and cannot do," he said with a wink. "Although, I warn you, I'm quite willing to try anything," he added as he poured her tea.

His voice was teasing, seductive. He knew exactly how to respond in the game of amour. She almost wanted to say, *thank you*, for so facilely rising to the lure, for reminding her that this was only sport. "How charming you are, Gazi. I hope you don't mind me calling you that. I don't know you yet as Darley."

"Perhaps later," he said, looking up from pouring himself a brandy, the decanter dwarfed by his large hand. "You can practice tonight."

How smoothly he'd done that. Double entendre—with such finesse. She felt quite unaccomplished.

"One or two sugars?" He indicated the sugar bowl.

"Two please." She met his gaze. "And thank you for everything."

"I should thank you," he said, picking up two

sugar lumps with silver tongs and dropping them into her cup. "You bring me pleasure." He smiled. "In any number of ways—most of them curiously innocuous. I'd forgotten such pleasures existed."

"We've been at war too long."

"Perhaps that's it," he said, sitting down across the table from her, sliding down on his spine into a comfortable sprawl. Lifting his glass to her, he grinned. "Personally, I think it has something to do with magic."

She laughed. "A most benign magic if it is."

"One we should enjoy while we may. We reach Kulali in two days." He hadn't meant to speak so gruffly at the last. But she must be told and better now than after several brandies when his mood would be less predictable.

Aurore set her cup down and looked at him. "Not Eupatoria first?"

It took him a moment to reply. "Your brother sailed for Marseille yesterday."

"You're sure?"

He nodded.

"Why didn't you tell me?"

He drained half his glass before he answered. "I wanted to avoid a fight."

"He's on his way to Paris then." She could be civil; why fight with Etienne already gone.

"I would assume."

"Am I that difficult?"

"No, of course not."

"Liar."

He grinned. "Only when necessary."

"When you're placating a lady."

"I suppose," he said with a shrug. "Don't say you haven't told a lie or two for dalliance's sake."

His smile was quite beautiful. She found him hard to resist. "You're sure about Etienne now." Irrationally, she didn't wish to think about Gazi's former amusements.

"I'm sure. The message came from a reliable source. Are you hungry?" A man's attempt to avoid conflict, or in Darley's case, his intent was twofold. He *was* hungry. "I can't remember when we ate last."

"Last night at Adlberg's."

"I drank instead to allay the tedium." He pulled himself upright. "What do you want to eat? These tiny sandwiches are not going to suffice for me."

"You decide. Your cook has his hands full I expect with the ship full to capacity."

"He'll find us something." Darley rose to his feet. "Excuse me—I'll be right back."

Aurore barely had time to drink her tea and sample a sandwich before Darley returned. "They found you a cabin, and cook promises me some food before long." Moving to the table, he tucked some sugar into his jacket pocket, picked up the decanter of brandy and the teapot and nodded toward the door. "Take your cup and the sandwiches and follow me."

He led her down the passageway, past several cabins to the bow. Tucking the decanter under his arm, he opened a small door and stood aside to let her walk in.

"They cleaned out the carpenter's storeroom," he said, bending low to avoid the lintel, following her and shutting the door behind him. "Tait is a wizard at overcoming difficulties."

"It's lovely." A folding officer's bed had been balanced between the two portholes, the coverlet an elegant Turkish silk in shades of green. Her valise was set on a chair beside the bed and a small pot of cherry blossoms was hanging from a hook nailed into the hull planking. "You must thank him."

"I already have. He brought up your valise, I see. He can find your trunks if need be, or," he said with a smile, "I could lend you one of my robes tonight."

"Will you be sleeping here too?" There was no evidence of male clothing or accoutrements—no shaving things or personal items.

"It's up to you. I wasn't certain what you wished with so much company aboard. If you'd prefer I didn't, I'd understand."

"I don't care about that—about what people say." Not that she ever had, but certainly now with people dying all around her, and displaced as she was from her former life, social custom was paltry stuff.

"You don't know how grateful I am for your—hospitality," he gently said.

Did personal pleasure take on greater significance in times of crisis? She was rather of the mind that it did. "Perhaps you might show me your gratitude in bed tonight," she said softly, her smile a siren's smile old as time.

His smile, in contrast, was lush with promise. "I would be honored."

"Lucky me," she purred.

"Au contraire, darling. I am the lucky one. In the meantime, please be my guest," he said, motioning to the bed. "We'll finish our tea while we wait for further sustenance."

They both took off their boots and, sitting on the bed, finished the tea—or in Darley's case his brandy—talking of nothing as Darley so easily did.

In short order, two cabin boys carried in trays of food.

"Put them here," Darley said, pointing to the foot

of the bed, and after exchanging a few comments about mutual acquaintances, the boys left, each richer by a gold sovereign. An enormous sum.

"You are extremely generous," Aurore said.

"I have advantages few people do," he said, handing her a napkin and flatware. "Why shouldn't I share my fortune?"

Her brows lifted slightly. "You are not the norm for your class."

He smiled. "A position I have never aspired to." He surveyed his cook's offerings. "Hmm . . . wild asparagus. We are fortunate. Here," he added, offering her a plate. "See what you think of Apostolo's omelet."

It was delicious. Like the tea dainties had been. That Gazi had only the very best staff was not unexpected.

They ate omelets first, then shrimp in white wine sauce with scallions, mustard, chili pepper, parsley, lemon juice and some excellent feta cheese. Rice with chickpeas and currants was delicious as well, and a small walnut cake with honey glaze finished the meal.

Darley ate all of his and whatever Aurore didn't want, washing it down with a local wine. "What do you think of the wine?" he asked, as he poured them both another glass. "Rather good if I do say so myself."

"Yes, it's quite nice."

He looked at her. "Now *that* was a qualified response."

"I make wines. I'm fussier than most, but it's very pleasant, really. I don't mean to impugn your wine."

"It's not mine, so impugn away."

"I'm sorry. I don't know why I even said that when you have been so gracious in every way—helping Etienne and me in any number of ways. And now this great comfort you offer here." She lifted her hand in an encompassing gesture that indicated their small abode. "I am completely beholden."

"How beholden?" he murmured, both his smile and roguish comment teasing by design. Her voice had held a note of melancholy. He understood; she was leaving her entire life behind.

"You are predictable at least, my darling Gazi," she murmured, faintly sardonic.

"Forgive me. It was a crude attempt to divert you. Sleep if you wish. When you wake we'll be that much nearer Paris."

"Divert me instead."

A plain spoken request, impossible to misconstrue. "It would be my pleasure," he said with infinite gallantry. "Let me have these trays taken away." After rising from the bed, he walked the few steps to the door, opened it and bellowed. "Sorry," he said, turning back to Aurore with a rueful smile. "But the din on the vessel drowns out a normal tone of voice."

He apologized to his cabin boys as well when they came running. "Not a problem, sar," the oldest one said with a wink. "You have yerself a right nice night."

"Eff'en you be need'n anything, sar," the younger boy said, "I could sit outside here and wait."

The boy received a scowl from his companion for his comment.

Darley only said, "Thank you, Bobby, but that won't be necessary."

Shutting the door, Darley turned and stood entranced by the sight of the lush, nude beauty in his bed. "Now what if we'd forgotten something," he said with a smile, "and one of those boys would have had to come in?"

"I trust you would stop them," Aurore said with an answering smile, arching her back slightly so her plump breasts rose temptingly, slowly spreading her legs in an even more enticing invitation.

"Damn right I would." He was stripping off his shirt as he spoke. "You are for my eyes only," he said in a low growl.

"I just *love* when you're autocratic."

No, you don't. But apparently she did tonight—for the aforementioned diversion he surmised. "You must do as you're told, Miss Clement, or I'll put you to work in the kitchen. Do you understand?" He unbuttoned his breeches.

"Yes." A delicious lustful jolt raced through her vagina. "Although, I confess, I don't know how to cook."

"You can scrub the pots and stoke the fire. Apostolo wouldn't let you cook anyway. But if you please me, I'll keep you in my bed instead. You must please me though. Is that clear?"

She nodded.

"Say, yes, sir. You must address me as sir."

"Yes, sir," she said with feeling, for Darley suddenly stood naked before her, his breeches at his feet, his erection at the ready.

He lifted his chin the merest distance. "Come here." He stood at the foot of the bed, two steps from the door, or from any other area in the minuscule space.

Coming to her knees, she moved down the bed, stopping before him, trembling slightly as the pulsing between her legs heated her senses, her brain, her seemingly insatiable appetite for Gazi.

"You must pleasure me first and if I find you satisfactory, we will consider your pleasure next."

She took a small breath in an effort to tamp down her lustful cravings and offered him a look of inexpressible innocence. "What would you like, sir?"

"If I have to tell you, you're of no use to me. Perhaps you'd prefer scrubbing pots."

"No—no, sir. I'll think of something."

"One would hope so," he muttered. "I doubt a seductive little piece like you is undefiled."

"I have known a man, sir."

His gaze narrowed. "Indeed. *A* man?" Even playacting, the thought offended him.

Her lashes drifted lower for a moment before she met his gaze once again. "Perhaps more than one, sir."

He bridled at her words while perversely his cock surged higher in lecherous response. "If I wanted conversation," he grunted, "I'd call in my chaplain."

"I'm sorry, sir. I was just answering your question." She was liquid with longing, shivering faintly, that which would give her surcease within reach and splendidly roused. Dare she ask for it?

"I'm losing patience, Miss Clement."

She hesitated the merest fraction of a moment, not sure who was most impatient, the throbbing deep in her core echoing in her ears. But uncertain of Darley's response in his current peremptory mood, she obliged him. Reaching out, she ran her fingertips up his towering erection and, grasping it with both hands, bent her head and slid the tumescent crest into her mouth. Then drew it in deeper and deeper still.

His eyes went shut as his cock slid into her mouth and he gave himself up to carnal sensations—her caressing tongue, soft skimming lips, the grazing friction of her teeth. The gratifying feel of his cock gliding in and out of her mouth. Shoving his fingers through her golden hair, he held her lightly captive as she serviced him, as her head moved slowly up and down in lascivious submission.

But before long, no matter how inspiring her performance, Darley found himself distracted by the sight of Aurore's ripe bottom swiveling and dipping in a highly erotic oscillation. As the sway of her derriere quickened, he debated degrees of tactile friction apropos mouths and cunts as though it was a technical exercise of equivalents. When obviously it wasn't, he decided after only a few moments of contemplation. Passion and partiality got in the way. At which point, he eased his fingers past her lips and freed his erection.

"Turn around," he ordered, gruffly. "And hurry."

She willingly did, positioned on her hands and knees. And two seconds later he had his hands on her hips, her bottom was raised high and he was buried deep in her incredibly slippery cunt.

"No one can say you're not ready for sex," he whispered, withdrawing, swinging his hips forward once again, holding himself against her womb with practiced delicacy for a tantalizing moment. *While she whimpered, fevered and overwrought.* Repeating the slow, smooth penetration and withdrawal in a languid, sequential flux and flow he offered her ravishment and rapture in equal measure.

Over and over and over again—practiced and deft.

Slowly in and as slowly out. Then less slow, more forceful and compelling.

She matched his rhythm with an intuitive synchronism, yielding and tractable—deliriously unrestrained, gasping and whimpering impatiently as he withdrew, always eager for more. Waiting each time with wanton abandon to be filled full of his cock again, to be stretched taut, and pleasured.

There was something about her lustful, panting neediness that grated on his nerves, jealousy perhaps, although Darley was not about to acknowledge so aberrant an emotion. But something made him want to subordinate her excessive, gushing fondness for cock to himself alone. "Tell me your hot, fevered cunt is only mine or I'll stop." His voice lowered to a growl. "Do you hear?"

"Yes, sir, I mean, no, sir . . . that is . . . I'm only yours, sir!" Aurore cried, delirious, quivering, weak with desire, literally hovering on the brink of orgasm; she could feel the first tremulous flutters begin rippling up her vagina.

"If you dare fuck anyone else, I'll lock you away," he snarled, ramming full bore into her in a hard driving downstroke, marking her as his like some demented beast.

"I won't, I won't, I woooonnnn't!" Her climax abruptly washed over her with such violence that her scream filled the room in a long, protracted, delirious sound of hysteria.

Hard-pressed as Darley was to contain his own orgasm, it seemed ages until she at last went silent and limp. But gentleman that he was, he managed to wait.

Just barely.

A second after her last orgasmic sigh died away, he jerked out and came on her back. *If this was an apoplexy, he thought, it was a damned satisfying way to die.* Gasping for air, his chest heaving, his heart pounding against his ribs, he blissfully absorbed the incredible pleasure.

Braced on her hands, rational thought having returned to Aurore before Darley for obvious reasons, she was currently involved in a losing debate with herself. How could she possibly live without the sumptuous sexual pleasure Gazi dispensed so freely? And yet, surely she must—for this wild rapture would soon be not only beyond her reach but irrevocably lost. "Are you awake?" she asked, because putting some distance between herself and Gazi's talented cock was seriously required.

"Yes. Sorry." Darley blew out a breath. "Let me find something to wipe you off." Reaching for his shirt, he performed the requisite service with a kind of professional competence, then wiped himself and tossed his shirt under the bed. "I'll have to find us some towels," he said, easing her onto her back and dropping down beside her. "By the way, that was very, very, *very* good," he drawled. "Matchless in fact."

"Mine was in the superlative range as well. For which I thank you." She was pleased she was capable of similar urbanity.

Drawing her into his arms, he lightly kissed the golden curls atop her head. "You make me feel that there is genuine goodness in the world."

"While you, darling Gazi," she whispered as she rested in his arms, "are the absolute master of diversion."

"*Your* master, if you please," he teased. "And don't forget it."

"And why would I want to when you offer such enchantment," she answered in the same playful vein. "I am yours . . ."

For a startling moment he found the idea attractive. That she would be his and conversely, he, hers.

But he had lived alone too long to succumb to such conceits; he quickly dismissed the notion.

She realized in the small ensuing silence that she had overstepped her bounds. "I meant it in play only," she said, arching up to drop a light kiss on his cheek.

"I know," he said, his smile full of charm. "You are a most lovely playmate, darling. I mean it."

"Tell me about these," she said, tracing one of the scars running down his torso, wishing to change the subject. "Where and when and how did you acquire these marks of combat?" She touched another deeper laceration under his arm.

Perhaps because he too preferred speaking of things less fraught with emotion, he answered her question when normally he was reticent about his dueling. "That one," he said, in reference to the scar she was exploring under his arm, "was over a senseless, drunken argument. I was young and stupid, quick to take offense. Someone alluded to my parentage in a disparaging way—you know how that goes. I damn near died, we both damn near died," he added with a grimace. "I was laid up for nearly three months. Merjani, who has since become my good friend, almost lost his arm. He didn't fortunately, and we are both older and wiser now. As for the others, the stories are about the same. I was operating on a hair trigger years ago." *Because he didn't care if he lived or died.* "The mountain warriors are obsessed with honor. It wasn't a good combination."

"You have given up dueling?" Hopefully, he had, she thought, his body marked with scarring. Lifting up on her elbows, she half lay across his chest and smiled at him. "If you haven't, you should."

"I have. No more foolishness." For a second, he thought he was looking at Lucia, Aurore's face in the twilight triggering a brief déjà vu memory. But the moment passed and he understood that while similarities might exist, the differences were vast. "Are you tired?" he asked, perhaps wishing to focus on other things, or perhaps responding to her heavy-lidded gaze.

Aurore smiled. "Not too tired. Why?"

"Just wondering." At which point, apparently, his penis was wondering the same thing, for it began to rapidly rise to the occasion.

Her smile widened as the twitching crest of his erection brushed her rib cage. "I can tell."

"So?"

"Need you ask?"

He was both pleased and displeased with her answer, but he chose to say in roguish sport, "What was I thinking?"

"I have no idea."

"Since I have several, it's not a problem." Rolling over her, he settled between her legs and said, soft and low, "How about something conventional while we're resting? Then later on, I'll work you a little harder."

"Promises, promises. I see why all the ladies adore you."

"Hush," he said, not sure he liked her coquettish tone. And then he kissed her and wooed and seduced her until she was no longer able to flirt and play, until she was capable of feeling only what he was feeling.

That night for the first time in a decade or more he recognized a pleasure of another kind. Attachment perhaps, or an ardor beyond the norms of passion, the kind of feeling that warmed his heart. He even contemplated tomorrow and future tomorrows instead of concentrating on the heated moment.

Or he did for a time.

Until cooler reason prevailed.

Chapter

20

When he first heard the muted sobs, he thought he was sleeping. He'd had a reoccurring dream since the first bloody battle at the Alma opened this spurious war—the screams, cries, moans and lamentations of wounded men; the deafening gunfire; the flocks of crows rising into the gray sky.

It never went away.

Like now. *No . . . not like now.*

Darley suddenly came awake. They were lying front to back, his arm around her, the small stirring of Aurore's body echoing her plaintive weeping.

"Darling, darling," he whispered, gently turning her so she faced him, wiping away the wetness on her cheeks with his fingertips. "Tell me what's wrong," he said, chivalrous and gallant, "and I'll fix it."

"You can't." Dewy eyed, sniffling, inconsolable.

For one of the few times in his life as he gazed at a tearful woman, he was inspired to seriously question how he might help. "Tell me what you need, darling. I'll make everything right, you'll see."

"I don't know what I need." The merest wisp of sound, doleful and desolate to the core. Sick at heart, Aurore had been trying to come to terms with the grim reality of losing her home, telling herself it wouldn't be for long—attempting to further bolster her spirits by reminding herself that unlike so many soldiers onboard, her limbs were all intact and she was in good health. But in the dark hours before dawn, her emotional defenses had reached a low point and she was no longer capable of believing the optimistic lies. That she and Etienne would return one day to the home of their birth and re-establish their lives.

That the passion she shared with Gazi would be easily forgotten—relegated to nothing more than fond memory.

"Your brother is safe if that's what you're worrying about," Darley whispered, wiping away fresh tears.

She shook her head and wept some more.

"Are you missing home?" He could empathize; he had had his moments over the years.

She nodded this time, her bottom lip trembling, her sobs intensifying.

"Would you like some brandy?" His first choice for temporary oblivion.

She shook her head again, a fresh torrent of tears pouring down her cheeks.

Now what? He was at a loss. He didn't suppose she was interested in sex, although he'd always found lust an effective opiate against cheerless memory. He doubted she would find it so, he decided, surveying her tearful face.

He groped for some remedy.

It suddenly came to him—prompted by recall of a mother's touch perhaps or by other cues he chose not to recognize. Sliding up into a sitting position, he lifted Aurore onto his lap and leaning back gingerly against the flimsy headboard, he drew her close. "There, there," he whispered, softly consoling. "Things will be better soon." Offering various nebulous phrases of comfort that he could recall, he gently rocked her in his arms.

Inspired by his tenderness, she wept even harder.

As he continued to wipe away her tears with the sheet or his fingers or with a kiss, he racked his brain for some other means of bringing her relief. But tearful women had been rare in his life. He was nonplussed.

Silvery moonlight streamed through twin portholes in the bow, illuminating the small cramped space. It glossed Aurore's fair hair, shimmered over her pale flesh, highlighted her liquid eyes and quivering mouth—the boundary between dream and reality briefly coalescing in magical imagery.

Her hot tears were cool on his chest, however—a rebuke to magical thinking. And Darley was never uncertain about the boundaries of reality for long. The sky was changing color outside, he pragmatically noted. Morning was hovering on the horizon. Perhaps the dawn of a new day would bring Aurore comfort.

"How long before we reach Paris?"

Her voice was barely audible. He stopped rocking her and bent his head low. "Did you say Paris?"

"Will it be long?"

Her eyes were huge, and dark in the half light. She looked sixteen. And desperately unhappy. "We could take the train from Varna. It might be faster. Would you like that?" He felt an inexplicable impulse to add, *"Tell me what I can do to make you happy again— anything at all . . . just tell me."* Not yet lost to all reason, though, he didn't.

She sat up a little straighter. "I'd like that."

Her voice held a small hint of purpose, and her woebegone expression was a modicum less forlorn. "Then we shall," he said, feeling as though he'd accomplished some signal feat.

"I need a kiss," she whispered, lifting her face to his.

He obliged, but tenderly—a brotherly or cousinly kiss.

"More," she said a few moments later in the softest of little purrs. And twining her arms around his neck, she leaned in closer.

Perhaps sex wasn't out of the question after all, he thought, aware of her hard, peaked nipples brushing his chest, conscious of the delicately altered tempo of her breathing.

His kiss this time was a kiss of seduction—teasing at first, a light back and forth motion of his lips against hers, unruffled, soft as silk, sweet as clover, indulgent in a cloudless sky sort of way.

But very shortly her idea of indulgence apparently differed from his and she opened her mouth in a slow, tantalizing spur to seduction. Willingly conceding to her charming provocation, he slid his tongue past her lips, over her teeth, and deeper still until he felt the yearning little sigh rising from her throat.

Her arms tightened around his neck and she moved her hips ever so slightly, sliding her soft bottom over his thighs in the merest little wiggle.

He knew what she was asking for, but having served as handkerchief so recently *and* protractedly, he lifted his mouth and asked, "Are you sure?" It was an astonishing question for a man who had amused himself in the game of amour for a very long time. He was not usually so fastidious.

Her eyes widened the minutest degree and she shifted back enough to survey his face. "You're not actually thinking about refusing me, are you?"

"I'm trying to be polite, that's all." His shoulder lifted in the smallest of shrugs. "You've been crying for quite a while."

"For that precise reason, I would appreciate your taking my mind off my troubles. If you don't mind. *If* I'm not imposing on you." She wrinkled her nose. "Good God, Gazi, you of all people to be put off by a few tears."

He laughed. She was back in form—the assertive little tigress he found so fascinating. "That's the last time I'll try to be tactful. Look, darling, I don't mind if you don't."

She snorted. "Such false modesty. As if any woman would. You know you're good."

"I could say the same of you."

"I'm not sure that's *comme il faut*." She smiled. "But then so little is in this charming arrangement of ours."

"I didn't know we *had* an arrangement," he drawled.

Her gaze narrowed slightly. "We do until Paris. And don't you forget it."

"Yes, dear."

She grinned. "A submissive Gazi. Let me mark the day and hour."

"I am always yours to command, darling, you know that," he smoothly replied.

"All I know, my sweet, is that your lovely *cock* is always interested and at the moment, he and I are of accord. I suddenly, and sensibly I might add, no longer wish to dwell on unpleasantness and misery. It must be because you're an excellent kisser," she added, her voice sultry and low. "So if you don't mind, right now, I only want to feel the pleasure of your cock inside me and count orgasms."

"Ah—so I'm simply here to play stud?"

He was grinning. She glanced at his erection standing at full mast. "Why don't we say to Varna at least. And then after that we could renegotiate if you wish. I would be willing to make it worth your"—her gaze dropped to his crotch—"splendid friend's while to accompany me through to Paris however."

"Done," he said.

She smiled. "I adore how you never quibble."

"And I adore how you make me feel like fucking 'til I drop. I'm not seventeen anymore; this state of constant rut is not in a normal day's work for me."

"So you think of this as work?" Her pout was sugar sweet and very close.

"Not in the least, darling." He grinned. "More like heaven on earth."

"That's better."

"No, this is better . . ."

They played some Kama Sutra games, a certain wildness in the air. Darley had worshiped at various temples in India and had been recognized as an industrious acolyte in the arts of love. Aurore had read the texts in a Greek translation, a beautifully illustrated version. While not as accomplished as Darley, she was in the mood to escape the world. And her partner was more than willing to accommodate her.

"That's why you can last so long," Aurore whispered, much later, half-breathy and momentarily replete. "I have only read of such accomplishments."

Darley kissed her lightly as she sat on his lap, facing him, her legs wrapped around his waist, his rigid erection filling her still. "Practice, darling. I spent one hot summer at a temple in northwestern India. And as you see," he added with a quirked grin, contracting his gluts and flexing his hips slightly, "I have very good muscle control."

"I am so very pleased," she whispered with an answering grin.

"I gathered you were by that last high-pitched scream," he murmured.

"Oh dear . . . do you think anyone heard?"

"We're practically at the waterline. Don't worry, no one heard," he lied. It was his yacht, after all. He could cajole Aurore from her tears in any fashion he chose.

And he had.

And he continued to do so—until they reached Varna.

It was not a hardship.

Chapter

21

Two days later, they took their leave of Captain Harris. The *Argo* was sailing on to Kulali while they would travel overland. Hiring a fiacre at the docks, Darley instructed the driver to take them to the train station.

"The war has disrupted the train schedules," the driver warned, speaking in a lingua franca common to commercial travelers. "War matériel being transported east is clogging the rail lines."

"A delay could be problematical I suppose," Aurore said, taking note of Darley's frown.

"A prompt departure would be better," he muttered. "But I know some people in town where we can wait." Leaning forward, he said to the driver, "The Hotel Europa." Preferred by business travelers, the lobby should be bustling with activity. There was safety in the midst of a crowd.

On their arrival at the hotel, Darley asked the driver to wait, and escorting Aurore into the busy dining room, he ordered tea and writing materials. After composing a brief note, he handed it to a servant with instructions for its delivery. Knowing Turkish custom was averse to visitors dropping in unannounced, Darley had tactfully conformed to convention. "Hopefully, Rashad is in town." He smiled. "If not, we'll try someone else." They needed a safe location in which to wait for the train and, more important, a private railcar for their journey.

His friend Abdul Rashad could supply both.

Fortunately, Rashad was at home and promptly replied.

Darley and Aurore arrived at the Turkish diplomat's home a short time later and were welcomed with great warmth.

"Come in, come in!" Abdul Rashad greeted them at the door of his home, brushing aside his major domo to vigorously shake Darley's hand. "What a pleasure to see you again, my friend! It's been too long!" He glanced at Aurore and smiled.

"Allow me to introduce Miss Clement," Darley said. "We are both in flight from the Russian authorities."

"A pleasure to meet you, my dear," the sultan's envoy to France said, offering Aurore an exquisite bow. Then with a glance for Darley he added, "I was wondering what brought you to this little outland. You are perfectly safe here, though, never fear." His brows flickered in amusement. "My guards prefer dead Russians to any other kind, and they can smell one a mile away." He beckoned them toward a drawing room visible across the hall. "Come, have tea with me and tell me of your adventures."

Abdul Rashad was a tall, striking man, past middle age, but lean and fit, his hair graying, his dark eyes imperturbable. He had seen more than his share of the inequities of the world. A Croatian by birth, Rashad had served in the Austrian army before joining the Turkish army where he had risen to prominence. His marriage to one of the richest heiresses in Constantinople also had been instrumental in advancing his career.

"Naturally," Rashad added as they moved toward the drawing room, "my home is at your disposal for as long as you wish."

"Thank you. The hotels are too dangerous," Darley replied. "The Third Section is, we assume, in active pursuit."

The diplomat half turned and met Darley's eyes for a moment. "Espionage?" *He had rather thought an irate husband.* "Although, I shouldn't be surprised with England in this war."

"Raglan can use all the help he can get," Darley drily replied.

"So I have heard. Our Omar Pasha has distinguished himself, however." Omar Pasha, like Rashad, was a native of the Balkans.

"Perhaps a relative of yours?" Darley quipped.

Waving them to chairs, Rashad said with a smile, "He might very well be with a father such as mine."

Once they were seated and a servant had poured them tea and left the room, Abdul Rashad lounged back in his chair. "Now then, supply me with all the interesting details of your espionage activities."

Darley explained briefly all that had transpired prior to his and Aurore's meeting in Simferopol, then in slightly more detail described how they had been discovered in Adlberg's study, their subsequent escape and his concern for their safety. "We still have most of Europe to cross and several more days of travel facing us. And if the trains are delayed, who knows?"

"I have a number of informers in my employ as well as a sizeable troop of mercenaries at my disposal. Why don't we eliminate your pursuers before you leave Varna?" Leaning over, Rashad offered Aurore a plate of sweets as if talk of murder was inconsequential. "It's a simple enough matter and then your journey would be uneventful. Try an apricot pastry, my dear," he added with a smile for Aurore. "I recommend them."

"Even if we liquidate some of the agents," Darley said in a considering voice as Aurore obliged their host, "there are bound to be others."

"True, but the subsequent ones will be more wary," Rashad noted, offering Darley the plate of sweets.

Darley shook his head, excessive sweets a Turkish obsession he forbore. "I'd prefer staying ahead of the Russians instead—if possible. The more distance we can put between our pursuers and their superiors in Russia the better. Third Section agents generally are not allowed to operate independently. In addition, Miss Clement is rather inclined to reach Paris quickly." Darley turned to smile at Aurore. "She is concerned for her brother's safety. I was hoping, in fact, that we might make use of your private railcar— as a security measure—and leave as soon as possible."

Custom railcars offering luxury, comfort and privacy were in common use by those wealthy enough to afford them.

"Unfortunately, the governor of the Danubian Principalities took my railcar to Bucharest yesterday. But I'll send him a telegraph and have it returned immediately. It should be back in Varna by noon tomorrow. We'll have the train for Paris delayed for you." Another prerogative of wealth.

"Perfect." Darley exhaled in satisfaction. "We are in your debt."

"Nonsense. Actually," Rashad noted, "my wife is in Paris as we speak. I was planning to send the car west soon anyway."

"We are very grateful, nonetheless," Aurore noted. "I hadn't realized we would be pursued even outside Russia." She shot a critical glance at Darley.

"I didn't see any point in alarming you."

"Nor should you be alarmed, Miss Clement," Rashad interposed, stepping in to allay a possible argument. "I have considerable troopers under my command. Your journey home will be safe, I assure you. Now, if you would care to refresh yourself or rest before dinner, I could have you shown upstairs."

"Thank you—how kind. I would like that immensely." The last few days had been turbulent. She was feeling fatigued, and arguing about who knew what when would serve no purpose at this late juncture.

A short time later as the sound of her footsteps faded on the stairs, Abdul Rashad looked at Darley, one brow raised in query. "A female spy. Unusual." He smiled. "As is the lady. She is quite out of the ordinary—assertive too," he added with a smile, "and more than an acquaintance I surmise. Brandy?" Coming to his feet, he moved toward a liquor table.

"Yes, she *is* out of the ordinary and more than an acquaintance. And yes, a brandy would be most welcome." Sinking lower in his chair, Darley relaxed for the first time in days, the remainder of their journey likely to be undisturbed thanks to his friend's resources.

"Are you involved with the lady—beyond the superficial?" Rashad inquired as he poured two drinks. "I ask out of curiosity. I couldn't help but notice an intriguing look pass between you two occasionally."

Darley shrugged. "She's a charming companion—nothing more. I continue on to England from Paris."

"Ah." The older man approached with their drinks. "I rather thought I might have detected a love match."

Taking the offered glass, Darley smiled. "She is loveable certainly."

Rashad's lashes drifted lower. "But not loved."

"You of all people are hardly capable of recognizing tender passion." That Abdul Rashad had married for reasons other than love was universally understood. And while he had chosen not to take additional wives as Islam allowed, he *had* devoted considerable time to sexual amusements.

"My son has fallen in love," Rashad murmured, taking his seat opposite Darley. "I find myself envious—thinking of all that might have been had I chosen another path in life." He smiled faintly and shook his head. "Old age. I am more inclined to melancholy I'm afraid. Tell me now," he went on, his voice suddenly brisk, "how does the incompetent Raglan?"

Darley explained all he knew of the ongoing operations at Sevastopol and, when asked, detailed why he feared that they were being followed. "Do you know a German named Hausmann?"

Rashad nodded. "He has crossed my path from time to time. A man of considerable experience to have survived so long in his chosen profession."

"So I understand. He pointed out a little man to me one day. The Third Section agent in Sevastopol—a dogged type he said, ambitious too. Not that they all aren't, but some aspire to more than monetary gain. This Kubitovitch was such a man, he said."

"Would you recognize him?"

"Of course."

"Give me a description and we'll have the harbor watched. Whether he arrives before or after you depart, I will see that he is eliminated."

"Again—thank you."

"An invitation to your wedding will suffice."

Darley laughed. "I don't suggest you wait for that."

After another brandy, Rashad called in a servant and dictated a number of orders, after which he suggested he and Darley speak to the leader of his guard troop. "I'll send some of my men with you, so you can enjoy your journey to Paris rather than having to concern yourself with assassins. You'll like Stephan. He's a countryman of mine—a cousin of sorts." The Ottoman empire offered opportunities to ethnic minorities under the sultan's suzerainty. While central power presided in Constantinople, the government was served by a meritocracy as well, where ability rather than nationality was recognized.

"After we've spoken to Stephan, I'll introduce you to a couple who will accompany you in the capacity of cook and maid. They've become my personal bodyguards when I travel. Very competent. Circus performers at one time. You'll like them."

While Darley and Aurore were enjoying the hospitality of Abdul Rashad in Varna, Kubitovitch was disembarking from a coastal steamer in Odessa. The British navy controlled the Black Sea, but steamers plying the coast with cargo and passengers were allowed to operate under her majesty's supervision.

Fortunately, false identity papers posed no problem for a Third Section agent. Kubitovitch had several forged identities.

Kubitovitch hired a carriage and had himself driven to Third Section headquarters where he closeted himself with the director of the secret police. He presented his case in a version in which no blame for Darley and Aurore's escape accrued to him, explaining at great length that Osten-Sacken had been a considerable hindrance to his investigation. "Those nobles look at you with a sneer or worse—you know what they're like," he said, meeting his superior's gaze. "They own the world."

"Maybe not forever." In his position, Ershov was fully aware of revolutionary politics, and while he didn't favor such heretical leanings, he was, still, the son of a dockworker. To even scores was bred in his bones—that retaliatory sense of personal justice not only useful but an asset in his trade.

"We can see that the patrician Osten-Sacken suffers for his actions if these spies are eliminated. He will be obliged to answer for his blunder. But before we can even think about retribution for the general, we have to stop these spies from escaping." Kubitovitch leaned forward slightly, unable to suppress his agitation. "Telegrams should go out to our stations in Varna, Kustenje and Constantinople, warning them to be on the outlook for the yacht *Argo* and the male and female spies. It will be a feather in your cap, Ivan Michaelovitch," Kubitovitch went on, careful to keep his voice cordial rather than toadying. They all lived a life of lies, but unseemly sycophancy raised suspicions. "If these two spies are captured, you will surely be rewarded with a post in St. Petersburg."

"You will be compensated as well." Blunt, hard words. The director was a brawny, stevedore of a man, his childhood on the docks of Odessa etched on his face and liver. Altruism didn't exist in his world.

"I agree. But there is more than enough glory to go around, Ivan Michaelovitch." Time pressures didn't allow a lengthy, tactfully phrased discussion. Kubitovitch was beginning to sweat. "If you chose not to act, however," he added, knowing every minute the director hesitated his options diminished, "and these spies escape, our superiors will require explanations that we *may not* survive."

The director grunted. He knew how errors were dealt with—death was often a blessing. "Give me your messages. I will see that they are sent."

"I need a swift cutter as well and a bank draft for five thousand roubles."

"Five thousand roubles?" The director scrutinized Kubitovitch, trying to decide whether the five thousand roubles might be funding his agent's personal escape plans.

"It could be on *your* head if they escape," Kubitovitch warned, the distrust in the director's eyes transient but revealing. "I could explain that you thwarted my plans to capture them."

Mistakes simply were not allowed. Uncertain or not, Ershov couldn't afford to take chances. Time enough to throw Kubitovitch to the wolves at some later date should it become necessary. "Very well. I hope for both our sakes you do not fail."

Kubitovitch met the director's gaze with one as chill. "I like to live as much as you."

Chapter

22

Rashad's private railcar arrived in Varna shortly after noon, thanks to lavish bribes showered on various railroad officials en route from Bucharest. Trains carrying war supplies had been shunted off to feeder tracks and spurs while the private railcar and engine sped past, its fireman shoveling hard to keep the firebox stoked red hot.

The railcar was joined to the Bucharest–Vienna–Paris train that had been waiting ten hours at the station. Rashad's factotum bestowed further largesse on the railway functionaries at the Varna station while his employer bid adieu to his guests. With the engineer checking his watch and cursing aristocrats who thought the trains ran to accommodate their personal schedules, Rashad and Darley exchanged promises to sail the Agean islands in the fall.

Darley and Aurore boarded a few moments later, at which time, the engineer immediately signaled to the conductors who swung themselves up onto the train. Working his levers, the engineer blew a long blast on the whistle and, at last, the train moved slowly out of the station.

Darley and Aurore settled into the comfort of Rashad's elegantly appointed salon, accepted coffees from Tereza the maid and exchanged smiles across the expanse of exquisite silk carpet fit for a pasha's palace. Where it had been at one time before Rashad had ousted the recalcitrant subject of the sultan and had taken over the governance of the region himself.

"You are well connected, my lord," Aurore teased. "We travel to Paris in great comfort."

"Rashad owes me some favors."

"I gathered you were old friends."

"I've known him for years."

"And?" She was curious about every facet of Darley's life—when she shouldn't be, of course. An affaire was, by any measure, superficial.

"And—nothing much. We met in Constantinople years ago." *In a luxurious brothel.* "We found we had much in common." *Beyond amorous proclivities.* "Perhaps we both have traveled the world for the same reasons—ennui at times, the search for adventure . . . curiosity mostly, I think."

His usual bland answer, giving away nothing. "Rashad has a family?"

He nodded. "A number of children—six, I believe. He said his eldest son is marrying soon." Like Rashad, Darley experienced a small twinge of regret at thoughts of love and what might have been. "Speaking of young men marrying," he said, wishing to change the subject, "does your brother have any young ladies in Paris angling to join your family?"

Aurore smiled. "No, I'm happy to say. He is *not* ready for marriage."

"I did rather get the impression he was enjoying his youth."

"Oh yes—in every conceivable way."

"And do you have friends waiting for you in Paris?" He meant men friends, although he wasn't so gauche as to say it. Or admit it actually mattered.

"Yes, far too many at times. I am not enamored of what passes for social amusements. It's such a waste of time in most instances."

He had met women of accomplishments before, but none with the breadth of Aurore's interests. "You prefer your vineyards"—he smiled—"and spying."

"On the contrary," she said with a faint shrug, "my spying came about willy-nilly. Once Etienne enlisted, I felt a certain obligation." She smiled. "Then, I found out that I was good at it."

He liked her smile. It was open and unaffected—like she was—in so many delectable and adventuresome ways. "Apropos things you're good at," he murmured, his appetite for her never long suppressed. Unquenchable actually—for reasons he chose not to dwell on. "Would you be interested in an afternoon nap?"

"A nap?" A velvety soft query.

"Eventually," he said, as softly.

"I would, of course. You tempt me every minute, Gazi, my sweet." Unlike Darley, she admitted her need for him. As she recognized that he would soon be gone from her life. "Just a warning, darling. I may not let you sleep."

He grinned as he rose from his chair and held out his hand to her. "It's remarkable how much and how often we agree . . ."

Rashad's bed was large, the mattress fashioned from the finest swansdown, and in very short order they were cocooned in a cloudlike softness as they lay entwined, and blissfully joined.

"It wouldn't be out of the question to indulge in a little foreplay from time to time," Darley teased, having been admonished to enter her posthaste.

"Why would I want to when this"—she gently swiveled her hips so every heated nerve involved in their close contact sport fully appreciated her point—"feels so really, utterly perfect."

His smile was very close and amused. "So I should just stay here for the duration?"

"What a lovely thought," she purred, sliding her palms over his muscled shoulders in delight and appreciation. He held his weight lightly suspended above her, the warmth of his body palpable, a sensation of hard, tensile strength held in abeyance for her pleasure infinitely arousing. "Ummm . . . nonstop sex from here to Paris . . . how gratifying."

"Greedy puss."

But a proprietary intonation tempered his hushed reply. And when in the past she might have taken issue with such blatant authority, her traitorous body melted around his hard, rigid prick in utter submission instead.

He, of course, noticed, and taking advantage of the increasing pliancy of her vaginal tissue, he eased forward a fraction more and then yet again—another piquant, provocative distance.

She screamed in a wild, feverish exaltation.

He caught his breath, hit by a wave of gut-wrenching delirium.

For the next small interval, silence reigned while the glittering carnal splendor slowly faded and brains reasserted their supremacy over pure, unadulterated feeling.

As Darley lay motionless inside her, they could both feel the rhythm of the train, the slight, pulsating oscillation of vaginal and phallic membranes matching the cadence of the wheels. A subtle, tactile friction perhaps best appreciated when a certain level of stimulation has oversensitized the nervous system.

"How do you do it?" she murmured at last, her gaze lifting to his, her smile beguiling.

"It's you," he graciously replied in lieu of saying, *One learns what women like after years of fucking*. And in all honesty . . . she was extravagantly appealing.

"Then you don't mind if I'm perhaps unreasonably demanding on our journey to Paris?"

He lightly kissed her smiling mouth. "God, no, I'm more than willing." An understatement of sorts when he was, in fact, feeling a rare, intoxicating fever in his blood. When contrary to past custom, he was in no hurry to reach their destination. "Let me know when you've had enough."

"Thank you," she said sweetly. "I will."

Although, when it came to sexual willingness, their appetites were well matched. Some would say voracious. Or personally endearing.

Or both or all.

But life was dear and time even more precious.

At some level, they understood that all too well.

Chapter

23

After receiving a ship-to-shore signal from their man in Varna, a swift cutter flying an Italian flag had docked south of the city, sliding into a private slip on private land and offloading five men shortly before noon. Within the hour, those men, carrying Austrian papers, had boarded the Paris train—and installed themselves in two private compartments. Commercial travelers one would say on first seeing them. They carried leather sample cases and wore salesmen's modest black suits and serviceable brogues.

On second look though, four of them appeared uncomfortable in their business suits. The width of their shoulders and arms strained the cheap fabric, giving them the appearance of peasants dressed up for a village wedding.

In contrast, the little peanut of a man with them looked as though he was gingerly herding lions.

The men had all received their instructions from Kubitovitch on the voyage from Odessa, although once onboard the train some reconnoitering would be required. In the course of the afternoon, each man walked through every car in the event their information was incorrect and their targets were traveling in public.

They weren't. The Varna agent had been correct.

Then again, Abdul Rashad was an eminence in the city, easily recognized, particularly when he traveled with his entourage as he customarily did. The Varna agent had given them a description of the occupants of Rashad's private railcar and the state of their security. Four guards—one front and back, the other two apparently alternating shifts. It shouldn't be difficult to overcome the guards with the men at his disposal, Kubitovitch reflected. He had four Bulgarian assassins—professional and nerveless.

After a light supper carried aboard with them, the Bulgarians slept the evening away while Kubitovitch smoked one cigarette after another, too nervous to eat or sleep with so much at stake. Both Gazi and Miss Clement were not from the usual common herd of informants. They were high-profile spies. If this operation proved successful, he was assured the notice of his superiors in St. Petersburg—the only ones who really mattered. Formerly, he had only dreamed of seeing the capital city. The prospect of actually living there had been beyond his imagination.

Until now.

He must have checked his watch fifty times before it was time to set out on the mission. Although, as the saying went, he didn't shoot the gun, he only bought the bullets; the assignment would be carried out by the professional killers.

After waking his companion, he woke the three men in the adjoining compartment and, after a

glance at his watch, offered a final word of confirmation. "If it becomes necessary to leave the train, we
meet in Vienna. You know where." The men had
been paid the first installment of their fee; the con-
cluding payment would be delivered on completion
of the assignment. Either here or in Vienna.

Kubitovitch watched the four men walk away with
a sense of trepidation, suddenly feeling as if his entire life lay in the balance. Optimism and dread
struggled for supremacy in his thoughts. *Would all go
well? What if it didn't? Why shouldn't it, he admonished
next. These brutes were Ershov's best.*

And having reassured himself, he imagined the
gratifying scene in St. Petersburg: he would smile
humbly as he received the medal of St. Andrew for
his triumph; he would offer grateful thanks, give
credit for his success to the superb training and disci-
pline of the Third Section Academy. He would be
dressed in a new uniform from St. Petersburg's finest
tailor, perhaps a hint of scented pomade in his hair
in imitation of the prestigious guardsmen. He half
smiled at the image.

But his hands were shaking when he unscrewed
the cap of his brandy flask, and he spilled a drop or
two lifting the flask to his mouth. Soon, though, the
brandy quelled the worst of his agitation, and after a
second drink his calm was restored. He was able to
contemplate the sweetness of victory and its ensuing
rewards with blissful equanimity.

Darley was lying beside Aurore, half dozing, when
his eyes snapped open and he glanced up. Footsteps
on the roof. In a flash, he put a finger to Aurore's

mouth, waking her. Lifting his chin upward, he gave silent explanation for his actions, and at her nod of acknowledgment, he rolled off the bed and grabbed his trousers.

She watched in silence as he jerked on his trousers, jammed a revolver and kinjal into his waistband and bent low to kiss her. "Lock the door behind me," he whispered against her mouth, then sliding a small handgun under her pillow, he disappeared through the door like a shadow.

Locking the door behind him, she forced herself to shake off sleep and deal with the threat. She hadn't heard a thing, and listening now, not a sound was evident above. Who had been on the roof—or more pertinently, how many? She had considered themselves relatively safe this far from Sevastopol. Apparently, an error on her part.

After slipping on a dressing gown, she quickly knotted the tie at her waist, picked up the handgun and, sitting on the bed, debated whether the door or windows would be the most likely point of entry. Pushing herself upward until her back was against the headboard, she was in a position to guard both. Fully awake now, her finger rested lightly on the handgun trigger.

Darley met Stephan near the front of the car. The door had been shoved open, so the wind rushed in, and the black forests of the Transylvanian Alps swept past in a blur.

"I was coming to check on you," Stephan murmured. "We have one less assassin. I cut his throat and tossed him overboard."

"Footsteps on the roof woke me." As Darley was speaking, a struggle exploded at the rear of the car, the clang of pots and pans and curses coming from the kitchen.

Both men sprinted toward the conspicuous sounds of a skirmish.

Before they'd passed down the length of the railcar and reached the kitchen, quiet had been restored. Vasile, the ostensible cook, was dragging a body by its feet through the back door of the railcar, a trail of blood following in its wake. The huge head had been nearly severed from the body, the arterial blood literally gushing from the corpse.

Vasile, once a weight lifter in the circus, picked up the limp, bloody form once he was on the platform outside and threw it over the rail.

"The bastard bled like a pig," Tereza muttered in functional French as she eyed the mess on the kitchen floor. Diminutive and slender, testament to her former life as an acrobat, she was barely five feet tall.

Blocking the doorway with his bulk, Vasile offered his wife an astonishingly gentle smile. "I'll clean this up. Make us some coffee as long as we're all awake," he added in a mix of bad French and Romany. He nodded at Stephan. "Georgh was garroted by some bastard who dropped from the roof, but he fought him off. Killed the prick with that cannon he carries. He's sitting on the platform out back, thanking his saints and trying to catch his breath."

One of Stephan's men approached them from the front of the car. "Everything's clear in front. I sent Alex up on the roof."

"Good. Help Georgh." Stephan nodded toward the back door. "He took out another one of the—"

The small, muffled cry had the impact of a rifle

shot. They all looked up or turned, the ominous sound filling their hearts with dread. An all too familiar sound to those in the kitchen who had seen their share of life-and-death struggles.

Aurore was in the grip of a bull of a man, one of his arms around her throat in a stranglehold, his other hand holding a gun to her head. Her face was ashen as she fought for breath.

"No one move," the Bulgarian growled in his native language, "or she dies."

Darley didn't understand the words but the meaning was clear.

"Easy," Stephan said under his breath to Darley.

"He's mine," Darley muttered, his eyes narrow slits.

Even with lack of air making her dizzy, Aurore was berating herself for missing her target and only grazing the man's arm. He'd swung through the bedroom window, feet first, with such explosive force the shock of it had ruined her aim.

The Bulgarian took note of the people grouped at the end of the railcar who apparently had been discussing something and understood from their inactivity that his partners were no more. The slick of blood on the floor was further confirmation.

He'd seized the woman as a precaution—a hostage always beneficial in situations like this. But deprived as he was now of any possible assistance, she had become indispensable to his escape. Not only would she serve as his shield, he would take this woman with him as he leaped from the train.

She could cushion his fall.

Moving backward, he dragged Aurore with him toward the doorway.

Aurore had no illusions about the man's intentions. She was disposable once her usefulness was at an end—that occasion fast approaching.

Darley was waiting for a clear shot or, that lacking, *a* shot. He too was aware of the diminishing time frame.

Knowing she had only seconds left as they approached the open doorway, Aurore gathered her strength. Gasping for air, she managed to twist marginally within the man's harsh grip and jerk her knee upward into his crotch.

She might have been a fly for all his reaction to her blow.

But for a millisecond he was distracted, and in that fleeting moment Darley's hand swept up and a second later a large caliber round buried itself between the man's eyes.

Darley was already sprinting down the length of the car when the man's shriek rent the air. As the brawny assassin staggered backward through the doorway, his powerful upper body twisting in free fall toward the platform rail, his arm was still ruthlessly clamped around Aurore's throat in a death grip.

Terror-stricken that Aurore would be flung off the train with the man's fatal momentum, Darley flew headlong through the doorway.

The dying man teetered for a moment on the cusp of the rail, and as he tumbled backward into nothingness, Darley frantically lunged. Catching Aurore's outstretched arm, his fingers closed like a vise on her forearm. She hung for a moment like a rag doll in the wind before he seized her other arm in a firm, hard grip. "Now," he grunted, as the forest rushed by them in a blur, and bracing his feet for leverage, he swung her up over the rail with adrenaline-spiked strength.

Pulling her against his body, he pinioned her in his embrace, and trembling, she clung to him, their hearts beating like drums, the pale moon shining above indifferent to the crisis only narrowly averted.

"It's over," he whispered.

"All of them?" she croaked, her windpipe bruised, aching.

"Every one gone," he gently replied.

Still shaking like a leaf, she didn't ask for details, content to know that there was certainty in Darley's use of the word *gone*.

When Aurore's breathing returned to a semblance of normal, Darley quietly said, "I'm leaving you with Vasile and Tereza for a few minutes. They're both armed. I want to check the rest of the passengers. It's only a precaution," he added, as she gazed at him with alarm. "We'll be back soon."

She wished to say, *Don't go,* but knew as well as he that he had to ensure another assault force wasn't on the train. "Hurry back," she said instead.

Kubitovitch heard the sound of compartment doors opening and shutting in ever-closer proximity and quickly gathered up the envelopes of money he'd packed in his valise. Stuffing the packets into his coat pockets, he eased open the door of his compartment and glanced up and down the passageway. A group of men were talking to a conductor at the far end of the car. There wasn't time to debate his options. He slipped out the door and ran.

Stephan noticed the running figure and nudged Darley.

Darley took one look, shouted, "Stop!" and fired.

Kubitovitch had zagged and ducked at the shouted order, the diversionary tactic second nature after years in the shadows, and Darley's shot parted the agent's straw-colored hair at the top of his head, leaving a bloody furrow.

Not about to stop, too petrified to even feel the pain of his wound, Kubitovitch literally ran for his life, slamming through the doorway separating the cars and jumping from the metal stairs without thought. Tucking into a roll—one of the lessons in escape maneuvers learned in the academy—he hit the ground in a tumbling somersault and landed by chance in the soft muck of a marsh. His clothing was somewhat the worse for wear from his swift decamping, but more significantly, he was still alive. Which, he suspected, was not the case with the Bulgarians.

As he rose to his knees and surveyed his position, a rivulet of blood slid down his forehead, and for the first time he felt the sharp, throbbing pain. Cautiously examining the top of his head with his fingertips, he realized he was an enormously lucky man. The shot had grazed his head, slicing through the skin but doing little enough damage as far as he could tell. Coming to his feet, he stood ankle-deep in marsh water and muck and debated his next move.

The train was miles away by now, those who would harm him becoming more distant by the minute. He still had four thousand roubles left after paying the Bulgarians, an auxiliary plan to fall back on, only a minor wound and a few bruises.

Returning to Russia was out of the question, of course. The operation had been an unequivocal failure.

He glanced up at the moon to get his bearings and began walking west.

When Darley returned, Vasile and Tereza went off to bed.

"I won't be able to sleep," Aurore said, "but you sleep if you wish. I'm not frightened, only restless."

"Do you want to sit here?" Darley indicated the salon with a flick of his fingers. "Or would you rather lie down? The other bedroom is undamaged."

"Here, I think." There was a feeling of safety in the well-lit space, the image of the man smashing through her bedroom window still looping through her brain.

"Would you like coffee or tea—something to eat?"

"Don't bother Vasile. I'm fine."

"I'll get us coffee and one of those apricot pastries." Darley began moving toward the kitchen.

"I'll go with you."

Turning, he held out his hand and smiled. "I'm going to keep you in my pocket until we arrive in Paris."

"That would be very nice." She slid her fingers through his.

"They really are all gone now, darling," he said, wishing to reassure her, gently squeezing her fingers. "Kubitovitch was the last of them and he jumped off the train. With any luck, he's dead from the fall."

She smiled. "You may tell me that with great frequency for the rest of our journey."

"Maybe I could think of another way to take your mind off your recent ordeal," he said, smiling faintly. "When you're feeling better, of course."

"Food would help, I think. I'm starved. It must be the aftershock."

"Food first, my lady. Let me amaze you with my expertise in the kitchen," he teased.

She *was* amazed as it turned out. Coming from a home where food was prepared by servants, she was at a loss in the kitchen. Darley, on the other hand, made excellent coffee, and a tasty dish of eggs and peppers served on bread he stuck on a knife and toasted over an open flame.

"There is no end of your talents," she murmured, having finished her eggs and toast to the last morsel. "Do you perhaps play the violin as well?"

He grinned and pushed his plate aside. "No, but I play in other ways you might enjoy."

She smiled. "As to that, I am most grateful for your ability to make me forget. There has been too much malicious mischief about with the war and all."

"We reach civilization soon. The mischief will cease."

"Are you sure?"

"Yes," he lied. "I'm sure."

She set aside her napkin and came to her feet. "In that case then, let us think only of pleasure and"—she grinned—"particularly my pleasure."

He laughed. "You're feeling better, I see."

"You always make me feel ever so good, darling Gazi," she softly said. And to that end, she wished to delight in him while she could—a thoroughly selfish impulse, but better that than a life of regret.

Chapter

24

Three days later, Darley and Aurore stood on the train platform at the Gare l'Est in Paris.

Darley should have been completely fucked out and more than ready to say good-bye. But instead, he was very close to saying to Aurore, *Why don't I see you home?*

A lavender twilight colored the city and sky beyond the train sheds, the March air was cool, the bustle of travelers passing by them on the platform an unseen flurry of movement. Everyone was in a hurry, travelers in a rush to reach their homes or businesses, their families and friends—their mistresses. This was Paris after all.

"We should find you a cab," he said.

"Yes."

They had spoken briefly on the train about their plans. Darley would continue on to Calais from Paris. He was going home to England for a visit, and after that he wasn't sure, he'd said. He didn't explain that his life went where it may—or at least it had for eighteen years. And at thirty-eight, he considered himself too old to change.

Aurore was looking forward to seeing her brother once again, and as soon as the war came to an end, she hoped to go home. Unlike Darley, she had spoken of her uncertain future—but without melancholy. She had become reconciled to the fact that outside events were in control. At least for now.

She suddenly wrinkled her nose. "What a terrible odor." Strange—the smell of roasting chestnuts had never struck her as unpleasant before. Perhaps the long train trip was to blame—the ever-present, belching smoke when one went outside or opened a window, the bouncing ride over marshland or mountain terrain, the occasional odd item of food. *Taste some so Vasile won't cry. He's been cooking all day,* Darley had said once as she'd hesitated over a strange dish brought in by Vasile. *I'm only kidding,* he'd added at the look on her face, *but try some anyway. It's good.*

But unlike Vasile's eastern European dishes, this smell was making her nauseated. She must be coming down with something.

"Are you feeling all right?" Her face was white.

"I don't know. Is that smell disgusting to you?"

"The chestnuts?"

She nodded. "The oil must be rancid."

She was asking the wrong person; he liked the smell. "It could be." But he politely said, "Why don't we go inside and get away from the odor. You should sit down. You look pale. Would you like me to get you a tisane or a lemonade—a glass of wine perhaps?"

Clamping her gloved hand over her mouth, Aurore swallowed hard. "Please, don't talk about food," she said through her fingers.

"Sorry."

After taking a few deep breaths, she let her hand drop from her mouth and smiled shakily. "Forgive me. I rarely feel nauseous like this."

"You're probably just tired after the long trip." *With little sleep and almost constant sex, why wouldn't she feel a bit under the weather?* "Come, we'll go inside and find you somewhere quiet to sit."

As they moved down the platform toward the station, Aurore fought fresh waves of bile rising in her throat. The coal fumes from the trains, the strong aromas of cooking rising from the many food stands, even the sight of refuse on the tracks beside the platform provoked a queasiness.

The smell of cooking crepes drifting out from the station proved to be the last straw. Turning, she raced for the platform's edge and, on reaching it, immediately doubled over and vomited on the tracks below.

Darley was right behind her, fear beating at his brain. Holding her around the waist, his other hand on her forehead, he steadied her as she retched and heaved. This was how cholera started, he thought. And three days later you were dead. Half the armies of England and France had died of the disease last year.

When there was nothing left in her stomach to eject, she stood up and he handed her his handkerchief. She wiped her mouth and handed it back. "Thank you," she whispered, deathly white. "I would like to sit if—"

He had her up in his arms before she finished

speaking. "I'll find a quiet corner," he said, carrying her into the station in long, swift strides. "Would you like some water now?" With cholera, dehydration ultimately killed you.

Still fighting off a billowing nausea, she shook her head.

He found them a bench as far away from the bustle and food stands as possible. They sat side by side in silence, Darley watching her like a hawk his last surviving chick, while Aurore tried to suppress her urge to vomit.

Five minutes passed, then ten. Feeling as though the worst had passed, Aurore turned to speak to Darley—too soon or too quickly apparently, for her stomach rebelled. Breathing slowly through her nose, she sat utterly still and waited for the queasiness to subside.

Neither spoke. She couldn't and he didn't want to.

Darley was thinking about sick women who became sicker. And died. Disturbed and agitated by the damning images filling his brain, he abruptly sprang to his feet and walked away, feeling as though he needed to physically distance himself from the quicksand of morbid memory.

Aurore squealed and flinched as he'd leaped up, and shutting her eyes against the turgid recoil in her stomach, she fought down another wave of nausea. When she opened her eyes sometime later, he was seated beside her again, his expression shuttered. The shop of memories behind his eyes was closed and he was keeping it that way by sheer will.

"When you feel up to it," he said, speaking softly and slowly, fully aware now that sudden movement was distressing to her, "I'll carry you to a cab and take you home. We'll send for the luggage. Don't argue, please."

"Won't argue," she said so low, he had to bend his head to catch the words.

"You tell me when you're ready. We'll sit here as long as it takes."

"The smells," she whispered.

"We should leave now?"

She nodded.

"If you feel the urge to vomit, just do it. We can find other clothes tomorrow."

"Very well," she said, beginning to sense a lessening of her stomach complaint. Although, she was also aware that Darley's word, *tomorrow*, had brought with it a truly heavenly sense of joy. Was it possible the two were a balmy matter of cause and effect?— because she felt *ever* so much better suddenly. She could even move without feeling nauseous, while the thought of food no longer made her want to vomit. In fact, she might be just the tiniest bit hungry. Not an unusual sensation for someone who had just emptied her stomach, she decided, choosing to look upon her restored health with less whimsy and more pragmatism. "You know, I feel a little like eating," she said.

While Darley's use of the word *tomorrow* might have been remedy for Aurore's queasiness, her *feel like eating* phrase was like music to his ears. Cholera victims did not have appetites. He could feel the tension leave his shoulders. He also experienced a sudden rush of happiness that he chose not to acknowledge.

That she was improving was enough.

That he would be staying in Paris tonight was just an added bonus.

And if Aurore was in the mood for food, what better city in which to indulge her urges.

"Do you want me to carry you?"

"No. I feel quite"—she smiled—"*quite* well."

He stood and offered her his arm. "Shall we?"

She smiled again, thinking how effortlessly he pleased and enchanted. "I would like that immensely." Rising, she placed her hand on his arm.

"Would a private room at Voisin be to your liking? We are neither of us dressed for the evening, although," he quickly added as they moved toward the main entrance, "it's entirely up to you. I have no compunction dining publicly in travel clothes either."

She grinned. "So it's not that you don't want to be seen with me?"

"Hardly. I would be the envy of every man in the room."

But once in the cab and resting against Darley's shoulder, Aurore changed her mind. "Would you care if we dined at home instead? My staff will manage something I'm sure."

"I would be content with bread and butter if you were with me, darling."

"Indeed, and if my stomach becomes a trial again, perhaps that's what we will have."

"It makes no difference to me. You do have brandy, I presume."

"You are welcome to drink yourself into a stupor."

He smiled into the twilight shadows. "Now why would I do that when I have you to sleep with tonight?"

She felt rather than saw his smile. "You might want to reconsider. I can't guarantee I won't vomit on you," she teased.

"If you have a wash basin near, be my guest."

"I have modern plumbing, I'll have you know. We are very up to date."

"How big is your tub?" A sudden tantalizing warmth infused his voice.

"Very."

"In that case, I look forward to whatever you might spew on me."

She laughed. "You bring me joy, Gazi." Her voice was teasing but her gaze was not. And for a brief moment she thought of his leaving with great sadness.

"You make life worth living, sweet puss. I'm thinking I might stay in Paris for a time. My family isn't expecting me. Do you mind?" By force of habit, he chose not to examine the reasons he was reluctant to leave her.

"I would adore it if you stayed." She didn't even care that he might think her hopelessly enamored.

"I have an apartment in the city. I could have my things sent there if you're concerned about propriety."

"I don't care in the least. And consider, darling, this is Paris."

"Ah, yes, Paris in the spring. Even better. Perhaps we should thank the Adlbergs for driving us from the Crimea."

"For now, I agree. Although, I do want to go back. If the Allies win, of course. I expect the Crimea will become theirs in the treaty settlement. After all, one of the major reasons France and England went to war was for the naval base at Sevastopol."

"I know you want to return. I didn't mean it otherwise. And there is a good possibility the Crimea will change hands. Plans for a spring offensive are *en train*; I expect you already know that. The Allies will make a major assault on Sevastopol no later than June—a successful one I don't doubt." He diplomatically included the French, who were in truth the superior force. He particularly wished to avoid any controversy tonight.

"I'm not privy to Pelissier's plans, but I'm pleased to hear it. I might very well be home by fall then."

"It's very likely."

He told her what he knew of the assault plans as they rode to the outskirts of the city. She asked definitive questions and he answered as well as he could. While Pelissier had not taken her into his confidence, she had an excellent grasp of battle strategy.

As they approached the Bois de Bologne, Aurore said, "Now that we're almost there, what would you like for dinner?"

"You decide. I eat anything." He was pleased to see that her appetite had definitely returned, although his cholera fears would not be completely quelled until several more hours had passed. But for now, he was mildly optimistic. Her vomiting had been likely due to some other cause.

The moment the carriage swept through the gates and moved up the drive, Aurore opened the window and hung out her head like an impatient child. "The lights are all on! Etienne must be home already!" she exclaimed. "Isn't that wonderful!"

"It is indeed." Darley found that he actually meant it, when in the past, he would have preferred not having company for the evening. But Aurore was so obviously excited and happy, he took pleasure in her delight.

Even as he rejoiced with her, a small niggling unease raced through his senses. He hadn't felt this way since—*No! Don't go there!*—he silently admonished.

He abruptly dismissed the unwelcome thought.

Chapter

25

Darley had thought he'd seen guards in the trees bordering the drive, and as they alighted from the carriage, he was pleased to see that he had been right. Two armed men immediately approached them. Etienne must be here, he decided. And the boy was sensible about the danger.

"Good evening," Aurore said, nodding at the guards. "I am Miss Clement. I assume my brother hired you."

"Yes, miss. Just being careful." The men stepped away.

"I was right," she said, turning to Darley as they walked toward the entrance. "Etienne is home."

"And the premises are secure. Good boy." He was saved the trouble of finding credible men in an unfamiliar locale.

Her brows lifted slightly as she ascended the low bank of stairs. "Is this still really necessary?"

"It never hurts to be cautious," he said, choosing an innocuous reply. He didn't want to unnecessarily alarm her. Regardless, the men on the train had been disposed of, unless the Third Section had altered their methodology, it was inevitable that there would be more.

The door opened on their approach, as though they had been observed by unseen eyes.

"Welcome home, Miss Aurore."

Old Bizot, who had served the family since her father's youth, was frailer than last she'd seen him, but his smile was as warm as ever. "Thank you. It's good to be home."

"The young master thought you must have been delayed somewhere."

"We took the train. There are always delays. Has Etienne been here long?"

"Three days, miss. I sent a footman to tell him of your arrival. He is about to go out for the evening. Will you be wanting dinner?"

He spoke as if she'd never been gone. As if she'd come in from a day of shopping or visiting. "Yes, perhaps in an hour or so. The marquis will be staying with us."

Bizot finally deigned to look at Darley, surveying him with the presumption of an elderly retainer who had served and supported two generations of Clements in all their endeavors. "Very good, miss," he said at last, offering Darley a faint nod of acknowledgment—a probationary acceptance. "Would the gentleman prefer the Richelieu room or the India room?"

"The India room, thank you, Bizot. And some brandy in the drawing room."

"Champagne as well?"

Aurore smiled. "Yes, to celebrate our homecoming."

"Indeed, miss." A smile creased his ancient face. "And may I say how gratified we are to have you and the young master with us again."

As the major domo bowed and walked away, Aurore took Darley by the hand and said under her breath, "Ignore Bizot's scrutiny. He's protective."

Darley smiled. "I thought I might be called out."

"He'll warm up to you. He always does."

"What does *always* mean?" He understood the French were more blasé than most about love affaires. Had Aurore often brought lovers home?

"Really, you're being ridiculous." She knew what he meant. She was not so sure she *liked* what he meant.

"About what?"

"About what you're thinking."

"So do you?" He was pressing her. He didn't know why.

"Why should I answer?"

"Peace of mind for me."

Her brows rose. "Really. My love life is a concern for a man like you who considers sex a casual amusement. Like say, with Zania."

Once she brought up Zania, he understood he wasn't going to win this argument. "Forgive my boorishness," he said, his smile full of grace.

"Gladly." She too was thin-skinned when it came to sharing. It made no sense, of course. Gazi was not hers to share. "Come now. I'll show you our cherry blossoms. Their fragrance was in the air as we came up the drive. This turned out to be a perfect time of year to arrive."

Either that or be hung from the nearest gallows. "I agree," he said. "It couldn't be better."

They left the flamboyant baroque entrance hall with its elaborate vaulting and colorful marble pillars and moved down a corridor lined with portrait busts displayed in shell-shaped wall niches.

"Relatives?" Darley queried, the variety of head-dresses, hairstyles, collars and ruffs covering several centuries of fashion.

"My father's family," Aurore replied. "My favorite is the woman over there." She gestured toward a bust of a ravishingly beautiful woman, the execution so realistic her eyelashes were visible. "My grandfather brought home an Italian wife after Napoleon's Italian campaign. Canova did that."

"She looks like you."

"Do you think so? I don't see the resemblance. She died before I was born so I never met her. Here we are." She stood before double doors bordered in a broad frame of carved, green jade. "Prepare to be dazzled. The cherry blossoms are quite spectacular."

They entered a room decorated in chinoiserie style from a century ago.

Not just the cherry blossoms were dazzling. "You have a very beautiful house—this room included," Darley remarked, surveying the colorful hand-painted wallpaper, the delicate faux bamboo furniture, a silk carpet of vast dimensions.

"My father's family served in some diplomatic capacity or another since the reign of Louis Quartorze—my grandfather's brief flight prior to the revolution notwithstanding. Every ancestor brought back beautiful things from their travels. Including the cherry trees," she added, pulling him to the bank of French doors overlooking a formal garden.

"Impressive," he murmured a moment later as he

stood beside her and gazed out on a vista of magnificent flowering trees. The ancient trees formed the boundaries of the garden, long straight rows framing the parterres, each tree heavily ladened with pink blossoms.

"I'm grateful one of my forebears traveled to the Orient and brought these home. It wouldn't be spring without the cherry trees scenting the air."

"And yet *your* family decided to stay in the Crimea."

"My grandfather and father both served the French foreign service there as well."

"Ah—so your involvement with the French army was not out of the ordinary."

"I suppose not. Although I did not commit myself prior to Etienne's enlistment, as you know."

"Did I hear my name?"

At the familiar voice, Aurore spun around to find her brother standing in the doorway, looking handsome and fit. He was dressed in full evening rig, ready for his night on the town. "I was telling Darley about our family's diplomatic service."

"Which service will end with me," her brother said with a grin as he strode toward them, his footsteps silent on the plush carpet. "That kind of life is too boring by half," he added, reaching out to hug his sister. Stepping back, he put his hand out to Darley. "Always a contentious issue between Rory and me."

"Etienne is too busy amusing himself," Aurore noted with a smile as the men shook hands. After almost losing her brother, however, she had no quarrel with anything he did so long as he was happy.

"And why shouldn't I. Plenty of time to do stodgy diplomatic work when I'm old and gray. Speaking of which, I'm about to go out. Drinks at the club, then a quick look in at Countess Esterhazy's ball." He winked at Darley. "The Hungarian women are the most beautiful in Europe—no offense, Rory. After that there's a gypsy club with more beautiful women. If anyone would care to join me . . ."

Darley dipped his head. "Thank you, no."

Etienne glanced at his sister. "I know you're not interested. Rory dislikes society functions as a rule."

"As a rule—they are extremely boring," she sardonically noted.

"Except for the beautiful Hungarian women."

"I'm sure you're right, darling," she replied, indulgent in all things to her brother.

Bizot entered the room, followed by two footmen carrying trays.

Aurore glanced at Etienne. "Do you have time for a drink before you leave?"

"Certainly. A whisky for me, Bizot."

"Right here, sir." A good servant anticipates.

A few moments later the three were seated in chartreuse-painted armchairs cushioned in scarlet, embroidered silk. Their drinks had been served, the servants had departed and they were snugly in Paris well beyond the war's reach.

"It's good to be back, isn't it?" Smiling, Etienne raised his glass. "To successful escapes and the very best of sanctuaries."

"Amen," Aurore murmured, grateful to be sitting in the comfort of her home instead of a prison somewhere—or worse. Lifting her glass to her mouth, she took a sip of champagne.

"Agreed." Darley drained his glass of brandy before turning to Etienne. "Although I see you have taken precautions and hired some guards."

Etienne smiled. "I assumed you and my sister would have the hounds on your trail. The Russian secret police has a certain reputation," he added with a flicker of a grin. "This place is an armed camp."

"Very thoughtful of you. And much appreciated," Darley said in the way of understatement. "Your journey to Eupatoria went smoothly, I gather?" Lifting the decanter from the tray on the table before him, he uncorked it and poured himself another drink.

"Absolutely. My black racer was in the mood to run. We made record time."

"When we reached Sevastopol, we heard that you had already set sail," Aurore noted. "We assumed things went well."

"The point was to stay ahead of our pursuit. Which we easily did. My stallion is a sweet goer and your men, Darley, ride like the wind." Etienne refilled his glass. "How was your journey? Uneventful, I hope."

"Yes," Darley replied, careful not to look at Aurore. "Uneventful." Nonstop fucking and assassins aside. "Did you bring your racehorse home with you?"

"I wouldn't think of leaving him behind."

"Etienne raised him from a foal." Aurore smiled at her brother. "He won a tidy sum racing him."

"I'm thinking of running him at Longchamps. He's better than most of the bloodstock in the field."

Etienne spoke of his hopes for his stallion as well as the events of the following day that revolved around the races at Longchamps. He also shared gossip about their friends with Aurore, explaining that everyone had insisted she call on them the moment she reached the city. "Not that you're likely to do so," he added with a grin. "But I didn't tell them that. And don't you dare wait up for me tonight." He gave his sister a warning glance. "She does, you know," he noted, turning to Darley. "I'm too old to be monitored."

"I shall see that she doesn't," Darley pleasantly replied.

"Excellent!" Pouring his second whisky down his throat, Etienne came to his feet. "I will see you two tomorrow," he said with a bow. "Briefly at least—I leave for the races at noon. Are you staying long, Darley? If you are, I'll take you shooting. I just bought the most splendid shotgun."

Darley shrugged faintly. "I'm not sure. I'll see."

"Well, if you do, you'll have to try my Holland and Holland 8-bore double barrel." He was already moving toward the door. "It's superb."

"He misses me terribly as you can see," Aurore mockingly noted.

"He's young."

"And self-centered."

Darley smiled. "That's part of being young." He nodded toward her glass on the table beside her. "You're not drinking."

"I thought I'd wait to eat something first. Just in case," she said.

"Probably wise. Do you mind?" He picked up the brandy decanter.

"Not at all."

"I don't get drunk."

"I don't care if you do."

He smiled. "Such unfettered license."

Her brows rose slightly. "Why would I want to govern your drinking?"

"Some women do."

"Don't tell me what some women do with you."

"Jealous?" Perhaps he knew of what he spoke.

Less reticent, more outspoken, or perhaps touched by fatigue, Aurore said, "Yes. Don't ask me why. I have no idea when you're sure to leave before long." She smiled. "Don't be alarmed. I have no intention of being difficult about your departure." She might even have meant it. She wasn't sure.

"I don't know when I'm going."

"I understand."

"I didn't want to leave tonight and it had nothing to do with you feeling unwell. But I tend not to stay anywhere too long." He didn't want her to think otherwise.

"Really, there's no need to explain."

They were both exceedingly civil. The end of a love affaire was a subject that required civility. There was no point in making things uncomfortable.

"I'm going to wash up before dinner. Would you like to see your room?"

"Certainly."

He took his glass with him as they left, finding himself in a mood to drink. They spoke of general things as they moved down the corridor and ascended the broad marble staircase; they were both well bred enough to speak of trifling subjects with aplomb.

But Aurore found herself wondering how long he'd stay. When she shouldn't.

Darley was thinking he should leave. But not tonight.

She showed him to the India room, an apt designation for the flamboyant display of hot colors, sumptuous fabrics and furniture clearly made for a palace somewhere in the Punjab.

"I like the decor—somewhat familiar," he said, standing in the middle of the room, turning slowly to survey the riot of pattern and dazzling color accosting his eyes. "Nice size bed too," he added with a nod toward a monstrous canopied bed. Made to accommodate a dozen harem ladies and their master he knew.

"My great-grandfather had it sent back."

"And where are you sleeping?"

It was softly put, but even then she felt a small pleasurable ripple slide up her vagina. "Down the hall," she said, trying to suppress the tremor in her voice. She wanted him too much; it would never do. He was too assured, too familiar with obliging women, certain to leave soon. "I have to consider the servants," she lied, needing time to sort out her tumultuous feelings.

"You're not serious."

"Maybe I am."

It was obvious she wasn't. "Surely you needn't stay in your room all night?" A velvet soft invitation to pleasure.

"I'm not sure," she coolly said. Unfortunately, a shiver of longing raced up her spine, proving her duplicity.

"What if *I* am?"

"You could be wrong." Oh dear—she should have been more firm.

"No, I'm not." His voice in contrast was assured. Three days on the train from Varna gave him a fairly good idea of what the lady wanted. "And consider, darling, how you like to come all night long. I could help you with that."

Abruptly turning away, Aurore bolted for the door before it was too late. "I'll meet you downstairs in an hour," she said, flustered and rattled, careful not to look back.

His words, *I could help you with that,* were ringing in her ears.

Chapter

26

Dinner was subdued.
Even the servants were soft footed and quiet.

Darley drank most of his meal, although he ate
when the roasts and game were served. Still chafing
at Aurore's feeble excuse about the servants, vexed
at her senseless equivocation, he'd already drunk a
half bottle before dinner. He was perhaps slightly less
reasonable than he might otherwise have been. But
it didn't show.

Aurore had spent the interval before dinner in
her bedroom trying to come to terms with her feelings for Darley. Her much too enamored feelings.
Not that she'd come to any meaningful resolution.
But then matters of the heart did not easily yield to
reason.

In terms of more mundane matters, she was
pleased to find that she could eat again without feeling ill. So aside from the mild tension in the air, Aurore enjoyed her cook's festive menu. Every dish was

a special favorite of hers: tomato and shrimp bisque; a delicious pot-au-feu that had been cooking since morning—the only way it comes of age; woodcocks flamed in rum; a roast beef for her gentleman guest, she suspected; macaroni a la menagere—a dish from her childhood, as was the violet ice cream and almond cake for dessert.

Conversation was desultory. She would bring up some topic of discussion or ask a question of Darley and he would answer with courtesy—and brevity.

Aurore finally gave up trying to make small talk. A relief in a way. It was difficult enough trying to disregard Darley's stark beauty, dressed as he was in his fine evening clothes with diamonds sparkling in his cravat. Ever efficient, Bizot had seen that their luggage was delivered forthwith and now she was forced to behold the spectacle of the Marquis of Darley lounging in his chair like some prince of the blood. He wore a half smile on his face, the devil was in his eyes, and despite his fine tailoring and formal attire, he *flagrantly* exuded male virility.

Which flaunting exhibition of brute sexuality made it even more difficult to control her ardent longing. She knew exactly how virile he was, how long he could last, how sumptuously blissful he made her feel. How he could maintain her sexual desires at fever pitch. How he was—bar none—her aphrodisiac of choice.

Jolted from her musing, she glanced up to see Bizot.

"Forgive me, miss. Count Choiseul and Monsieur Nolhac are in the drawing room. I told them I would see if you were at home."

Bizot must have spoken to her before. He would not have touched her shoulder otherwise. Looking down the length of the table, she observed Darley's sardonic smile, as if he somehow knew that she had been thinking of him. "Would you like visitors?" she asked.

"Not particularly."

His insolent drawl annoyed her or perhaps it was the degree of certainty in his voice. That assurance that she would accommodate his wishes—that any woman would. Particularly when she was struggling to maintain some independence in their heated relationship. "Certainly I'm at home to them, Bizot," Aurore declared, a doctrinaire note in her voice. "Show the men in."

Darley's gaze narrowed.

Rankled by his critical gaze, fighting for a certain personal autonomy, she defiantly raised the bid. "Bring up the Napoleonic brandy, Bizot," she added. "It's a favorite of the count's."

Darley poured himself another brandy and drank it in the silent interval before their guests appeared. "Some people rate Napoleonic brandy I see," he murmured as a footman hurried in with two bottles from the cellar.

"I didn't know you liked it," she replied a trifle coolly.

"But you know the count does."

"We're old friends."

"Friends like we're friends?"

Her nostrils flared slightly. "I don't see that it's any of your business."

"An answer in itself."

"Don't jump to conclusions," she said stiffly.

"Why would I not, having met you under such impromptu circumstances and spending that very same night in your bed."

"That's quite enough," she murmured, indicating her servants with a sideways glance.

"I didn't know you were so proper."

"And I didn't know you were so rude."

"If your guests stay too long," he said softly, "you'll see just how rude I can be."

"I don't answer to you," she snapped.

"I beg to differ with you in that regard. If the servants weren't here, I might explain in more detail."

"For heaven's sake, Gazi!"

"Darley," he said, cold and brusque. "We are long gone from the mountains."

"As you say, and with that distance you seem to have altered," she returned with equal chill.

"You as well," he curtly replied. "Now that you are with your friends."

The door to the dining room was thrown open, curtailing their verbal skirmish.

Aurore offered a dazzling smile to the two men who entered. "Philip, Bertrand, how nice of you to call," she said, gracious and affable. "Do come and join us."

"We met Etienne at the club," the count explained, walking toward Aurore. "He said you were in Paris so we came to see for ourselves. May I say, you are looking magnificent as ever, my dear."

"*More* magnificent, Rory," Bertrand Nolhac noted with a wink as he kept pace with his friend. "It must be the Crimean air."

Aurore laughed. "Hardly. At the moment the air is alive with gunshot and cannonballs."

"Then, how nice that you are safely here," the count said.

"With us," Nolhac murmured as they reached Aurore.

Both men made their bows and kissed her hand with the exquisite grace of Frenchmen born and bred.

"Allow me to introduce the Marquis of Darley," Aurore offered. "Darley, Count Choiseul and Monsieur Nolhac. Darley was kind enough to escort me home from the Crimea."

Darley should have risen to his feet. He didn't. "A pleasure," he said in a tone of voice that made it clear that it was not in the least a pleasure.

"Sit please," Aurore quickly interjected, waving her guests to chairs held out by her servants. "And tell me what has transpired in Paris in my absence." She smiled. "Bizot brought up your favorite, Philip. The '05."

"Ah, it's a real pleasure to have you home, my dear," the count drawled. "Along with access to your cellar I might add. Now, as for the latest gossip," he said, and went on to elaborate on the current state of the Parisian haut monde.

The men were handsome, cultivated and obviously friends of long standing. They chatted about mutual acquaintances, disclosed the latest gossip at court, brought up amusing stories from their childhoods. The three had often spent vacations together at Deauville. Plans for future entertainments were discussed, the spring round of social engagements in full swing.

And all the while, the Napoleonic brandy continued to be poured.

A tic appeared over Darley's high cheekbone as he listened to the conversation. It was not a discussion for the uninitiated. The talk was of family, common memories, mutual friends.

Perhaps by design.

That the men were vying for Aurore's attention was plain.

That she was rashly flirting was plainer still.

No one could deny that Aurore's visitors were handsome, young men of the world—easily amused and amusing, relaxed, convivial.

And becoming increasingly annoying to Darley.

He probably shouldn't have said what he said. If not for the considerable brandy he'd consumed before their arrival and the subsequent imbibing of the fine '05 vintage, he might have held his tongue. On the other hand, his temper had been under severe duress for quite some time as he listened to the intimate, warm exchange between friends.

That there would be the devil to pay was inevitable.

Abruptly pushing his chair back, Darley came to his feet and in a voice smooth as glass, said, "I'm so very sorry, but we had plans for the night." He met Aurore's startled gaze, held it for a taut moment, then turned to the two men with an icy smile. "Perhaps you would like to come back some other time. Tomorrow for tea, perhaps. What do you think, *dear*?"

On hearing the word *dear* spoken in that hard tight voice, Aurore understood that the situation would only get worse if she balked.

The word *dear* also made it abundantly clear to Philip and Bertrand that the Marquis of Darley was something more than a friend. Not that either man would consider deserting Aurore should she need them.

"We are at your disposal, Aurore," the count said with exquisite courtesy. That they were friends and champions should she need them was also exquisitely clear. "Whatever you wish, of course. It was not our intention to impose."

"You're not imposing, but Darley and I *were* invited out," she lied. "Perhaps tea tomorrow would better serve."

"Of course," Bertrand murmured, immediately rising. "Say at five?"

"Five would be excellent."

"Should you need us for anything beforetimes," Bertrand murmured, shooting a dark look at Darley, "you need but ask." It was a formal offer of assistance.

"No, no, I'm quite comfortable." The men were all glaring at each other; she did not want the situation to escalate into a duel. "And with Etienne here, should I need anything he will oblige me."

Understanding that Aurore's brother would protect her should she require it, the men respectfully made their bows and left.

The door closed on their visitors.

Silence descended on the room.

Darley sat down, reached for the brandy and filled his glass.

"That will be all tonight," Aurore calmly announced, giving a nod of dismissal to the servants in attendance.

She waited until the last footman exited the dining room before turning on Darley. "How dare you," she hissed, seething with fury. "How *dare* you embarrass me in front of my friends."

"You invited them in to piss me off." He scowled at her. "What the hell did you expect."

"I expected you to act like a gentleman."

"Maybe we could have shared a foursome," he said with icy malice. "Would that have been polite enough for you?"

"Bastard."

"Bitch. Admit, you were trying to make me jealous," he growled. "Well, you fucking succeeded. Are you finished eating?"

"Whether I am or not is no concern of yours," she snapped.

He laughed—a sharp, caustic utterance. "That might work in a drawing room somewhere, but I'm long past drawing room manners. It's all the killing of late," he said with silky derision. "One loses one's fine sense of deportment."

She stared him down, her hands flat on the table, her diamonds at her ears and throat incongruously sparkling brightly. "You don't frighten me if that's what you're trying to do."

He shook his head, took a deep breath, counted to ten, then counted to ten again. "What I am trying to do," he said with soft restraint, "is get you upstairs and into bed. Are you finished?"

"I have no intention of going upstairs and getting into bed with you." Each word vibrated with distaste.

"Suit yourself." He nodded toward the servant's door. "I'd suggest you tell your staff not to come in and clean up then."

Her astonishment showed for a second. "I'll do no such thing!"

"Then I will." He stood.

"No, stop." She jumped to her feet. "That won't be necessary." She couldn't possibly involve her staff in this row.

Darley was drunk. Unpredictable. And suddenly she was sorry she'd lost her temper and invited Philip and Bertrand to join them. It had been childish and petty of her.

Standing at opposite ends of the table, they watched each other.

Breaking the obstinate silence first, Darley lifted his glass to her. "My compliments on your cellar." Tossing down the liquor, he set down his glass.

"I'm pleased you enjoyed it."

"Who wouldn't."

They both spoke with stiff civility.

Darley flexed his fingers, clenched his jaw, softly exhaled, then drawing in a breath, he said, half to himself, "I was going to pick you up, toss you down on the floor and have my way with you, but now I'm not so sure."

Aurore lifted her chin. "I was going to order you out of my house, but now—"

"I wouldn't have gone," he interrupted.

"That's what I was thinking."

He dropped down into his chair. Still moody, in a voice more testy than penitent, he muttered, "I apologize for my temper. But you shouldn't have flaunted your friends in front of me. Notice, I'm being polite. I didn't say lovers."

"That's a leading remark, I presume. You don't actually think I'm going to respond to such impudence."

He gave her a glowering look. "You are an extremely difficult woman."

"In contrast to what—all the obliging ones?"

"Damn right." A sullen grunt.

"You're not exactly the usual fawning suitor." *Au contraire.*

"Please, the word *usual* always offends me with you."

She smiled despite herself, liking his jealousy. Understanding the feeling. She would keep him locked away for herself if she could. "I'll probably regret telling you this"—she was no different she supposed than all his other obliging women now—"but if you must know, the word *usual* refers to nothing more than casual suitors. I have not slept with countless men like you have women. There have been some, not many, and I was engaged to a lovely man who drowned while out sailing. You were the first since then." She smiled again. "Which may have accounted for my impatience that night in Sevastopol—although it might have been your allure. I still have not decided which."

He was astonished how his mood instantly improved on hearing her explanation. He was even more astonished that her impatient desire for him pleased him so. He sat up straight, his sudden smile like a bright rainbow after the storm. "You have made me a very happy man." He grinned. "Happy as a king, as a lark, as the day is long and every other gratifying analogy." He gracefully dipped his head. "Now, if you would allow, I would like to make you happy in return."

"I should refuse. You've been embarrassing and shamelessly rude."

"And yet," he whispered, rising to his feet, recognizing capitulation when he heard it.

She nodded. "And yet . . ."

"The craving remains," he murmured, moving toward her. "I have no explanation. Nor do I care." Reaching her, he took her hand and smiled his glorious smile. "Your bed or mine?"

"I should say neither," she said with a pretty little pout.

"Don't. I will make you happy."

Arrogant man, she thought. But she couldn't fault his assurance. She smiled. "Perhaps I'll give you a list of my requirements tonight."

"The mood I'm in you may carve it on my body if you wish." He tugged on her hand and smiled. "Talk to me upstairs—of this list."

As they walked up the stairs, hand in hand, she allowed herself to contemplate how lovely it would be if he stayed. They would go to bed like this every night and he would wake beside her and make her happy as he'd promised. She had never before given herself up to fantasy. Even with Petros, she had thought of him as a companion first, a lover second. They had shared common interests, family ties in the area, a love of the land. She had never trembled at the sight of him or been roused to passion by his merest touch.

Yet with Gazi—she half smiled at such wistful daydreams.

Fortunately, she understood the difference between wanting and having.

And with Darley perhaps part of the excitement was in knowing there was nothing lasting. She must seize her happiness while she may.

A sensible maxim for life in general, she decided, the war having driven home that unvarnished truth.

Darley had noticed both her smile and her contemplative air, but he'd learned long ago not to ask a woman what she was thinking. It might oblige one to hear or do something one would rather not hear or do. Nor did he ask her again which room she preferred.

Rather excessively focused, he chose for them, understanding from her silence that she had relinquished that decision.

Opening the door to the India room, he followed her in, shut the door and locked it for good measure.

Their recent guests may have made him cautious or maybe he simply chose not to be interrupted.

"There's another entrance to the room," Aurore said with a small smile, taking a seat in a nearby chair as though they had come here for conversation instead of sex. "In the event you're thinking of keeping me captive. Although I doubt you'll find the door."

Darley quickly scanned the room. "Since it's apparently well hidden, I must see that you don't wish to run," he murmured, taking a seat opposite her. It was early. They had all night. If she wished some style of conversational foreplay, he was more than willing. As for her running, he rather doubted it. Her cheeks were flushed that rosy pink of arousal, her breasts were swelling above her decolletage with each breath. With each tempestuous little breath. "Family diamonds?" he casually inquired, indicating her jewelry with a flick of his hand. He was willing to sit here as long as she wished.

"Yes." She touched the glittering necklace. "A prerevolution remnant."

"Lovely." He smiled. "You keep a wardrobe here as well, I see. I like your gown." She was stunning in embroidered Lyon silk, a pale creme confection embellished with flower garlands. "Very—virginal."

It took her a fraction of a second to respond, his dark gaze predatory and compelling. "Thank you," she said a moment later, the tremor in her voice only faintly heard.

But heard nonetheless. "Are we going to sit here long?" His voice was silken, his lounging pose serene. "If so, I might bring a bottle closer."

"I can make you wait." A small pettish sound.

He smiled. "Yes, I know."

"And I intend to."

"In that case," he said, imperturbable and urbane, "pardon me while I avail myself of that brandy over there." He rose, walked to a table outfitted with decanters, lifted one stopper, then another, before finding what he wished. Walking back to his chair, he sat down again, said, "Pardon my manners," and lifted the decanter to his mouth.

"You've already drunk a good amount tonight," she said, her gaze critically assessing.

"You needn't worry. I am quite sober. What were we discussing, now?"

His languid drawl annoyed her. He had been here like this a thousand times before, she suspected. Calmly waiting, certain of the outcome. "I thought I'd make my list of requirements."

His brows rose an infinitesimal distance. "Ah. Would you prefer a pen or a knife, then?"

She gave him a jaundiced look. "Very amusing."

"I've been carved up for much less pleasant reasons," he murmured. "Feel free."

"You mean it?" No reasonable person would.

"If you wish, of course."

She didn't quite know what to say. Obviously, he meant what he said. There was a nervelessness about him that was undeniable. And irresistible. "You're mad," she said. "Although I expect you know that."

"Mad for you," he softly replied.

She sighed. "I don't know what made me think I could resist you."

Conscious of the merits of tact in situations like this he chose not to reply.

"Say something." A little huffiness underlay her words.

"I have wanted to make love to you since we arrived"—he glanced at the clock—"four hours ago. I
even sat through that unpleasant visit with your
friends without killing anyone. I believe I have been
penitent, polite and obliging." His smile was unutter-
ably sweet. "Have pity, darling."

She smiled. "You're begging?"

"I am," he simply said.

"I have been struggling to curb my obsession with
you." She shrugged. "I don't know why. But the feeling persists."

"We are both battling vexatious feelings. I suggest
we set them aside and enjoy what we have. You talked
about carpe diem pleasures in Simferopol if I recall.
I don't see why Paris should be any different."

"You are very reasonable."

"I like to think I am." *And so he had been until Aurore
entered his life.*

"Very well."

He laughed. "This is not the guillotine, my dear."

"I know, but my brain is awash in irksome contra-
dictions."

He placed the decanter on the floor and rose
from his chair, having decided that Aurore would
feel better if her brain was awash in the heat of passion instead. And he certainly would be happier.
"Tell me what's first on your list," he said, lifting her
to her feet. "Anything as long as it doesn't involve animals."

"I didn't know you had scruples," she quipped,
amusement in her eyes.

There had been times when he hadn't, but bringing animals upstairs tonight would have taken too
much effort. And he rather doubted Bizot would

allow it anyway. "Indeed I do have scruples on occasion," he lied, turning her around to unhook her gown. "So you needn't fear for your honor."

How pleasant it was to let Darley take charge, she decided. How gratifying to know that soon she would be transported to that wonderland of pleasure she only knew with him. And it was infinitely easy. She had only to give herself up to him and he would do all the rest.

Gifted, endowed by nature with distinctive attributes—sizeable attributes—he offered sexual largess and lavish satisfaction beyond what she had formerly known.

Although, initially, that night, he operated without his usual self-control.

After discarding Aurore's gown, with a rare impatience he ascribed to considerable drink, he murmured, "Forgive me," and picking her up, walked to the bed, sat her down, and unbuttoned his fly. Without removing her drawers—they were conveniently open at the bottom—he lifted her into his arms again, wrapped her legs around his waist, positioned his throbbing cock against her pulsing slit and thrust upward with hot-headed haste.

He stood perfectly still for a moment, engulfed within Aurore's steamy heat, ensconced in the exact location he'd most wanted to be all these many hours past. Buried as he was in the sweetest cunt, the tightest, most exquisite, most glorious cunt, he experienced concurrently both a wild arousal and a curious serenity.

Until he suddenly felt Aurore's hands gripping his shoulders, felt her slide up his erection and was graphically reminded of his companion's spirited impatience.

He moved then and she did in reply and so it went—but not for long. His lengthy wait had taken its toll.

"Don't you dare!" he heard her cry as though from a great distance and with considerable effort, he dragged himself back to reality and precipitously curbed his orgasm. Fortunately, his time in India had not been wasted. He refocused his attentions then and once the greedy Miss Clement had had her way with him, he immediately dropped her on the bed and came on her stomach.

"Ick," she said a moment later, her silk drawers stuck to her skin.

"Consider the alternative, darling," he calmly said, his orgasm having brought with it a certain tranquility. "I could have come inside you." He reached for a pillowcase.

"I suppose I should thank you," she grumbled. Then, she smiled. "I do, actually, thank you most profusely. I always think it can't get any better and yet, it always does with you. You are truly gifted."

"And you are temptation itself," he said, charming and urbane. He'd wiped himself off and was dabbing at her drawers with a clean portion of the pillowcase. "Don't move. I'll take these off."

He was completely unaffected, with an openness about him that belied the seductive genius so much a part of his nature. And he was truly a genius when it came to sexual pleasure. Surely, she would be the greatest fool to question why she was here doing what she was doing.

From that point on, she no longer did, reveling instead in the euphoric rapture he bestowed in limitless measure.

* * *

Much later that night, she pettishly wailed, "Wake up! Don't do this to me!"

Sprawled on his back, his arms over his head, Darley slowly opened his eyes and muttered half-asleep and edgy, "What the fuck . . ."

"Please, Gazi—I beg of you! Don't fall asleep!"

He must have dozed off for a minute. Blinking, he tried to focus his gaze—finally succeeded. Aurore was kneeling beside him, her breathing labored, her eyes pleading, her hands clutched between her legs, as though trying to contain the fire within.

Dragging himself awake, he glanced downward, then up again before meeting her gaze. He smiled. "You have to talk to *him*."

In her current frenzied state, she was more than willing. Her mouth was immediately inspiring, his fatigue quickly banished. In short order, he chivalrously set about relieving the lady's sharp-set lust in what turned out to be a long, drawn-out, heart-stirring exercise in prolonged delay.

"Now, now, now," she'd cry.

"Not yet." And he'd withdraw until her trembling stopped.

She threatened him and whined, tried artifice and subterfuge.

But he did what he did, intent on amplifying and heightening her resulting orgasm.

When he finally allowed her to climax, she was visibly shaken.

Pale and overwrought, drained.

He drew her close then and she curled up against him and slept.

* * *

Wide awake now, disquieted when he shouldn't be, he watched over her as a formless confusion filled his brain. He shouldn't be here. Perhaps he'd known that from the first. Sex aside, of course.

But there was always sex somewhere else.

And he had known that too from the first.

Chapter
27

He was gone when she woke in the morning, which turned out to be fortunate since the moment she rose from bed nausea overwhelmed her.

She raced for the bathroom and reached it just in time.

Lying on the Punjabi bed afterward, she scanned the room for any sign of Darley's things, although she'd known last night he wouldn't be here in the morning.

He hadn't said anything. He hadn't had to.

She'd known. He'd made love to her with an unusual solicitude, kissed her with great tenderness, indulged her every whim. Always gallant, he'd been even more unselfish last night, taking great pains to please her and succeeding masterfully.

But beyond the sensual euphoria and enchantment, the playfulness and soft caresses, had been the unspoken, inevitable good-bye.

Realistically, she had never assumed he'd stay, nor

had that ever been her intent. This was a love affaire, after all—by definition a fleeting thing. And yet . . . Aurore sighed and smiled at the same time. Darley was not the sort of man easily forgotten.

Which brought to mind affairs of another kind—a delicate little affair in this case. She made a small moue. One could only postpone and procrastinate for so long, she ruefully mused. The time had come, perhaps, to confront a significant consequence of the pleasure Darley so charmingly dispensed.

While her stomach upset last night could have been explained by fatigue, lengthy travel, strange odors, this morning's recent bout of nausea could not be so easily dismissed. She was not obtuse, nor ignorant of the principles of reproduction. She had also known friends with this common complaint. Most incontrovertible, however, in terms of confirming any suspicion she might have had was the fact that she had not had her menses since she'd met Darley.

Six weeks ago.

She wasn't blaming him. He'd always been careful. Not that she expected anything different—a gentleman knew better than to come in a woman. But however cautious their efforts, with unremitting sex the risk of failure increased.

Seminal residue occasionally intruded and infiltrated where it shouldn't.

In this case, into her womb.

In a way, she was grateful that he'd left. The situation would have been awkward this morning—an excuse for her bout of morning sickness wouldn't have been convincing. They both would have been embarrassed by the disclosure. She felt a hot flush warm her cheeks just thinking of the floundering conversation that would have ensued. Thankfully, the need for clumsy excuses, tactful politesse or perhaps—wrathful displeasure—had been avoided.

Although she rather doubted Darley would be so scurrilous as to reproach her. On the other hand, he had chosen not to marry for whatever reasons—although a dearth of women pursuing him was not one of them, she suspected. He very well may have faced such a situation before. If he had, apparently he'd avoided any repercussions. She was not inclined to attempt to coerce a man into marriage in any event. The thought was repugnant. And she rather doubted Darley would yield to coercion anyway.

They would be in agreement there, she decided.

So now—she was here, he was not and there was a child to consider.

What to do first?

It was opportune that she was in Paris, far from anyone who might have known that she was previously unmarried and unattached. When it became necessary, she would fabricate a story about a husband killed in the war and assume the role of widow. A familiar-enough ploy. Although, since Philip and Bertrand had seen her with Darley, she would have to take them into her confidence; but they could be trusted.

As for the aristocratic world, overlooking little imbroglios or delicate situations was normal. Discretion was a prevailing principle and not just in terms of pregnancies. In the haut monde, everything from mistresses to political graft was countenanced with politesse and tact, subterfuge and illusion—overlooking indiscretions not only de rigueur but a sign of good breeding.

And there was no need to tell Etienne or _anyone_

until absolutely necessary. Her brother would only feel obliged to interfere and she was determined to avoid his meddling. What he would consider an honorable solution would not suit her. Nor did principles of male affront have anything to do with her or her child. She wasn't particularly worried about Etienne, however. She could handle him. She always had.

She stretched lazily, all the pertinent issues nicely arranged in an orderly format that would unfold in time. And in truth, the thought of a child—Darley's child—warmed her heart. Would it be a boy—a girl . . . perhaps both, she mused, smiling faintly at the notion. A boy would look like Darley, of course, although what if a girl looked like Darley—very large and strong . . . or if a boy were fair like her and not large at all. She giggled softly, knowing it mattered not at all—large, small, fair, dark—as long as the child was theirs.

She had never allowed herself to think of her relationship with Darley in terms of love. Such a notion would have been beyond the pale of rational thought. But she was not inhibited by similar restrictions when it came to her child, and she would love and hold dear this child they had created together. She would be outrageously doting, she decided with a grin.

Which meant a certain attention to detail soon must be considered. She would need a layette prepared, and the nursery freshened and decorated, a nurse employed—several would be better, she reflected. Was it too early to interview tutors and buy ponies? Don't forget a doctor would be required. She would ask her friends and find out who was best. Or maybe a midwife would be more useful, she thought in the next second. Another question to ask her friends—when the time was appropriate. Heavens, so much to do and for such a lovely purpose.

And in truth, it was much better that she was dealing with this child alone. Darley might have proved difficult in any number of ways.

For instance, neither England nor France were particularly amenable to mother's rights, and should Darley decide to lay claim to this child, the courts would likely allow his claim. That was a fight she preferred avoiding.

She would have to make that clear to Etienne when she spoke to him; Darley should not be told about the child for practical reasons.

Although, in her current blissful mood, even thoughts of paternity claims could not curb her good humor.

And she was feeling just a little bit hungry too.

Why not, though? She had just thrown up.

Mmmm—what did she want for breakfast?

Chapter

28

Darley reached London that same evening, the train to Calais and the trip on the channel packet testimony to the efficiency of the transportation system. Hiring a coach at Dover rather than take the train, he seized the opportunity to doze on the last leg of the journey. His sleep the night before had been nonexistent.

Westerlands House in Portman Square was open, although the entire family was not yet come down for the Season. The social festivities would not commence until late April—the first to arrive in town, those mamas most anxious to marry off their daughters.

Darley was welcomed home with great warmth, the butler and two flunkys on duty in the front hall delighted to see the prodigal son returned.

"His Grace is just back from Brooks, sir," the butler, Simpson, said. "He will be most happy to see you."

Following Simpson down the hall, Darley inquired of his family. His mother, sisters and nieces were in Paris, he was told—a mild shock hearing that. Fortunately, he'd not stayed long enough to run into them with Aurore at some entertainment. The others in his sisters' families were planning on coming to town in a fortnight—no, there were no new additions to his siblings' families since last he'd visited. His brother and his household were in residence at Oak Hill. They had no plans to come down 'til the Season was well underway. Stopping before the library door, Simpson smiled at Darley. "This will be a most pleasant surprise for His Grace." Opening the door, he announced with relish, "The marquis is come home, Your Grace."

The duke was up out of his chair before Simpson finished speaking. "Welcome, welcome home, son! What a bloody delight to have you back!" Smiling broadly, the Duke of Westerlands advanced on Darley, arms open wide.

"It's good to be home," Hugh replied, his smile very like his father's.

As the men hugged, Simpson delicately shut the door and proceeded briskly down the corridor. Everyone below stairs must be apprised of the marquis's arrival, his suite must be quickly aired and readied; the cook would want to make something special in honor of Darley's wondrous appearance. He had last been home two years ago, and then only briefly for a nephew's baptism.

Young Hugh as he was still referred to, although he had long been a grown man, had always been a favorite of the servants. He'd always made it a point to know every servant's name from the lowliest scullery maid to the august steward, had taken time to chat with them all, knew their families and friends, and as a child, he was more apt to be found in the kitchen than anywhere else.

"Sit, I'll get you a cognac," the duke cheerfully declared. "And tell me to what do we owe this surprise visit? I thought you'd be up to your ears with Cattley's work for some time yet."

Dropping into a wing chair by the fire, Darley slid into a weary sprawl. "Lord, it feels prodigious good to be home," he said with feeling, stretching his legs out before him. Paradise took many forms. "As to my work in the Crimea"—he grimaced faintly—"we were caught in the act as it were at the Russian governor's house in Simferopol and had to run for our lives. It's a little too hot there right now with the Third Section on the prowl for us."

"You and whom? Anyone I know?" Returning with their drinks, Duff handed Darley his and took the matching wing chair across from his son.

"A French spy. She came into the governor's study while I was pilfering his desk. With the same object in mind. We barely escaped."

"She?" The duke arched one brow. "That's a bit unusual, isn't it?"

"Her family has diplomatic ties with France going back several centuries. Her brother had enlisted in the French army and she became involved as a result." Raising his glass to his mouth, he drank half the cognac in one draught.

"A French woman in the field. That still must be rare."

"Her family has lived in the Crimea for some time. Fifty years or more—something like that. I'm not entirely sure." He purposely spoke in vague terms.

"She must be at risk from the Third Section as well."

"I dropped her off in Paris. She has a home there."

"I see. Well"—the duke smiled—"fortunately you are here safe and sound and for that we are grateful. Will you stay for some time now that you are persona non grata in that part of the world?"

Hugh shrugged. "For a while. I'm never sure."

"We must see that you are entertained then, so you will be inclined to extend your stay," Duff replied warmly. "Your maman will be ecstatic that you have arrived. She and your sisters are scheduled to return in a few days. They're shopping for the Season so one never knows precisely how long fittings and such will take, but I'll see that a telegram is sent to your mother immediately. She'll be anxious to see you, I know."

Darley smiled. "And I her—and everyone else. The family has not expanded, Simpson tells me, since last I was here."

"No, but the children are all growing like grass. In only two years, Emma's oldest will be coming out."

Darley's eyes flared wide for a transient moment. "Good Lord. It can't be true." Emma was two years younger than he.

His father laughed. "You'll see how true it is when you see Maude. She's become quite the little lady. With a mind of her own, I might add. Not that that's unusual in this family."

"You taught us well, Papa. There are no sheep who blindly follow in the Westerland brood." Grinning, Darley raised his glass to his father.

"I won't take all the credit. Your mother *insisted* on raising independent children." Annabelle Foster, the greatest beauty of her day, had been an actress and playwright, the latter profession exceptional for a woman.

"Assuredly, it makes life more interesting."

"What of your plans after this visit? Where do you travel next?" While the duke would have preferred his heir marry and raise a family, he was inured to his son's wanderlust after so many years. Or at least respectful of Darley's inclination.

"I don't have any plans at the moment. At least nothing specific." Aurore was still very much on his mind—enough so that the practicalities eluded him. "You're looking well, Papa," he added, intent on recasting his thoughts. At sixty-six, his father was still fit and trim, his tall muscular frame evidence of good health and vigor.

"Thank you. As are you, although you could use some sleep, I suspect." His son's eyes were half-lidded, a faint weariness evident in his lounging pose.

"It was a long trip. We were in transit nearly a week. We took the *Argo* to Varna, then the train to Paris. I stayed at Miss Clement's last night; her brother had preceded us by a few days," he quickly interjected, not wishing to suggest anything more than a mutual working relationship.

"Miss Clement is the French agent."

"Yes, her brother had been recuperating in Simferopol and had to flee when we did. He rode to Eupatoria. We reported to Balaclava first. We all met again in Paris."

The duke took note of his son's feigned crispness of tone when he spoke of Miss Clement. *Interesting.* Not that he intended to read anything more into Hugh's friendship with a woman when his son had studiously avoided female attachment since Lucia died. While he had had his own demons to overcome after Waterloo, Duff had never quite understood how Lucia's death had so lastingly ravaged his son's life. But then he'd never had the woman he loved die in his arms. Nor have his infant son follow his mother to the grave a few days later. He also had had the great fortune to meet Annabelle Foster, who had become the wellspring of all that was good in life.

How often had he wished such happiness might come his son's way.

The family had always given Hugh wide latitude in his manner of grieving. Everyone realized that despair took different forms, required different remedies. They could only offer sympathy and compassion, and that they had done. And yet Darley had been seriously afflicted since that tragedy. "Another?" Duff asked, nodding at Darley's empty glass. He wasn't going to spoil the joy of his son's return with painful memories. "And I hope you're hungry, because we both know cook is busy in the kitchen right now preparing your favorite dishes." Standing, he reached for Darley's glass.

Darley grinned as he handed it over. "As it happens, I *am* hungry. I didn't eat much last night and left early this morning. As you well know, the food available at the train depots leaves much to be desired. Do you suppose cook has any of those rum cakes somewhere in the larder?"

Duff glanced over his shoulder as he stood at the drinks table, filling their glasses. "Ten guineas says she does."

"Perfect. With clotted cream?" Darley was salivating at the thought, all the pleasures of home enveloping him in a warm, glowing content.

Not the kind of content he'd experienced last night, he thought when he would have preferred those memories be less fresh and vivid in his mind.

What was Aurore doing now? he wondered next, that too an unwelcome but reoccurring thought.

He felt his stomach tighten at the disquieting notion that she might be entertaining their visitors from last evening. "Sorry," he said, looking up, realizing his father had been standing there for some time. "There had been plans afoot for a full-scale assault on Sevastopol. I was wondering if it had been undertaken yet," he lied.

Inspired by a father's intuition, Duff almost asked, *Is it a woman distracting you?* because Hugh's reply wasn't the truth or was barely the truth. And his eldest son generally opted for candor. "Drink up," the duke said instead, handing over the glass.

Taking his drink, Darley stared into the glistening liquid for a moment, as if some truth might lay therein. As if some palatable answer to the tumult in his brain would be revealed.

He knew why he'd left Paris. If he'd stayed it might have meant something he didn't want it to mean. To himself. To her. To everyone.

Then why this burning discontent?

It wasn't as though leaving women was unusual. On the contrary, it was the rule rather than the exception. *Although Aurore was indeed exceptional in every way—in ways he couldn't forget . . . or didn't want to forget. Merde.*

His father silently watched him. There was something different about his son this time. His mother would know what it was, he thought. Annabelle was prescient about their children.

Looking up, Darley found his father's gaze on him. "Sorry, my mind is wandering. I must be more tired than I thought."

"It's no wonder you're tired if you've been traveling for a week. Sleep late in the morning. Now, come, let's eat in the kitchen for old times' sake." Duff smiled as he came to his feet. "And to please Mrs. Baillie as well."

"How is she?" Darley asked, rising. "She never seems to change."

"She's healthy as an ox. I think her medicinal wee dram of whisky each night is the secret."

Darley chuckled. "I think I'll share one with her tonight. I could use an elixir myself."

Chapter

29

In the following month, perhaps Mrs. Baillie's elixir could be credited for the ease with which Darley's days flowed one into the other.

The marquis was caught up in renewing old friendships. He fell into a familiar camaraderie with his siblings who were all in residence, the house awash with nieces and nephews as well. With the Season gearing up, his mother and sisters saw that additional festivities were planned in his honor, while his friends at Brooks needed no such excuse to welcome him with wild enthusiasm. Within days of his first appearance in public, female enthusiasts were all atwitter as well. Scented billets doux addressed to the Marquis of Darley began arriving at Westerlands House in colorful profusion.

An eligible young bachelor of great fortune and title was naturally in high demand. And Darley, specifically, was even more coveted. The Westerlands were a handsome family, good looks and great beauty unfairly disposed on one and all, those less fortunate grumbled. Furthermore, Darley could personally charm the birds from the trees, not to mention—titillating gossip and ladies of all stripes confirmed—he was monstrous good in bed. Needless to say, in terms of *social intercourse,* the phrase was given a literal interpretation by the marquis.

His parents would exchange small smiles as a flood of scented missives arrived each morning, his sisters would pester him unmercifully for details, while his brother, James, would grin and say, "Some things never change."

As to some things never changing, Darley found himself in an all-too-familiar and awkward position one evening. Out of courtesy, he had agreed to attend a dinner party to please his sister-in-law who was sweet, amiable—the perfect spouse for his brother who relished his life as a country gentleman. Her bosom friend was hostess that night, and Clara had explained that Lavinia Blunt would be especially pleased to see Darley again.

Unfortunately, Lady Blunt had made her designs expressly clear the moment he'd arrived. "Lord Darley," she had exclaimed, with a dulcet smile. "How lovely to see you again. I don't believe you have met my daughter. She is *most* anxious to hear of your world travels—aren't you, Samantha," she had added with a meaningful look at her lovely daughter who stood beside her in the receiving line. "As we all are, of course." She smiled brightly. "But Samantha's governess always said she had such a flare for geography, didn't she, darling?" Another glance at her daughter who was surveying Darley with a connoisseur's eye.

"Yes, Mama." A heedless, inattentive reply—Samantha's gaze fixed on the marquis.

Now, Darley enjoyed beautiful women—and Samantha was blond, curvaceous—and clearly available, he understood, after meeting her startlingly sultry gaze. But she was also unmarried and in the market for a husband—two formidable obstacles to any possible friendship between them . . . Samantha's provocative glances notwithstanding.

He was courteous throughout the usual tedious dinner—naturally, she had been placed beside him at the table. And naturally, she had no conversation save for the gossip that passed for conversation in the beau monde. He heard more than he cared to about her bosom friends, the very best dressmakers, her mother's annoying habit of selecting completely unsuitable beaux for her—present company excepted, of course. That declared with a dazzling smile, a come-hither wink and another enticing view of Samantha's impressive bosom—her flirtatious posture of choice. Regardless that frequent display of her cleavage throughout the numerous courses, however, he had no intention of touching her—or them.

To wit. He had just recently escaped her oppressive company and the boredom of amateur theatricals that served as the evening's entertainment and had retreated to the library for a moment of respite.

With thoughts of escape prominent in his brain.

He had just poured himself a brandy when the door opened.

Even before he turned around, he knew whom he would see.

"Lord Darley, I do believe our theatricals have bored you," Samantha cooed. "And I couldn't agree more," she added with an understanding little smile. "I told Mama no one wishes to hear Letty Newsome's awful monologue." Shutting the door behind her, she rested back against the carved oak panels—literally barring egress from the room.

"I confess, theatricals rarely engage my interest."

"Nor mine. We agree on everything," she cheerfully noted. "Although, the moment I saw you"—her voice drifted lower, shifted into a heated undertone—"I just knew we would."

"Perhaps we could talk again some other time." Darley spoke in a deliberately neutral voice. "I was about to leave. I promised Harcourt I'd meet him for a game at Brooks." Wondering how much time he had before Lady Blunt would appear and feign affront that he and her daughter were inappropriately secreted away, he quickly surveyed the room, looking for a clock.

Ah, there. Not on the mantle as usual, but practically hidden on a small side table, the timepiece itself even smaller. He'd give the mother ten minutes. She would want to wait until her daughter had fully exerted her charms.

Samantha seemed not to take offense at Darley's talk of leaving, smiling at him instead. An alluring smile—much practiced and generally effective. "Do finish your drink first. I'm sure Harcourt won't mind waiting a minute or two." Pushing away from the door, she glided toward him, a young enchantress on a mission. A bankable one if all went well. "No one will even notice we're missing," she murmured softly as she drew near.

Now that was carte blanche license—should he have somehow missed all the previous signals apropos her availability.

Far from a novice when it came to dinner party amusements, Darley had, on more than one occasion, found himself closeted in some hidden nook with a lady who had her heart set on assuaging her carnal urges. So it wasn't that he was averse to fucking Samantha in the library. It was just that he was averse to fucking Samantha in the library while she was unmarried.

Raising his glass to his mouth, he tipped it back and swallowed the lot in a single gulp. "Forgive me, but I do have to go," he murmured, glancing at the clock once again before setting the glass on the liquor table and turning toward the door.

He had not taken more than two steps when he found his way blocked by a determined young lady.

"My dear Darley," Samantha purred, taking another half step so her magnificent breasts were pressed warmly into his chest, "at least give me one little kiss before you go."

He inwardly groaned. Even if time wasn't an issue, he was decades past virginal kisses. Or in the case of Samantha, perhaps not entirely virginal kisses, but unwelcome nonetheless. "This is not wise, my dear," he said with cultivated grace, glancing at the door over her shoulder. "You're much too young for me."

"I'm old enough to know things," she whispered, raising her limpid glance to Darley's wary gaze. "I know everything about making love, what a man likes and how to give pleasure—how to satisfy you." Slipping her fingers under her decolletage, she began to slide her dress down over her plump breasts.

Darley moved in a flash, caught her hands before her nipples were fully exposed and said gruffly, "Don't be foolish." Peeling her fingers from the lace-trimmed neckline of her gown, he placed her hands at her sides, quickly covered her breasts and stepped away.

"I could say you tried to undress me," Samantha sulkily asserted, peevish that her plans had gone awry. "I could say I resisted and you tore my gown." She clasped a bit of the lace trim decorating her decolletage and lifted one brow in challenge.

"I don't suggest you do that, but"—Darley shrugged, the indifference in his voice marked—"do as you wish. I don't care."

She glared at him, pouty and resentful; men were generally more amenable. Always, actually. "Papa could *make* you marry me when we are found alone like this."

Darley stifled the impulse to say something rude. "No, he couldn't," he simply said.

"What if my mama comes in and sees me with my clothes in disarray?" Samantha had not yet completely given up on the Darley fortune. She could bare her breasts in a second when the door opened.

"My dear young lady," Darley said with more civility than she deserved, "I don't care if the entire dinner party were to arrive and see you *naked* with me. I'll be leaving London soon. You won't. Use a little sense for Christ's sake." His voice at the last was sharp. "It's your future at stake, not—"

A delicate knock on the door stopped him in midsentence.

Darley nodded toward the door. "I suggest you tell your mother you've changed your mind."

"What if I don't?" Samantha snapped, tantrumish and scowling.

Good God, the little bitch was irksome and, moreover, incredibly naive if she actually thought he could be coerced into marriage. "You'll only embarrass yourself. I'm past caring about this kind of stupidity."

His eyes were so cold that even Samantha began to question whether she could prevail with a man like Darley. A first as it were, for a young lady who had always captivated and charmed by fair beauty and shapely form. "You are most unreasonable," she sniffed.

"And you are a self-seeking bitch." His patience was at an end, and if she wasn't going to open the door soon, he would.

"How dare you say that!"

"You have no idea what I dare," he said, each word ice cold. "But I suggest you call off your mother or you'll rue the day you questioned my audacity."

Samantha quailed before Darley's fierce gaze, a chill slid up her spine and she realized with another little shiver that he was not the type of man who would succumb to threats. In fact, he was more than willing to join battle against those who threatened him.

Spinning around, she ran for the door.

He heard her say before the door shut behind her, "Darley wasn't here, Mama. I don't know where he went."

He left soon after, stopping only long enough to make his excuses to his sister-in-law who was winning at bridge now that Letty Newsome had quit the stage. "I had a lovely evening," he said blandly, his smile equally mild, "but I have another appointment. I'll see you at breakfast."

Standing on the pavement a few moments later, he was reminded of the reasons he avoided society. It was suffocating in its banality, while the desperate quest for a husband that engaged so many young ladies, mothers and female relatives was grim and relentless.

For a moment, he considered leaving the city. In

the past, as well as now, he often felt as though he didn't fit in—an outsider in a fashionable world that held little interest for him. A world where foolish little coquettes like Samantha thought any man would sell his soul for a look at her tits. Although Lavinia Blunt was even more of a simpleton for not knowing better. *Merde* and double *merde*.

He shifted his stance, debating whether to decamp for places unknown.

Then he softly exhaled. Unfortunately, his mother and sisters had a full compliment of parties scheduled, and he was expected to join in the family festivities.

So then—where now? Quitting London was temporarily out of the question. It was too early to go home. There was no Harcourt waiting at Brooks. Thank God, at least there were always married women looking for diversions.

With Samantha's marriage trap fresh in his mind, he vowed, in future, to restrict his female entertainments exclusively to women of unimpeachable profligacy. And he did.

But in the coming days, even as Hugh was busy partaking of amorous trysts with carefully chosen females—opportunistic women need not apply—he found himself thinking of Aurore with a certain unwanted frequency—thinking she was like him . . . living in Paris but wanting to be somewhere else. But he thought about her in other ways too. Ways that unnerved him. Ways that occasioned increasingly lustful cravings and offered particularly voluptuous delights to whomever he was currently fucking.

* * *

While Darley was intent on seeking respite from boredom and banality in countless boudoirs, Aurore was reaching the point in her pregnancy when Etienne would soon have to be informed of his impending unclehood.

Her tummy was beginning to show—very faintly—but her maid had already noticed. And soon, others would as well.

Her morning sickness had dissipated, for which she was grateful. Etienne had never been aware of it since he rarely came home at night and when he did, he slept until noon. By which point, Aurore was always feeling hale and hearty.

It took a certain self-possession and grim resolve to finally have the difficult conversation with her brother. She stopped him one evening as he was about to leave, having decided that evenings were always less unsettling for her stomach even now. "Might I have a moment of your time," she said. "I have something I wish to say to you."

Etienne looked up, his hand—clasping his gloves—arrested above the hall console. "Good Lord, have I done something wrong?" He knew that tone.

"No, no, it has nothing to do with you. Come into the drawing room."

As Etienne followed her in, he said, "If it's about that young female who called the other day, I had no idea she knew where I lived."

"No, it has nothing to do with her, although she was very sweet to return your watch. She wouldn't have had to." The little milliner had blushed as she handed over Etienne's watch to Aurore. She didn't want Etienne to think she was a thief, she'd said. "I think the young lady was hoping to see you," Aurore added, in a softly teasing tone, recalling the pretty girl's obvious disappointment at not finding Etienne home.

"I brought her a reward for her kindness yesterday," Etienne muttered, not quite meeting his sister's gaze.

"That was very nice of you. I'm sure she appreciated it." And Aurore was struck afresh with the vagaries and vicissitudes of love. Who loved whom, when, how much, how long? It seemed the perfect amalgam of time, place and emotional receptivity was as elusive as the Holy Grail. "Would you like a drink?"

Etienne looked wary. "Do I need one?"

"No, no. Sit, please. This won't take long." And she sat so he would. She also sat in the event she might faint from the fluttering apprehension racing through her senses. Once Etienne sat down—although gingerly—on the edge of the chair, she said as calmly as she could, "What I am about to say may strike you as shocking, but I assure you, it isn't, nor need it be. The thing is"—she drew in a sustaining breath and then quickly before she lost her nerve said—"I am with child. It's Darley's. He does not know, nor do I wish him to know." She put up her hand to quell her brother's utterance. As he shut his mouth, she went on to explain. "Darley and I entered into a liaison we both knew would be transient. Surely, you understand the concept," she added, holding her brother's gaze for a moment. "In any event, I wasn't absolutely sure about the child until he had left. Not that I would have necessarily told if I had known. I intend to play the widow—not an uncommon pose in the *ton*—and raise the child myself. And please, don't talk to me of honor or principles. I don't wish to marry, nor does Darley. There, I'm finished."

"You can't possibly mean what you say—about raising the child yourself!" Etienne had jumped to his feet and was pacing. "It's not fair to you or to Darley. Have you considered he might *want* to know of this?"

"He doesn't. Trust me."

Etienne spun around and stopped. "How can you be so sure?"

"Because he made it clear that he is purposely not married. Which means that he does not *wish* to marry. You of all people can grasp the concept of bachelorhood."

Her brother expelled a large breath and dropped back into his chair. "Very well. I appreciate the parallels." Sliding down on his spine, he surveyed his sister from under half-lowered lids. "You're sure you can manage this subterfuge? People are bound to talk."

She shrugged. "I don't really care what people say. I will have to speak to Philip and Bertrand since they met Darley the night he was here. It was rather clear that we were more than friends. But Philip and Bertrand will be obliging. I'm not worried about them. You and I can discuss the particulars of the necessary fiction relating to my role as a widow some other time. It's early yet."

"When—that is"—Etienne was still young enough to be embarrassed by issues of birthing—"when will the child be born?"

"In November. Before winter sets in, I'm happy to say. And Darley *must not* know of this," she emphasized. "He might lay claim to the child, and the courts would rule in his favor. You understand?"

Etienne nodded.

"Please,"—she waved her hands—"go now. I didn't mean to spoil your evening. And, darling, this really has nothing to do with you. As for myself, I'm quite delighted about this child."

"Good. It's wonderful . . . really," Etienne said with polite exuberance as he rose from the chair. Gazing down at her, he hesitated for a second, then said very gently, "Whatever makes you happy is always fine with me, Rory. You know that."

"I know, darling," she said, swallowing hard to hold back her tears, her brother's unconditional love heartwarming. "I just hope you don't mind becoming an uncle."

"God, no!" Etienne grinned. "We could use a larger family now that there's just the two of us."

"That's what I was thinking." Grateful, happy, hugely content, Aurore smiled at her brother. "Now, go and enjoy yourself tonight. And if you see your little milliner, say hello from me."

"She thought you were very beautiful."

"She's quite lovely herself. Make sure you're kind to her."

"Of course I will be!"

Aurore fluttered her fingertips. "I'll see you in the morning."

"You don't need me tonight, do you?" he politely inquired. "I'll cancel my plans if you wish."

"Heaven's no! Have a wonderful time."

Etienne did.

First with his little milliner to whom he was especially *kind* so often and so intensely, she nearly fainted in ecstasy.

And then much, much later that night, when only

the diehard gamblers and drinkers were still at his club, Etienne walked in, woke up the porter who was dozing in a chair in the entrance hall and said, "I need a telegram sent. Right away."

His message to Darley was brief.

Aurore is with child. She says not to bother you, but I think you should do something about this.

He signed his full name, Etienne Andre Lepinay Clement.

At the same time in another club across the channel, Darley glanced at the clock on the wall of the gaming room at Brooks.

"Adelaide's going to be pissed," Freddy Richmond murmured, smiling at Darley over his hand of cards. "You told her eleven. I heard you clear as a bell even with that fat soprano bellowing in the background."

Darley shrugged faintly. "Old Palmer is up in Scotland anyway. Time isn't an issue, and"—he added softly, debating whether to draw another card—"I'm having a damned good run of luck."

"As always," Brummel muttered, scowling at his cards. "Give someone else a chance to win, dammit."

"Is Countess Palmer as good as they say?" a young viscount fresh in from the country asked. "She is the most stunning filly with her shapely form and glorious tits."

Darley turned a cool gaze on the fresh-faced youth.

"Pardon, sir, that—is . . . everyone says . . ." The young man's voice trailed off, his pink cheeks turned pinker; he shifted nervously under Darley's intimidating stare.

"Don't frighten the young buck, Darley," Freddy interposed. "He's just down from some hidden valley in Yorkshire—ain't that so, Ramsey? Somewhere just across from the Scottish border, I hear."

"Yes, sir. Just recently came into my title and come to town." He nervously bit his lower lip, the marquis's reputation for dueling formidable. It was said he had scars on top of scars.

"Stop glaring, Darley," Freddy drawled. A friend from childhood, he could speak bluntly to the marquis. "You're scaring the piss out of the boy. And admit, Adelaide figures rather widely in the broad sheets, big tits and all. It ain't as though she's come out of the convent last week."

Darley's brows rose, a small smile of forbearance graced his fine mouth. "Thank you, Freddy, for reminding me so eloquently of what passes for amusement in the fashionable world." A note of ennui had crept into Darley's voice. "My apologies, Ramsey. It's all pointless anyway—who fucks whom, when, where, how often." *Especially pointless after having lived through a war.*

"Easy for you to say," Georgie Brummel grumbled. "Women beg you to warm their beds."

"Give up gambling, Georgie, and you might have time for fucking," Freddy noted. "You practically live in the gaming rooms."

"Maybe I will." Unlikely that though. Georgie Brummel was addicted to gambling. Fortunately he had the fortune to sustain his passion.

A small silence fell as the men studied their cards, the large pile of markers in the center of the table a compelling reason for deliberation.

It really *was* all a pointless repetition from morning to night, Darley reflected. The races, a rout or dinner somewhere that required an appearance, Brooks for some gambling before the inevitable night of fucking. And so it went unceasingly. Christ, he'd been here way too long. After Emma's party to-morrow, he'd say his good-byes. Where he'd go, he didn't quite know. Someplace where he could breathe fresh air and flirtatious females were in short supply.

Freddy looked up. "Pon' my word, I finally have a winning hand."

"Not so fast," Brummel said, tapping his finger on the green baize for another card.

The young man from Yorkshire suddenly looked pained, his pink cheeks pale, a look of apprehension in his eyes.

"Stop while you're ahead," Darley said kindly, nod-ding at the boy in commiseration. "There's no harm in caution." His maman would appreciate him not losing the family fortune his first time in the city. "If you like I could introduce you at Joselle's instead. You might enjoy yourself more."

Freddy shot his friend a surprised look. Neither money nor title was sufficient to get past the door-man at Joselle's without her approval. Darley was of-fering this young bumpkin entree he never could have achieved on his own.

"I would be honored, sir! Most humbly honored!" Wide eyed, the viscount sat transfixed.

"Well, then—no time like the present." Darley smiled, set his cards on the table and came to his feet. "I'll introduce you to all of Joselle's ladies, but since I have other commitments, I'll have to leave you on your own. Is that all right with you?"

The viscount jumped to his feet. "Yes, sir. I shall be quite content, I assure you! Vastly content, sir!"

I can't keep Adelaide waiting too long, Darley thought. But Joselle's wasn't far from Mayfair. An hour at the most to see that the young boy was settled in and then the necessary apologies to Adelaide would be required. But, with Adelaide, as long as the sex was swiftly forthcoming, she never bore a grudge for long.

As the men walked from the room, Freddy turned over Darley's cards he'd left on the table and blanched. Four aces. He would have lost miserably with his pairs.

Chapter

30

The knock on the door was insistent as was the voice of his valet.

How did he find me, was Darley's first thought.

His second caused him to glance at the lady sleeping beside him.

A faint smile curved her mouth, as if she were having a pleasant dream, her breathing soft and regular.

Grateful she hadn't wakened, he slipped from the bed, quickly strode to the door and, opening it a crack, put a finger to his lips.

"Sorry, sir," his valet whispered. "I was told this was urgent." He held out a folded telegram.

Darley nodded, held up one finger as a signal to wait, took the telegram and, unfolding it, scanned the contents. Crumpling the telegram in his fist when he was finished, he dipped his head. "I'll be right out." Without shutting the door for fear the sound might wake his bed partner, he swiftly gathered up his clothes, shoving the telegram into his jacket pocket. The gossip sheets would run riot if word of this got out. Frowning, he scanned the bed-chamber, looking for his shoes. *Ah—there. By the door, where he'd kicked them off when Adelaide had pleaded, panting and flushed with desire, "Hurry, hurry, I can't wait."* After walking over to his shoes, he picked them up and quietly eased through the half-open door out into the hallway. Handing all but his trousers to his valet, he stepped into them, buttoned the fly and put out his hand for his shirt. "How the hell early is it?" he asked, sliding his arms into his shirt sleeves.

"Six, sir."

His brows shot up. "Jesus." Then striding away in the direction of the staircase, fastening his shirt studs as he went, he tried to get his sluggish brain around the devil of a mess facing him.

Standing barefoot on the porch a few moments later, squinting against the morning sun, he shoved his arms into his coat held out by his valet. "When was the telegram delivered?"

"A half hour ago."

"How in blazes did you find me?" More to the point, how did he manage to talk the Countess Palmer's servants into letting him in?

Georgie raised his brows as if to say, *What is a good valet for?*

"Well, thank you. This *is* urgent." His pulse rate concurred.

"His Grace thought it might be."

Darley shot a sharp look at Georgie. "He knows then."

"He sent me."

"Does my mother know?"

His valet shrugged. "The duchess knows most everything, sir."

"*Merde.*"

"The carriage, sir." Georgie nodded at the waiting vehicle. "His Grace thought you might prefer it." What the duke had actually said was, *Even if the marquis is dead drunk, carry him out from wherever he is, throw him in the carriage and bring him home. This looks important.*

His father was waiting for him in his study as Darley knew he would be, although it appeared his mother was not yet up. A small blessing, Darley decided, as he entered the room.

"Good news?" Duff murmured, leaning back against his desk chair, a faint smile on his face.

His father was dressed for riding, although his shirt collar and jacket were open, so he had already returned from his morning constitutional. "Very amusing," Darley muttered, moving toward the desk. "Does mother know?"

"No. Nor do I. I have no idea what was in your telegram, but with the Paris address, I thought you might like to see it with dispatch."

"Very perceptive of you."

"You have been more or less screwing yourself to death. I thought you might be compensating for something . . . or someone," the duke drawled.

"She's pregnant." Darley took the telegram out of his jacket pocket, smoothed it out on his jacket lapel, tossed it on the desk and sat down.

Picking it up, Duff read the few lines on the wrinkled paper, then read them again in the event there was some underlying message. "Her father—brother—which?" he asked, looking up.

"Brother." Darley shoved the chair back so he

could stretch out his legs and sighed—in exaspera-
tion, perhaps futility.

"You can't expect him *not* to take offense."

"No."

"She chose not to tell you. Why is that?"

"Fuck if I know," Darley muttered.

"I thought I heard you two downstairs," Annabelle
cheerfully proclaimed, gliding into the room in her
dressing gown and a cloud of jasmine scent. "Don't
get up, for heaven's sake," she added, waving the
men back in their chairs.

How could she have heard them when her suite
was across the house in the west wing, Darley wondered.

The duke didn't question his wife's statement.
Annabelle had a sixth sense about their children.

"So tell me, why are you two down here so early in
the morning?" The duchess glanced at her son's un-
shaven face and rumpled evening clothes as she took
the chair beside him. Taking note of Darley's stock-
ingless feet in his evening shoes, she added, "Whatever brought you home must have been urgent."

No one spoke for a moment.

The duke looked at his son. "These things happen," he said, good-natured and benevolent, leaning
forward slightly as though in empathy. "Would you
like me to tell your mother?"

Annabelle's apprehension largely diminished at
her husband's words. "Darling, whatever it is, your father and I have lived through worse." She smiled. "At
least no one in London has tried to kill you."

"Not yet," Darley replied, smiling gratefully. His
mother's reminder of the various hindrances in his
parents' courtship helped put everything into per-

spective. Reaching out, he plucked the telegram from the desk and handed it to her. "A lady I met in the Crimea is pregnant with my child. Or so her brother says."

Her mother's brows rose. "There's a question then?"

"There could be. I don't know her very well."

"Is this about money?" Having read the few sentences, the duchess placed the telegram back on the desktop.

"I don't think so. She has resources."

"Well, you must find out whether it's true." The duchess's expression and tone were dispassionate. Annabelle understood the machinations of society better than most.

"You are under no obligation," his father quietly said. "I know it sounds callous, but this woman—Miss Clement—may have ulterior motives. Or her brother may. Does he have gambling debts for instance, or—"

"No," Darley quickly interjected. "Etienne is a fine young man. And Miss Clement—as the telegram notes—did not wish me to know."

"Or so he says," the duchess murmured. Having been embroiled in the foibles of the aristocratic world at one time, she had come to believe less in what people said and more in what they did. And this telegram was asking something of her son. Something substantial.

"Would you like me to go to Paris with you?" the duke asked. "Or we could send Hamley from Plunkett's firm in our stead? To offer some—er—settlement perhaps. He knows well how to deal with sensitive situations like this."

Darley smiled at the thought of Hamley offering Aurore compensation in lieu of a father for her child.

"I see you think not," his father said.

Darley's smile widened. "She would throw him out on his ear."

The duke and duchess exchanged a meaningful look.

The Duke of Westerlands leaned back in his chair, pleased at his son's good cheer. "It seems you prefer dealing with this yourself, then."

"Yes." Darley stood. "Is your yacht still at Dover?"

"Indeed it is." The duke glanced at the clock on the mantle. "If you hurry, you should make the late afternoon train for Paris."

Twenty minutes later, the duke and duchess had seen their son off and were in the breakfast room having their morning coffee.

"The family will need to be told something," Annabelle said. "Not that Hugh hasn't come and gone precipitously before, but he was planning to attend Emma's dinner tonight."

"Why not the truth." The duke shrugged faintly. "Or some version of it since we don't actually know the whole truth. Hugh didn't seem indifferent at least. A good sign perhaps. Although, I suppose it all depends on the lady's motivation."

"Apparently, it's not about money." They both understood that angling for marriage in the *ton* was very much about money. Who had it, who didn't, how to get it. "Hugh said this woman is not without fortune."

"That doesn't rule out other machinations," Duff

murmured, the target of a goodly number of females in pursuit of a husband in his youth.

His wife smiled. "And you would know, wouldn't you, dear."

His smile was affectionate. "That was long before I met you."

She had never doubted her husband's love; it was the great joy of her life. "You know, darling, of all our children, Hugh reminds me most of you. He has always been more questioning perhaps, or less ready to accept the life of ease to which he was born."

"And troubled since Lucia's death. You needn't be tactful. I understand. You saved me. I wish our son would be as fortunate."

"Do you think"—the duchess smiled wistfully— "May we hope at least that this woman may make a difference in Hugh's life? I sent along that pink diamond ring. I hope you don't mind."

"Good idea. He can always bring it back if he wishes." But the duke had taken a hand in the situation as well, not that he felt inclined to disclose his actions—for the moment at least. Annabelle wouldn't approve.

"Do you think this child is Hugh's? I couldn't quite read his response."

"It sounded as though he'd been acquainted with her for some time. Although, he also expressed some doubts."

"Should you have this family investigated, perhaps?"

"I sent the ambassador a telegram with a few questions along those lines. I should hear something by afternoon."

"Thank you. It doesn't hurt to be cautious. Although, if Hugh brings this woman into our family, she will be welcomed regardless what the ambassador says."

His wife's tone was decided and firm. "We agree, darling. You needn't look at me like that," he added with a smile. "She could be a high-wire artist, and if Hugh wishes to marry her, our family will have a new talent in its midst and be much the better for it."

Annabelle reached over and patted her husband's hand. "You are without pretensions, darling, and I adore you for it. If only Hugh could be happy, now . . ."

"I have a good feeling about this," Duff said, winking at his wife.

Also, the British ambassador in Paris had been sent his orders.

Chapter

31

His mother had pressed a small jewelry box in his hand as he'd left, and exiting the hired carriage outside Aurore's house, he felt the shape of it in his pocket for a transient moment. Stepping down onto the gravel drive, he stood motionless as the carriage drove off, not sure he should be here. Not sure he *wanted* to be here. *Coerced in any number of ways, large and small.*

Henri, the captain of the guards, walked from the shadows and smiled in welcome. "Good evening, monsieur." Not a word about his absence. "Miss Clement is home and all is safe."

"Thank you. A pleasant night, is it not," Darley said as graciously. He had spoken to Henri before he'd left, suggesting the guard force be augmented at his expense. Extra insurance, as it were, he'd said, and he'd given Henri the name of his Paris banker.

"The young master is out—with bodyguards, of course," Henri explained. "Although, fortunately, we have had no incidents of any kind. Not so much as a stranger walking past."

"Good. Perhaps we are forgotten with the war taking everyone's attention."

"I suspect as much. For which we can be grateful, monsieur." Henri had commanded a troop of Algerian irregulars and seen his share of bloodshed before a leg wound had ended his career.

"Indeed," Darley murmured. He glanced at the house facade. "It doesn't look as though Miss Clement is entertaining tonight."

"No, sir. Miss Clement has been something of a recluse of late. She will enjoy a visitor. Now, if you'll excuse me, our rounds are at timed intervals."

Darley watched the guard leader disappear into the dark garden surrounding the house and, drawing in a small breath, surveyed the night sky as though an answer to his uncertainty lay in the stars. The moon was a sliver of gold above the trees, the stars faint, not sharp and brilliant like they were in the Caucasus.

But then this was Paris, not the mountains of Circassia.

Although he felt as though he were standing on a mountain precipice and the ground were sliding out from under his feet.

Merde.

Taking an *about-to-mount-the-scaffold* breath, he gazed up at the house facade, the main floor windows ablaze, the drapes open. Not a sign of life. Thank God she was alone.

This was not a conversation to have with guests in the house.

Or anytime, he bitterly thought.

While he'd had considerable time on his journey

to contemplate the complexities and limited options—what she might say, what he would—he really
would have *preferred* avoiding this confrontation.

The question of whether the child was his or not
would be awkward no matter how diplomatically approached. Add to that the challenge of whether he
could believe Aurore if she said the child was his—
something he seriously doubted. She obviously thought
differently however, since he was the recipient of Etienne's telegram. He swore again, something he'd been
doing with great regularity since reading the telegram. Although, in truth, the question of paternity
probably wouldn't be answered with any certainty
until the child's birth.

And perhaps not even then.

So no matter how the issues were discussed—tactfully or otherwise—this encounter would likely be
unpleasant.

Unlike the pivotal occasion in which the seeds had
been sowed for this fruitful result.

Whoever may have been involved.

Although, apparently, he had been cited as the
whoever. And during the hours of his journey from
London, after much chafing, thorny contemplation,
he'd come to a decision best characterized as an *if
worse comes to worst* solution.

If necessary he would marry her.

If *absolutely* necessary.

A chivalrous, admirable conclusion, he decided,
an unselfish decision arrived at for the sake of Aurore and her child.

Naturally, then, consider his surprise when he was
announced by Bizot, Aurore shot up from her chair

in the small sitting room and rather than welcome her knight-errant, she said, coolly, "What do *you* want?"

Darley's shaky grasp on chivalry and honor instantly evaporated.

"A pleasant good evening to you as well," he drawled, his French exquisite and mannered, his insolent gaze less so as it traveled slowly down her figure then up again, coming to rest at last on the faint rise of her stomach.

"Have you seen your fill?" Her brother had told her what he'd done. And *she'd* explained to him that she had no interest in a man who made an appearance out of necessity.

"With you, darling, as always, I'm not averse to seeing more," he murmured.

"Not likely that," she said in her same chill tone. "Now go."

He didn't. He sat down instead, very near where she was standing, and looking up met her gaze. "Your brother sent me a telegram," he said, soft as silk.

"I heard about it too late. He shouldn't have done it." Suddenly overcome by dizziness, she quickly sat down.

"Are you all right?" Shifting forward, Darley put out his hand in a gesture of sympathy.

Her head came up. "Don't touch me!" She had had a month to build the ramparts.

Leaning back in his chair, he flippantly observed, "It seems I may have touched you one too many times already. Or someone else did," he added, deliberately rude.

She looked at him, her gaze direct and unabashed. "I didn't ask you here and I have no intention of trying to convince you of anything."

"Try me anyway. I want to know." He stretched out his legs and leisurely crossed his ankles. "And you might as well speak your piece because I'm not going anywhere until I *do* know."

"I have—as you so quaintly put it—no piece to speak," she said, her voice tight with restraint, thinking how dare he condescend to her.

A taut, uncomfortable hush settled over the room. The gaslights seemed to flicker in the restive air.

Darley studied Aurore, his dark gaze probing, slowly sweeping her body, always coming back to her fecund center. This hadn't just happened, he decided. If it was the result of his night in Paris a month ago, the child would not yet be visible. And it was. "You knew before I left Paris, didn't you," he said at last. "The train station—the smells . . . it was this instead, wasn't it?"

She didn't answer at first, and then as though having come to some decision, she spoke, her voice tempered and constrained. "I wasn't certain."

"Why didn't you say something anyway?"

"Because I wasn't certain." Her voice was stronger now, her gaze direct.

"Do you know when it happened?" A hint of truculence beneath his agreeable tone.

She didn't care. She knew what she knew. "I haven't had my menses since that first night in Sevastopol."

"You're sure?" He thought he'd been careful; he always was.

"Yes."

"I'm not sure I believe you." He didn't say I *don't* believe you. He was not that discourteous at least.

"It was a rather lengthy interval of sex that night

in Sevastopol—not that our successive encounters weren't as well. Under those circumstances, no matter how cautious you were—and I realize you specialize in caution in that regard—there are vestiges of fluids that can remain. I have no other explanation for this lamentable event."

Curiously, her use of the word *lamentable* irked him.

Not that it altered the situation in any way. He could accept her word or argue the point.

"You needn't look at me like that," she said, sitting up very straight as if defying his presumptive gaze. "I am not obliged to meet some standard or measure of your making. In fact, I told Etienne in no uncertain terms that I didn't wish you to know."

"He apparently thought otherwise. He said in his telegram that I should *do* something about this."

Her nostrils flared. "So I'm supposed to be grateful you responded? You needn't have. I don't wish to be caught in the middle of some masculine posturing that has nothing to do with me," she said with a sniff of displeasure. "Consider yourself free of any responsibility, Darley. I mean it most sincerely. I am capable of taking care of this child myself." He was obviously here under duress. She wasn't surprised. She'd known what he was from the first.

"What if I wish to know"—he hesitated, not yet capable of taking ownership—"this child," he said, instead of *my* child.

She smiled tightly at his significant pause. "I'm sorry. It's not possible," she coolly replied.

He opened his mouth to speak and shut it again.

"Wise choice," she murmured. "If you'd dared ask me that," she added, heated and low, "I would have had my grooms horsewhip you within an inch of your life." She would not explain again that the child was his.

"I could have been asking something else." There was something about the fire in her eyes that was captivating—as always, he thought. Like she was willing to take on the world.

"Were you?"

He smiled for the first time since he'd walked in. "No."

"Exactly. You see, we are at quite opposite poles."

"But not on everything," he said, his voice velvet soft. "There are times when we are in complete harmony."

She finally smiled. "Everything isn't about sex, Darley."

"With you, somehow it seems to take priority," he said with a practiced charm and a smile that offered sexual pleasure and endless delight, that guaranteed it with a disarming certitude.

"I am not in the mood to be seduced," she said, even as her traitorous senses trembled in remembrance. "Run back to wherever you were and return to your little playmates. I doubt you've been monkish since last I saw you."

His skin was too dark to blush, but the poniard struck home. "And you *have* been?" Defensive or jealous, he wasn't sure which.

"It's no concern of yours whether I have been or not. Go now, before I have you thrown out." A small matter of self-preservation prompted her command.

"That won't be easy."

"It will be done, nevertheless." She would not allow herself to succumb to his allure. He was what he was—prodigal and licentious, neither a suitable husband nor father.

Aurore's pronouncement was firm, determined. Like the woman who had risked her life for the Allied cause, he thought. The same fearless, fascinating woman who had persistently filled his dreams since Paris, no matter whom he was fucking, no matter where he was or what he was doing. And if epiphanies did, in fact, exist, he suddenly felt as though such a transforming event may have taken place. Or was taking place . . . or maybe it was just that he was finally willing to acknowledge that he had been unable to walk away from Aurore and get on with his life. "Let me explain something," he abruptly said, pushing himself upward from his lazy sprawl, his former nonchalance gone, a gravity in his tone. "I want you to know why I left, why I didn't come back—or tried not to." He put up his hands, palm out, to deter her protest. "Listen at least."

Guarded. "Very well." She'd thought herself immune to him after so long. Not so.

With the urge to lay bare his thoughts, he realized that at a stroke, a door had closed on his past—without reason or motive, without explanation. *At last. Or maybe not. He didn't know.* "I want to tell you about Lucia," he said, knowing that at least.

Was there a woman alive who would have been incurious? Particularly in this case when Darley had cried out Lucia's name in the throes of passion? "I'm listening," Aurore said.

"We were both young," he began. "We were very much in love, we married, and when she became pregnant, we were elated." He took a deep breath, leaned forward, rested his forearms on his legs and stared at the floor.

It was a man's explanation of love—without detail

or texture. She wanted to say, what did Lucia look like? What did she do? How much did you love her?

"Lucia didn't die of cholera," Darley went on, each word measured and deliberate. "She died in childbirth. My son died five days later." He paused, swallowed, then continued in the same low monotone. "I was tortured with thoughts of what I might have done to prevent my wife's pain and torment, or help in my child's pitiful struggle to live. We had doctors everywhere and they were helpless—useless. Lucia bled to death, my son's breathing—" His voice faded away for a second before he gathered himself. "Something was wrong." He exhaled softly. "And it never got better. When it was finally over, I buried them together in a little cemetery near a convent were Lucia had played as a child." He could feel all the anguish and pain as though it had been yesterday. *Why did he think he could do this?* "The pregnancy killed Lucia," he murmured, looking up from under his dark brows, his voice no more than a whisper. "I vowed to never do that to anyone again." *And I haven't.*

A kind of hell-on-earth desolation shown in his eyes, and something more as well—an unspoken challenge.

"I'm sorry for your loss—truly I am." Aurore's eyes were bright with tears. "And I wish I had an indisputable answer for you. I don't, other than to say, there's been no one but you since Sevastopol." He looked so miserable she wanted to take him in her arms and comfort him. But she would be lost if she did.

Darley was here out of some misguided sense of duty, not because he loved her.

And to dare to love him was too painful to contemplate.

Unrequited love. An insupportable phrase.

"No one since Sevastopol," he softly said, his voice slow and considering, as though he were reviewing a conversation from long ago. Then he sat upright once again, beautiful as a god, his traveling clothes impeccable, authentic bachelor and libertine in a black frock coat tailored to perfection. "In that case, the child must be mine." A grudging assessment.

Aurore's temper flared for an instant, but it was impossible to fault a man who feared fatherhood for reasons quite beyond the ordinary. "Yes. Undoubtedly, the child is yours," she replied with the disciplined restraint that had sustained her throughout this interview. "But you needn't involve yourself in what would only be a painful reawakening of your past."

"The thought of a child frightens me."

She saw his fingers tighten on the chair arms.

He smiled ruefully. "It's not logical, of course. I understand the differences." *Yet, at times, Aurore reminded him of Lucia if she turned her head a certain way or smiled just so.* Struggling to suppress the images from Parma flooding his brain, he added, his voice raw with pain, "It was just so fucking unbearable . . ."

She didn't know how to respond. What platitudes could possibly redress such horrors?

The fire crackled uncommonly loud in the hush.

She should offer him a brandy, she thought, feeling at a loss. After all, he'd come a long way for nothing. Perhaps a cold collation, she reflected as though playing hostess would overcome the harrowing narrative recently revealed.

"Look, I have something for you," Darley said,

shattering the silence. His voice was crisp as though driven by a *t'were best done quickly* impulse that might as swiftly fade. Reaching in his jacket pocket, he pulled out a small red leather box. "Here." Half rising from his chair, he handed Aurore the box. "My mother thought you'd like it."

Her surprise showed.

"Etienne's telegram came to the house," he explained, sitting back down. "My father sent my valet to find me, so they know. And they're quite content with whatever you decide," he added. "Or we decide . . . or"—he blew out a breath—"forgive my clumsiness. I'm making a hash of this marriage proposal."

She had opened the box, and whether she was astonished by the size of the diamond ring inside or by Darley's mention of a marriage proposal, her breath caught in her throat. She stared at him.

"I know I'm botching the hell out of this. I also know it's sudden, but"—he smiled—"perhaps not sudden enough for all those who will be counting on their fingers. So say yes and we'll be married. I'll try not to be scared out of my wits, you can try to come to terms with me as your husband and we'll muddle through this one way or another." If nothing else, he was a man of action.

"And what of love?" She had her own fears. Muddling through might not be enough for her. She set the box aside.

"If love is thinking of you every minute of the day, I am so inspired." He smiled. "You fill all my dreams as well."

He didn't ask her whether she loved him, arrogant man. "Do you wish to know whether I love you?"

He did a quick double take but recovered almost instantly and said with grace and charm, "I would like very much to know. And if you're not entirely sure yet, I will do my very best to gain your affection."

"Such humility, darling. I'm quite astonished."

He liked that she'd called him darling; he particularly liked that her little scowl had disappeared. "You will find me meek as a lamb," he said, his gaze sportive.

"Not too meek, I hope." A sportive reply in return.

"You have but to define your desires, my sweet," he murmured. "I am amenable in all things."

Her brows rose, her blue eyes twinkled. "You're even willing to marry me."

"Indeed, that too."

"And I am to appreciate the great honor, I suppose."

"On the contrary, the honor is mine." The amusement was suddenly stripped from his gaze, his voice took on a deep tenderness. "I am the one to be grateful. You have made me whole again, or at least hopeful of the future. You have given me back my life."

"Perhaps we have both found new meaning in our lives," she said, thinking how large the world and how fateful their meeting.

"Yes," he said. A discerning man, he knew better than to argue. But in his heart, he knew whose life had been irrevocably lost and now found. "So then," he added, affably, "what do you think—your priest or mine?"

"Not tonight surely." She gave him a sharp look. "Don't say you brought one with you."

He had, not knowing at the time exactly why. Or more precisely, simply nodding as his father handed him the British ambassador's name and address in Paris and nodding again when Duff had said he was sending along Whiteside just in case. "I do have a priest in a hotel in town, but yours is perfectly fine if you'd rather."

She wrinkled her pretty nose. "I will *not* abide an authoritarian husband."

"You decide where and when, then," he quickly returned, his worldly prerogatives such that his self-esteem was never at issue. "I have no strong opinion either way, other than a consideration for the child's future. You know how people will talk. Sooner rather than later would be wise, darling."

"Hmmm," she said. "I have to at least wait for Etienne and he never comes home 'til morning."

"We could find him at his club or wherever."

She was reminded of the man she'd known in the Crimea, who lived by his wits, who made life and death decisions with ease. He could very well find Etienne, she decided. "Let's wait until morning. A few more hours can't matter." Her brother wouldn't appreciate being pulled from some woman's bed where he surely was at this time of night. "We probably could find something to do until then," she murmured, playful, tantalized as she always was with him, and admittedly now, deep in love.

He smiled back. "I might be able to think of one or two things you like," he said, this man who was known far and wide for his sexual endowments and expertise—who had miraculously found salvation in love. He held out his hand. "Come here and we'll talk about it . . ."

Epilogue

The Marquis of Darley and Miss Clement were married in the Chinoiserie drawing room the following afternoon, with the British ambassador as witness, along with numerous functionaries he had brought along to provide all the requisite forms for a British subject's marriage in France.

Two priests presided—Mr. Whiteside and Monseigneur Sagarin. Darley wished no questions about the legality of the ceremony.

Etienne was there as well, somewhat shaky after a night of carousing, but smiling broadly and vastly content with all that he had achieved.

It was a simple ceremony and brief.

The prerogatives of wealth and fortune.

The British ambassador said afterward to Darley, "I will telegraph His Grace, the duke, with news of your nuptials." He did not say he had been under orders to see that they were accomplished one way or another. Grateful it hadn't come to that, his present to the newlyweds was, as a result, extravagant. A Limoges china service for fifty, the marquis's and Aurore's entwined initials to be added at their convenience.

The newlyweds stayed in Paris until the birth of their son—a plump, healthy, robust baby. And it wasn't until afterward that Darley realized how truly terrified he'd been of the delivery. Aurore understood that her husband had stayed by her side throughout her labor out of love. She had not realized he was there through sheer willpower alone. But when their son was first put in her arms and she saw Darley look away, she knew. *We can't replace what you have lost. But we will love you too.* "Look, darling," she said, instead. "I think he's smiling."

And when Darley glanced back, she displayed their rosy-cheeked son who was indeed twitching his little mouth into what could pass as a smile. "Isn't he clever?" Aurore said, like every doting mother does.

Darley's strained expression lightened. "He's big," he said softly.

"Big and strong like you," she said, smiling at her husband.

"He has your eyes." They were ever so slightly tilted at the corners.

"Do you think so?" She studied the plump little face. "Perhaps he does. Oh dear, I believe he's about to cry." She glanced up at Darley and grinned. "Someone better tell us what to do."

As the midwife came running over, Darley leaned back in his chair for the first time since Aurore had gone into labor and allowed himself a roseate moment of hope. These moments followed one after another until a fortnight passed and hope turned to certainty at last.

Mother and child continued to thrive and prosper, enough so that the small family traveled to England for the Christmas season where the Westerlands household one and all greeted their newest members with exuberance and affection.

After the war, the necessary pardons were obtained—never an issue for those privileged few who lived in the rarified world inhabited by royals. Cousin Bertie talked to cousin Rupert who talked to cousin Sasha and so on and so on. Before long Aurore and Darley no longer needed to concern themselves with the Third Section. They were given leave to return to Aurore's Crimean estate.

So other than the horrendous loss of life, and the fact that the Black Sea was declared neutral, the war had little changed the map of Europe or Asia Minor.

From that point on the pattern of Darley family life was directed by the seasons. They would often spend summers in the Crimea, traveling to the Caucasus as well. Then in the fall after the grape harvest, home to Paris, followed by the Season in London with occasional holidays at their English country home.

The marquis's family led an idyllic existence—there was no other word for it.

Two more children were born—both healthy to Darley's great relief—and the rambunctious youngsters grew into adolescence in a world free of major wars. They all heard the stories of their parents' espionage activities—although the children's version was an account of adventure rather than perilous danger. And in truth, as the years passed, even the two principals involved recalled hazardous events with a certain equanimity.

Insulated by happiness and a privileged environment, that their memories were tempered by time was perhaps—inevitable.

Until one fall night in London as Darley and Aurore were leaving the theatre, the marquis saw a small, peanut of a man ahead of them in the crowd, and suddenly life and death issues came hurtling back with a vengeance. The shape, the height, even the man's hurried walk occasioned a spiking alarm. "I just saw an old friend the porter at my club tells me has been asking for me," Darley said. "You take the carriage home, darling, and I'll have a brandy with Faraday and be back shortly. An hour, no more," he murmured to allay the curiosity in his wife's eyes. "Faraday and I went to school together."

After escorting Aurore to their carriage, Darley was afraid he'd lost his quarry in the crowd. But, no—thank God—there was the shabby derby hat bobbing away in the distance. If necessary, he would kill the man with his bare hands, the marquis decided, pushing through the throng. But even as he hastened after the figure who might be Kubitovitch, he understood that had the agent wished to dispatch them, he or his cohorts could have made the attempt anytime this decade past. His family lived their lives openly.

As the crowd thinned and the bright lights of the Strand gave way to the lesser illumination of a neighborhood of small shops, the man looked back from time to time and quickened his pace. Lengthening his stride, Darley stayed with him, more and more sure that the man was Kubitovitch. Older, naturally, and slightly heavier perhaps, but there was something about the hunch of his shoulders that was unmistakable.

They traversed three blocks, then four, eventually five and six, the pace accelerating until the little man was almost running. They were moving into a less savory quarter where thieves brushed shoulders with men out for a night of pleasure, a place where personal safety was uncertain.

A fact, apparently, known to the little man. Coming to a stop under a streetlight, he spun around and waited with the resigned air of someone facing his doom.

"I can't outrun you," Kubitovitch said as Darley approached, "so we might as well get this over with."

His English was accurate but slightly stilted, like someone who more commonly spoke his native language. A large expatriate Russian community existed in London, Darley knew. What he didn't understand was why Kubitovitch was part of it considering his past. "I can snap your neck with ease, and am more than willing to do so if you don't tell me the truth. Do you understand?"

Kubitovitch cast a nervous glance around.

"No one will come to your aid," Darley observed. "As I'm sure you know." There were people on the streets but all were averse to any involvement for personal reasons having to do with indiscretions or the law or both. "So tell me, are you in or out of the Third Section? And if you're out, why are you still alive?"

"I am not alive as far as my former employers know." Kubitovitch answered with deference, even as he tried to gauge the marquis's intent.

"How is that possible? You look the same." Although, on closer contemplation, the agent had gained weight, his hair was longer, he'd grown a mustache and wore spectacles. Nonetheless—superficial changes that never would have deceived the Third Section.

"I may look the same to you." Kubitovitch smiled ingratiatingly, hoping to survive this encounter. "You still have the eye of a mountain man." In the Caucasus tribes, one learned early to follow a trail over dry rock with ease, or cull an individual sheep out of a herd by sight alone.

"Surely, someone in the Russian community here would have been suspicious." The expatriates were generally political dissidents—people wary by necessity.

"Russia's defeat in the war threw everything into chaos. Many in the Third Section did not survive the reorganization by the new, more beneficent tsar." Alexander II had, among other progressive reforms, freed the serfs in 1861. "My disappearance was incidental to the greater political upheavals." Kubitovitch was beginning to sense a possible reprieve, the marquis's expression markedly less ferocious now. "I am a violin instructor," he went on, a subtle cordiality in his voice. And when Darley shifted his feet so his stance was less confrontational, Nikolay Nikolaevitch casually added, as if they were acquaintances meeting on the corner, "A friend, who plays in the theatre orchestra, gave me free tickets for the performance tonight." Kubitovitch's aspirations for the finer things in life remained intact, although they were modified by his circumstances.

Darley held his gaze for a moment, and Kubitovitch's blood ran cold at the naked violence in the pale eyes. A brute barbarian in the flesh—despite the fine evening clothes.

"We were pardoned by the tsar in case you didn't know." A mild statement, softly put.

"I heard," Kubitovitch said, curtailing his impulse to shiver. And if he had had any hope of outrunning the marquis he would have bolted that instant.

A small silence descended on the island of gaslight illuminating the two men, large and small, the rest of the world passing them by without notice.

"If you give me your word you won't harm my family," Darley said slowly, as though he wasn't quite sure he was making the right decision, his expression shuttered and unreadable, "I have no quarrel with you."

Kubitovitch had always scoffed at the aristocratic code of honor and yet this man was asking for *his* word as if they were equals. For a dumbfounded moment Kubitovitch forgot his lifelong loathing for those of noble birth. But his survival mechanism resurfaced a second later and cold reality intruded. His answer was crucial to this man towering over him, even the manner of his reply would be scrutinized. "Let me assure you, my lord, I have no quarrel with you or your family," he said with utmost courtesy and a deferential bow. "Not now or ever."

"Then we are quits. I wish you a pleasant evening." Darley turned and walked away.

You had to admire a man of such courage, Kubitovitch grudgingly thought, watching the marquis walk off. Not knowing whether he was armed or not, Darley had turned his back on him without a qualm. Nor had he asked what name he was using or where he lived.

But the marquis was not so trusting that he dismissed Kubitovitch completely. He had the reinvented violin instructor, Vickers, watched for several years—until such a time as he was assured Kubitovitch was no longer a risk to his family. That appropriate moment arrived after Vickers married one of his violin pupils—a Miss Milbury from Chelsea.

Over the years, Aurore would look at Darley from time to time and with an affectionate smile, say, "Just think, darling, if not but for the hand of Fate. . . ."

He'd always agree.

But at base, Fate aside, the marquis understood that he had found his greatest happiness that cold February day outside Sevastopol. And he lived every minute of his life determined that nothing—whether divinity, destiny or fall of the dice—would threaten the love that he had found.

A Last Word—1914

On the eve of the Great War, two young men of fine family and fortune were lounging on the terrace of the Royal Yacht Club at Cowles after a preliminary run of the new racing yacht they had designed. They had been friends forever, having grown up on adjoining estates, attended school together at Eton, even spent some years at Cambridge in pursuit of a higher education uncommon in aristocrat circles.

But they liked astronomy, chemistry, the sciences in general. They not only shared an observatory built on land between their two estates, they had blown up any number of experiments purposefully or not in the laboratory adjacent to the observatory.

They were, in fact, so much alike that they were called the Wolf Twins both for their dark good looks and their reckless adventures.

"You're not leaving?" Neal Milbury looked up as his friend rose to his feet. "Have another drink. It's early yet. We don't have to be at Fraser's dinner until nine."

"I told my mother I'd fetch her from my aunt's." The two families were vacationing at their summer homes on the Isle of Wight. "Don't drink too much or Isabella will pout the entire evening," Lucien D'Abernon warned, waving as he walked away. "And she'll make us all miserable."

The two young men were both betrothed, having given into societal and family pressures at the age of thirty. But in their capitulation, they had not completely jettisoned their former ways. Not that young ladies of good family actually expected their fiancés or husbands to offer them complete devotion. It simply was not done.

Apropos that lack of devotion, rather than walk in the direction of his aunt's house, Luc turned left as he exited the Royal Yacht Club and made for a section of town close by the ferry dock.

Ten minutes later, he entered a narrow street of simple cottages and proceeding to the last one near the shore, walked up the path to the door and knocked.

The door instantly flew open, a woman's hand grabbed his arm, pulled him in and as he swung her up into his arms and kicked the door shut, he whispered, "I thought I'd never get away."

"You're here now. That's all that counts. How much time do we have?"

"Two hours, three if I make up some story, he said, setting her on her feet. What about you?"

"I have to be home by six or someone will notice."

They stood for a moment in silence holding each other close.

He was tall with dark hair and swarthy skin, she

was his opposite, small and fair with skin pink as rose-buds.

"I tell myself every day that we have to stop," she whispered, holding him tighter.

"I know. I do the same." Bending his head he kissed her gently. "But not today."

Her smile was bright with joy. "Thank you."

He grinned and, taking her hand, led her to the small stairway leading upstairs. "Thank me later, darling Lizzie," he said with a teasing smile. "When I deserve it."

Since Lucien D'Abernon and Elizabeth Milbury were both engaged to others, they were forced to meet clandestinely. Furthermore, Lizzie was sister to Neal, Luc's best friend, which made it even more difficult to sneak away.

They should or could or might have broken their engagements and carried on their relationship in the open.

If not for some deterrents.

Elizabeth's fiancé was the son of her father's business partner. To break off the engagement would possibly jeopardize her father's future. Not to mention her mother's overly sensitive notions of propriety.

As for Luc, his fiancée could possibly be disposed of—for a suitable sum, he suspected, and a plausible excuse for the public. If only Lizzie could be induced to change her mind.

But she had been, to date, unmoved by his pleas.

An added fillip to this problematic love affaire was the fact that the old Duke of Westerlands, who continued to protect his family's interests, knew that Lizzie was involved with his grandson.

Hugh had only recently learned of the liaison, and

although he and Kubitovitch had long ago put aside their differences, he viewed the relationship between the two youngsters as both interesting and ironic. While Kubitovitch's grandson, Neal, had been friends with Luc for a lifetime, there was now a possible merging of the two families should Luc and Lizzie contemplate more than a casual affaire.

A quixotic resolution to the past, was it not?

When Kubitovitch had married, he'd taken his wife's name, Milbury. He had also, through diligence and hard work, parlayed his father-in-law's small chocolate business into what was today a worldwide enterprise. One could purchase a Milbury chocolate bar most anywhere on the planet.

As the Milbury wealth had accumulated, a barony had come their way, as was often the case in England. Over the centuries, rich brewers and mill owners, merchants and bankers, had made their way into the nobility by outright purchase of titles or by befriending royal heirs or prime ministers—perhaps paying their gambling debts or pimping for them on occasion. It was all quite normal.

Perhaps it was time to pay a visit to his neighbor, Hugh decided. They could discuss how best to protect their amorously involved grandchildren. From gossip—or worse, should it come to that. Lizzie's father's business partner was an unsavory individual. The type who would take advantage of, say—a personal situation.

On the other hand, the love affair might play out in time.

So many did.

But why take chances? The duke bellowed for a footman. "Have the car brought around," he said when a flunky arrived. "And tell the duchess when

she returns from her tea that I have gone to the Mil-
burys."

A half hour later, he was ushered into Kubitovitch's aka Milbury's study.

Nikolay looked up from his newspaper. "I was wondering when you'd be over to discuss this interesting
situation with our grandchildren," he murmured,
folding up the paper. "Please, sit down. Brandy?" At
Hugh's nod, he rose from his chair with a grimace.
"Damn rheumatism," he muttered. "It's this English
damp."

Hugh grinned as he took a chair. "Better than the
cold of Siberia."

"True. But now you and I have lived long enough
to have this problem instead."

"Not a bad problem to have considering what the
alternatives might have been."

Kubitovitch laughed. "Some people are survivors,
eh—my friend?" Turning with two glasses of brandy
in hand, he moved toward Hugh. "So tell me, are
these two grandchildren of ours serious or not?"

"Who knows." The duke took a glass from Kubitovitch. "Excellent, as usual," he said a moment
later after taking a sip. "Your cellar is a testament to
your good taste. As is our grandchildren's taste in
partners, should it come to that." He grimaced
faintly. "The thing is though, I'm not as concerned
about this affaire as I am about your son's partner . . .
if you don't mind me saying so. Should Fisher get
wind of this, he could cause a considerable scandal.
And he's the kind that might."

Kubitovitch grunted. "I've been thinking for some
time—perhaps an assassin for him."

"Not so easily done anymore."

"Yet possible."

"True."

The two elderly men had survived a war where life was cheap, death was everywhere and whether one lived to see tomorrow was uncertain. And in the intervening years, human nature had not necessarily improved.

"Maybe we should wait until summer is over." Kubitovitch ran a hand over his thinning hair. "Luc and Lizzie might go their separate ways by then. As for my son's business partner, the end of summer is probably soon enough to resolve that issue as well."

But two weeks later, on August 4, 1914, England declared war on Germany, and mobilizing the country for the coming campaign took precedence over love affaires and business concerns.

Lucien and Neal were some of the first young men to take up arms.